BLIND THOUGHTS

THE ORDER OF THE HAWK TRILOGY
BOOK 1

C.L. SHARP

Cover Illustration and Design by Moonchildreams

Editing by Haleigh St. Paul at Page Perfectors LLC

ISBN: 979-8-9922229-0-6

AUTHOR'S NOTE

Greetings Reader!

Thank you for your interest in Blind Thoughts! This trilogy takes place in an urban setting and addresses many modern issues through-out each book. I believe in the importance of providing a warning in case any of the below topics can be triggering to you, the reader.

Content Warnings:

- Explicit language
- Descriptive sex scenes
- Violence and mention of torture
- Death of parents and loved ones in a tragic situation
- Brief mention of infertility
- Characters that deal with Anxiety and PTSD
- High School bullying

Safeguarding your mental health is extremely important, so please continue at your discretion. I hope you enjoy Talliana's story!

Wishing you a good read,

C.L. Sharp

To the ones who speak their mind and make no apology for it.

And to those who wish they spoke out more. That time is now.

By order of the Great Hawk, our people, made up of one hundred and forty-two bloodlines, are called to a high honor. We are called to guide humans onto the path of light and justice while removing all who wish to deceive and harm. We are called to protect nature and all its offspring, helping it flourish while guarding it against all who wish to destroy and cut down.

By the guidance of the wolves, with whom we have bonded, we are to live and work together; protecting one another so that we may not find ourselves alone and unable to complete what we are called to do.

Nature has bestowed upon us great powers that are to be used for our called purpose, not for our gain. May this order forever be carried out and light always be our guide.

- The Great Hawk & Our Call to Order

CHAPTER 1

August

THE SMELL OF SMOKE is enough to wake anyone from a deep sleep.

"Talli! Get up!"

Opening my eyes, I find Greer, my adopted sister, hovering over me. The air in the room is hazy, and the smell is strong. The siren starts blaring outside, and I note the sword clenched in her hand.

The Brethren are here.

Fear crawls up my throat as I throw off my covers, grab my phone and small dagger from my nightstand, and follow her out of our shared room and down the stairs to Dad's office.

"Get in, girls, quick," Dad says, motioning toward the hidden room behind his floor-to-ceiling bookcase. His eyes are bloodshot from exhaustion, the amber irises dull with sleep, and his bulletproof vest is haphazardly thrown over a white t-shirt. Mom grabs my arm from inside, and Greer and I quickly get in with her. Dad shuts the bookcase door behind us, locking us safely inside the hidden room and himself outside with the danger at our front door.

The adrenaline coursing through the three of us eases only slightly as the seconds tick by. Mom goes to the small brown leather couch that takes up half of the space in the cramped room and gently lowers herself to it. Her green fleece robe billows out around her as she sinks in. I join her, pressing my shaking hands into my lap and laying my head on her shoulder as we both breathe through the moment's stress. Her hair is a mess of dark-brown waves that spread out almost as much as her robe, and it cushions her shoulder underneath my head.

She turns her face toward me, giving me a reassuring smile. "I'm sure we'll be able to return to bed soon."

I return her smile and agree, "Dad will make sure of it. Otherwise, he'll have three sleep-deprived women in the house tomorrow." That's the least of Dad's concerns and we all know it, but I say it anyway.

It's hard to be positive in times like these, but I always find a way. It's the Hoffman specialty. Dad always finds a way to deliver hope to our people in the toughest of times. Mom always knows how to make people feel better. Greer has a much harder time being positive given her lack of Hoffman blood, but she *is* good at finding ways to take people's minds off of the negativity.

Then there is me. I enjoy making light jokes until people laugh and the mood lightens—definitely the most awkward out of the four of us.

Greer snorts at my joke and leans back against the door, sword still in her hand, but not clenched quite as tightly as before. Her mismatched oversized t-shirt and lounge shorts make the sword look out of place. She reaches her hand to her hair and tucks the long, raven-black strands behind her ears, while her pewter-gray eyes stay alert.

But that's my sister—a soldier guarding the door, ready to take on any threat even though the chances of danger reaching us here are minimal. I can tell Mom is fighting against the urge to ask her to stand down, but she has asked her that a hundred times before, and the result is always the same: Greer refusing to move. So instead, we all settle into our chosen positions, waiting for the siren to stop and for Dad to tell us it's safe again.

This room can't be considered a safe room, per se, but it's definitely more secure than sitting out in the open during an attack. The couch is pressed up against the far wall with a metal shelf next to it loaded with gallons of water and fire extinguishers. My feet are gently resting over top of a trap door that opens up into the crawl space under the house, which leads to the backyard in case the house catches on fire while we are trapped in here.

The need to break the silence in the room is overwhelming, but I push it down like I always do. These situations would be much easier and would go by faster if we did talk, but staying quiet and alert is paramount to our safety. We need to be able to hear if someone enters the house and ensure they cannot hear us. I trust Dad already has an officer outside the house to watch out for the Brethren, but we have to prepare for the worst.

My phone vibrates in my hand, and I look at it to see a text:

Trey: Are you safe?

A sense of relief floods through me and I reply:

Me: Yes. In the hidden room. You?

Trey: Yes. Currently watching over Ash. He's still asleep. These upgraded soundproof tiles really make a difference.

Me: Good! Stay safe.

Trey: Always. Love you.

Me: Love you.

My chest flutters, knowing he is worried about me. I have no doubt he would be sprinting down the road to get to me in the middle of an attack if he thought I wasn't safe. Treyton and I have been together for only three blissful months, but already, I know he would run into a burning house to get me if necessary. Unfortunately, in our community, the likelihood of the house over my head being set on fire is at a seventy percent chance, and that's being optimistic. I wish I could keep texting him, but I know he needs to stay focused on keeping himself and Ash safe.

An hour passes in agonizing silence and heightened nerves. The siren outside has long since blended into the background in my head until it stops suddenly. We all sit up straighter and wait another moment before we hear a distinct *click*.

The door opens, Greer ready with her sword just in case, and Dad appears. His face and light-brown hair are coated in black soot. Greer lowers her sword, and Mom and I stand up together.

"All is safe now," he announces.

"Who?" Mom asks, worry lacing her tone.

"The Brooks." A family who live only two houses down, and we are considered the middle of the community. The furthest away from all the gates and fences.

Greer's words echo my thoughts as she says, "They made it far this time."

"I suspect it was a test for them to see how far they could make it without us catching them. Our cameras caught them going over the fence, but by the time emergency services got there, they were hiding in the sea of houses. The officers on duty assumed they wouldn't stray far from the fence because they usually have some sense of self-preservation, but not tonight apparently." Dad runs his hand down his face and through his closely trimmed beard. Then he looks at his hand, realizing it's now black.

"Casualties?" Mom asks, getting his attention again.

Dad grimaces. "John is dead. Tarra and the kids are safe, but being treated for smoke inhalation. And two of our officers are also being treated for injuries."

My heart constricts knowing a neighbor died tonight, but I also feel relieved it was only one. The number is typically higher. Not all houses have hidden rooms, and a fire can catch fast on dry nights, trapping people before they can get out.

Greer and I make our way out of the room and toward our own again when Dad calls out to us, "Love you, girls."

We both say in unison, somewhat solemnly, "Love you too," and climb up the stairs.

Placing my dagger back in my drawer, I climb into bed and slide under my purple duvet. The smell of smoke has faded slightly, but it still lingers in the space.

"Greer?" I call out quietly.

"Way ahead of you." I hear her blankets rustle as she climbs out of bed, and then I hear the ceiling fan turn on, pushing the smell out of the air.

"Thank you."

I close my eyes, attempting the difficult task of trying to go back to sleep. How does someone sleep after a tragedy like what happened tonight? They either don't, or they sleep with nightmares plaguing them.

The next morning, Mom and I are hard at work doing what we can for the Brooks.

Luckily, their house is not a total loss, but there is enough damage that they are forced to move out until the house can be fixed and is considered safe again. Our community is set up so that in cases like these, we have a few empty houses for a family to move into until we can fix or rebuild.

A crew is already working on collecting any remaining un-damaged items and bringing them to the new temporary house. Another one is clearing out the mess left behind, and a third is assessing the damage to make a plan for repair. Mom and I and two other women from the community are collectively working on making meals, stocking their refrigerator with groceries, and buying or looking for donations for anything they lost in the fire that is an immediate necessity.

Whenever Mom and I help out like this after a fire, it still feels like we aren't doing enough, like there is more we should be doing to help. But to a family not only mourning the loss of a husband and father but also the loss of their home, every little bit of help counts. At least, I choose to see it that way.

Mom and I carry the last bit of groceries into the new house, and we've officially done as much as we can. On our way out, Mrs. Brooks catches us at the door. "Rose, I can't thank you enough for everything. You always go above and beyond for the people here. You too, Talliana." She smiles warmly at me, and I return it the best I can. Despite her soft words and warm smile, I can sense sorrow and heartbreak behind them. I quickly pull my senses back, not meaning to have pried into her emotions.

"Tarra, you and the rest of the community are not just people to me. You are all my neighbors and my friends. If there is anything you need, knock on our door anytime. Aaron and I will ensure it is taken care of," Mom tells her.

"You are truly the light of this community. May the Great Hawk bless you."

Mom lowers her head slightly in acknowledgment and then smiles genuinely at Tarra, her cornflower-blue eyes turning up at the corners.

I'm Mom's twin in so many ways. I have her thick and wavy hair, though mine still carries the red hues that have mostly faded from hers. My face is the same round shape, littered with almost as many freckles. But my eyes are a deep ocean blue instead of her bright color. Dad always jokes that he didn't know when I was born that he was getting a carbon copy of his wife. I don't share any of his physical features, but I did inherit aspects of his personality. Stubbornness and determination to always be right are the usual culprits.

We leave the house, and, looking up at the sky, I can tell it's already early-afternoon. Mom leans in next to me as we walk home and says, "You have worked hard today, Talli. Why don't you take the rest of the afternoon off and relax for a while? Take a dip in the lake or read. You'll feel better once you do."

"Really? Today is the last day of my internship, though. I don't mind going back to the medical center with you to finish."

Greer and I have spent the entire summer, minus the first and last week, interning at our prospective careers before our senior year of high school. Our whole class had to, as this is standard practice for our community to help us find the right fit. Greer has been at the police station working under one of the officers, while I have been at the medical center working under nurses like Mom and shadowing the doctors.

"Really. You're exhausted, and you've done enough."

"Thanks, Mom."

We get a few paces closer to the house when Ms. Molly, our mail delivery woman, approaches us. She greets us with a cheery smile framed by her short brown hair and says, "Rose. Talli. It's such a joy to see both of your faces out and about after the night we had."

"It's good to see you well, Molly. Talli and I were just on our way home from helping Tarra and the kids get settled," Mom replies.

Ms. Molly smiles brightly at me. "No doubt Talli is getting some valuable experience for her future as an elder's wife, as well."

My cheeks flush, but I answer, "Only time will tell."

"Oh yes, of course. I don't have foresight, but I have a good feeling that I will hear wedding bells before the end of next year." She winks at me and then continues, "Your mother is the best teacher you could have. I have never known anyone to match her grace and kindness. I'm sure you will do just as well when you and Treyton step into those shoes."

Her words are kind, but I can't help but feel self-conscious at the notion. Being an elder's wife like Mom was never a role I saw myself in before three months ago. Not that there is anything wrong with it. I just always planned to pursue my education, become a doctor for the community, and live a simple life—or, as simple as is possible for our people. But with Trey...It's a long way out, and he still has a lot of learning and aging to go, but it's clear he will be an elder one day, just like both our fathers, and I'll be the wife at his side. A role I realize now that I would be honored to have. As long as I have him.

"You are very sweet, Molly. I just do the best I can, and I'm sure Talli will do the same," Mom replies for both of us.

Ms. Molly either misses or completely disregards Mom's attempt to wrap up the conversation by saying, "You know, I saw Treyton following Aaron last week when I brought him his mail. I hate leaving it with the people downstairs because I don't like passing up the opportunity to say a quick hello." She lets out a laugh and continues, "Is he shadowing him now instead of Orsen?"

"Well, given his classification, taking over the mayor role from Aaron would make more sense for Treyton, rather than director of education from his own father. But I believe he is splitting his time between them both to learn different things," Mom answers.

Ms. Molly nods her head dramatically. "He is a smart young man. Well, I have to go! Nice seeing you both!" She bustles around us, her large messenger bag swinging wildly as she goes.

Mom and I continue walking, and when I am sure Ms. Molly is out of earshot, I ask, "Has anyone considered that having the worst gossip and biggest busybody as our mail person might not be a good idea?"

Mom laughs. "That is exactly why your dad likes her in that role. She tells him everything when she delivers his mail in the morning. He doesn't even have to ask."

Now I laugh. It's a clever and easy way to keep up with the community gossip.

"And Talli?" I look up at her again. "I trust you will follow whatever path the light leads you down, but you would make a great elder's wife one day."

Her comment warms me and I give Mom a side hug as we walk the rest of the way home together.

CHAPTER 2

THE FIREFLIES LIGHT UP the night sky like tiny symbols of hope.

That is why I love them so much. Nature created this beautiful insect to remind us that there is always hope where there is light. Light guides us out of the darkness and shows us where to go. It is warmth and safety. It is kind hands and a loving heart. It is the reason we are here, and it is the reason we fight. But we aren't called to follow the light. We are called to *be* the light, just like these fireflies. We are the Order of the Hawk.

Our community in the Commonwealth of Massachusetts and all its people are part of a hidden world spread out across the globe. Our ancestors date back to the fifteenth century, when the Great Hawk, nature's messenger, called our people into the Black Forest in Germany. There, It granted us our connection to nature, which allows us to protect it with the help of magic.

This magic gives us the ability to sense others' emotions. That is the fundamental skill that each member of the Order has, but depending on bloodlines—and, as some say, the intentions of our hearts—many of us manifest unique, specialized skills that range from mental to physical abilities.

"Hey," a familiar voice calls out from the darkened trail ahead.

My eyes work overtime to find him in the shadows of the large oak trees. There. Trey emerges from the path ahead, his brown eyes locking on mine as he crosses my backyard to where I am sitting on the edge of our back deck.

"Hey," I reply. He braces both hands on either side of me and leans in to press his lips to mine. Lips that are always soft and gentle, his kisses unhurried and savoring. He pulls back enough to ask, "Ready?"

I nod, the only response he needs before grasping my hips and pulling me off the deck to my feet. His hand encompasses mine as he leads me down the dark path to our spot. The one where we have spent most of our summer nights when he wasn't away on a mission. Now, we only have a week left before summer break ends and reality is knocking at the door again.

Trey adeptly leads me over every tree stump and rock in the path, his night vision impeccable. I know this path like the back of my hand, but when there is little to no moonlight peeking through the dense trees, it's easy to get tripped up. Thankfully, I can always rely on Trey to keep me safe in times like these.

In the back of our community is a large forest comprised of hundreds of acres of trees and wildlife. My house backs right up to it, and a mile north of the backyard is a large lake surrounded by willow trees. The drooping trees are uncommon in this area, and no one knows how they got there, making it a magical spot—our spot.

We emerge from the path and find the lake in front of us and our tree to the left of us. Under the tree, a blanket is already spread out with a lantern in one corner to illuminate the small space under it. The branches of the tree hang low, many brushing the ground, but there is one spot facing the lake where they are a bit higher, giving the illusion that you are in a cave when you are underneath it.

Trey and I settle in as I find a comfortable spot on his chest to rest my head and he wraps his arms securely around me. The calluses on his fingers brush up against the bare skin of my side, where my shirt is pulled up a little, and my body warms. Nothing is more comforting than being wrapped in his arms, listening to the steady rhythm of his heartbeat.

Breaking the quiet night, I say, "I had a nightmare last night after the attack."

"What was it?" He asks.

"Well, nightmare and memory. It was when some of the forest caught on fire when I was a little girl, but it happened again, and this time, the entire forest went up in flames," I explain.

"Nightmares have a way of bringing to light our biggest worries and I understand why that would worry you, Talli, but you know that it would take a lot for that to happen. The magic in this forest protects it. A small section may burn, but then the fire stops. That's what happens anytime the Brethren try to burn it down."

I know he is right, but I have a hard time shaking the fear that torments me anytime there is an attack like last night.

Trey sits us both up and takes my hand, placing it against the tree trunk behind us.

"Close your eyes and tell me what you feel."

I do as he says and concentrate. "I feel the tree...like it's a body beneath my fingers...There are layers of wood, like the tree's skin...There is water pulsing through it, like blood in veins...I feel life."

Opening my eyes again, I find his golden-brown skin glowing under the lamp light, while his thick, black hair absorbs it entirely. His smile is soft and perfect and...

"Exactly. Each tree is alive and full of magic. I know it's our job to protect it, but in reality, nature did a decent enough job protecting itself before we ever came along." He places his hand against the tree next to mine.

"What do you feel?" I ask him.

"Bark." He laughs.

"Why can't you feel what I feel?"

"Because you're a Healer. Your ability allows you to sense the inside state of a living being's body. You only need a touch, and you know if something is broken. It doesn't matter what it is—a human, an animal, or a tree—you can sense life in it. Me? I'm just an Intelligence Officer. I can't sense what's happening inside of a tree's body."

I smile at him. Knowing how much he admires what I can do warms my spirit, and he is always vocal about it. Trey knows how to make me feel seen and special when everyone else discounts Healers because we aren't a line of defense in this war. The war with the Brethren of the Flaming Sword, an organization built with the sole purpose of destroying the Order and burning us all to ash.

Deciding to change the subject, I ask, "What did you do all day? I barely saw you."

Trey's body tenses, not enough to be visible, but enough for me to feel it underneath my hand resting on his. I straighten my back and look at him, searching his eyes. "What is it?"

He scoots himself backward to rest against the tree trunk.

"They are sending me out again in the morning," he answers solemnly.

"No! Another mission? It's the final week of summer," I whine.

"I know. If I could control it, I would stay right here with you and never leave."

My cheeks flush, but it's not enough to rid me of the frustration I feel at his news. "Where are you going this time?"

"This one is classified. I don't even have all the details yet myself," he explains.

"This will be the third classified mission this summer, not to mention the other two non-classified ones you have been on. They don't have someone else they can send?"

"It's not that simple. All I can say is that it requires my ability. That's why it has to be me."

"Why do they need a Dream-walker?" I ask, confused. Before he can say it, I answer for him, "Classified, right?"

Trey nods in confirmation.

Trey's ability is dream-walking. This means he can consciously enter people's dreams and observe, manipulate them in small ways, or even fully take over and have a conversation with someone's mind. Old folklore about a "sandman" was created based on an Order's Dream-walker who attempted to help children sleep peacefully after a sickness came over the village. As weird or even as sinister as some stories can become over time, many are born from some level of truth. Unfortunately, our people are the cause of some, despite our efforts to stay hidden.

"How long will you be gone?"

"I'll be back before school starts, I promise." His eyes lock onto mine and I know he means it.

"I'll hold you to that," I threaten mildly.

He laughs, the sound full and wonderful and belonging solely to the man I love. "I don't doubt it."

Grinning at him, I turn, giving him my back, and then scoot until I am resting up against him. His warmth envelops me again. I spy one lone firefly dancing around in front of the tree before disappearing. Another reminder that feels sent just for me. One to be grateful for in this moment and maintain hope of a bright future with this man.

I feel Trey's fingers twirling around a strand of my hair, and I close my eyes, mentally letting go of my worries and fears.

"Mahogany," Trey says quietly to himself.

"Huh?"

"Your hair has so many different shades of brown and red in it. I'm trying to guess at them."

I giggle and feel him pick up another wavy strand. "This one almost looks like copper."

"I'm pretty sure it's all just considered auburn hair," I tell him.

"Auburn overall, sure. But there is much more to it than that."

His hand shifts again, and I let myself fade while I listen to him murmur random names of colors that quickly lose meaning.

CHAPTER 3

BEEP! BEEP! BEEP!

My alarm echoes through my head like the thumps of a heartbeat. I throw off my covers and turn off the alarm on my phone.

My eyes track to where Greer lies in her bed on the other side of our shared room. With one arm, she firmly holds a pillow over her head, while she tightly grips her light-gray comforter that meets the pillow's edge with the other. If I didn't know her so well, I would think she was trying to suffocate herself.

"Good morning, Greer!" I chirp excitedly in her direction as I open the curtains. She groans as her grip tightens, then reluctantly loosens.

"Good morning, Talli," she replies blandly. It comes out muffled because even though she has loosened her hold of the pillow, it still covers her face, leaving only a few strands of her hair visible.

"Well, I am not going to let your gloomy ass rain on my parade today. I've decided it's going to be a good day," I announce with a haughty tone. She pulls the pillow off her head and eyes me wearily.

"Nothing could rain on your parade right now, could it? Also, while we are on the subject, how late were you out last night?" The pointed accusation in her voice doesn't give me pause or dampen my bright mood.

"None of your business." I drag out the first word in a sing-song way. My mind flashes with the image of Trey bending down to give me one final kiss at our back door before he had to leave last night.

My skin grows hot with the ghost of his touch still lingering.

"Talli, your life is always my business. It's alright, though, it doesn't matter. My point is, I don't understand how you can be out so late doing I don't want to know what with your boy-toy, then wake up so bright and cheery. I'm exhausted just watching you bounce about this morning." Greer has managed to get herself up into a seated position on the edge of her bed while I have started rifling through the closet.

"Three things," I start while pulling out different outfit options to compare. "First, don't call him my 'boy-toy.' He has a name, which you know well, considering we all practically grew up together." Eyeing a fitted teal top with lace accents and a flowy pink one with a flowery print, I lift them both up to Greer and ask, "Mermaid or flower?"

"Mermaid," she answers, not thinking twice about me interrupting myself.

I put the pink shirt back in the closet and continue, "Second, I do not bounce, and your insinuation that I do makes me extremely self-conscious." I pause again, but only briefly, while I fish for my favorite pair of jeans from our clean laundry bin. "Third, don't be jealous because I have an unnatural amount of energy in the morning, and you have an unnatural lack of it."

She rolls her eyes at me, and on that note, I saunter into our connected bathroom, clothes in hand. I shower and get dressed quickly so that Greer can have a turn with the shower next.

Greer and I share a bedroom—not necessarily because we must, but because we want to. When Greer was adopted, she was a traumatized little girl in a new home with a solemn demeanor and little interest in talking. Mom and Dad thought it would be best for us to share a room so that I could keep her company and be there when she needed to talk. I quickly got used to it and was more than delighted as a young girl to do all her talking for her. We have been inseparable ever since and have had no interest in moving into separate rooms.

In truth, Greer and I are complete opposites in almost every way. She is tall and built like a ballet dancer, and I am short with an inconveniently large chest size. She is sleek and graceful, while I am soft in too many spots and not always great on my feet. Every color is my favorite color, and she is happy wearing her gray, drab hoodie every day, no matter the weather.

I stroll out of the bathroom to find Greer wearing said hoodie now while she lounges in her bed, phone in hand, looking at something. I guess she isn't in any rush for a shower. Without looking at me, she asks, "What are you doing today?"

"I promised Mrs. Hardy I would help with the kids." Mrs. Hardy is our community's daycare coordinator, and she is short-handed this week while Mrs. Leino is away visiting family in another community.

Greer's eyes crinkle. "Why am I not surprised? We finally finished our internships and got a week off, and you already have plans to work."

"I like staying busy! Plus, Trey is on another mission this week, so it's better than sitting around missing him," I explain in my defense.

Greer's face turns down. "Another one?"

"Yep."

She looks thoughtful momentarily while I finish getting ready, and then she asks, "Movie night tonight?"

"That sounds perfect." I smile at her, appreciating her offering something I enjoy doing that will also keep my mind busy.

"Enjoy your day being lazy," I call over my shoulder to her and then head off to start my day.

A beautiful day as a matter of fact. The sun is warm with a light breeze keeping me from sweating on my walk to the daycare center. But my pleasant mood dissipates slightly as I pass by the Brooks' house. The walls are still up, but the normally red-brown bricks are charred black from the fire. If Mr. Brooks hadn't been a Water Elemental, the house wouldn't be standing at all. Mom explained to me that he was trying to put out the fire as soon as it was set when a Brethren soldier attacked him from behind.

Such horrible people, the Brethren. How could someone feel that much hate in their hearts to do something like this? To kill with no remorse or hesitation. It wasn't always this way, but it's been this way for so long now, it feels like we have always been at war.

The Order did live in peace at first, spreading across Europe as our numbers grew, reading the truth of people's intentions to make the world a better place. We fought against people with dark motivations trying to take places of power, and we advocated for the preservation of nature. Until the late fifteen hundreds, when one of our kind residing in Scotland married a human man and told him the truth about what she was. As far as we know, this was the first time anyone had ever told a human outside the Order the truth. Her husband, being very superstitious, accused her of being a witch.

Realistically, we can be considered as such. We are born with abilities that we channel using magic. But we do not fly on brooms, cast spells, or eat children.

Thank god.

The Order managed to avoid the witch trials in Germany, but this misguided man became the founding father of the Brethren, and thus started the witch trials in Scotland. Trials that took so many of our lives, as well as many innocent human ones. In an effort to escape the Brethren, the majority of Scotland's community of Hawks fled to the Americas and settled in Massachusetts. There, a different incident involving some young human girls set off the Salem witch trials, causing enough of a stir for the Brethren to follow us here.

So, despite the widely held historical belief that the witch trials came to an end, they never truly stopped. The Brethren became a secret organization with the sole purpose of killing anyone who is a part of the Order of the Hawk. We are a whole other world living among humans who have no idea we exist, our original purpose mostly set aside to focus on our survival.

My stomach sours at my train of thought. I try not to think about what led our people to this war, but it's hard not to after an attack. Really, I try not to think about the war at all because all thoughts around it lead to depression, and I don't have time for that. There is too much to accomplish and a full life I intend to live.

So, I push away all the negativity and continue my walk, enjoying the sounds of a normal day: people walking to and from work in the community, a couple of cars driving slowly down the street, older children playing and shouting at each other, and someone mowing the lawn. A perfectly normal day.

I approach the daycare, a small bright blue building with a white picket fence, yellow shutters, and a matching yellow door. Once I finish doing a quick check on myself to make sure my mind and emotions are where they should be, I open the door and focus on the first sweet face I come across and make it my mission to ensure they have the best day possible.

"And finally, students, add a few drops of peppermint oil and stir the contents with your peacock feather for a full sixty seconds." I watch the second hand on the large wall clock move all the way around. He continues, "Pour into the vial. Seal it with the stopper, then shake."

I watch closely as Healer Weiss demonstrates. As he shakes the glass vial thoroughly, the contents turn from clear to burnt orange—a color that almost exactly matches the man's long, curly hair.

"This elixir can last at room temperature for about nine days, but can last in the refrigerator for sixty days. Beware, if the color comes out a shade darker or lighter than this, that means something is wrong in the measurement and it is not safe to use," Healer Weiss explains as he holds out the newly made elixir for everyone to observe.

He sets the vial down and straightens his light-blue scrubs as he studies all of our faces individually to make sure no one looks confused. Seemingly satisfied that everyone understands, he steps back and gestures to Mom, who is sitting in the corner of the classroom.

She stands and takes up a position behind the teacher's desk in the borrowed chemistry classroom. She smiles at everyone and addresses all the school-age Healers in the room. "Good evening, everyone. I have a couple of announcements, and then we can dismiss for the night."

Mom and I belong to the Healer classification of the Order. There are four classifications: Healer, Strategist, Intelligence, and Elemental. Depending on the unique ability the Hawk develops—if they develop one at all—they get placed in the classification that fits the best. This classification system helps with easy identification among our people and impacts what type of career a Hawk ends up in. Those who do not develop special abilities aside from being able to sense emotions have the luxury of choosing a classification and have a lot more freedom than the rest of us in what they do for the community.

Each classification has weekly classes outside of school, all year round. For Healers, these classes teach students new elixir recipes and what to expect from working at the medical center, help students learn to control their individual abilities, and much more. They are usually led by one of the community doctors, like Healer Weiss, and then Mom always makes announcements or shares news that is relevant to Healers at the end.

"First, there is a delay in shipment for our new cast iron cauldrons, so if your household was next on the list to get a new one, it will unfortunately be a couple more weeks. Second, since next week is the first week of the school year, we will not be meeting. If you have any questions or need help with something that cannot wait the two weeks until the next meeting, feel free to stop by the medical center at any time to request help. But that is all. Have a good rest of the week off," Mom concludes the meeting.

Everyone rises from their seats and vacates the classroom quicker than normal. I stay seated and wait for Mom to finish her conversation with Healer Weiss and then we head out as well.

"I've been asked to teach another first-aid class tomorrow. Would you like to assist me?" Mom asks after we get in the car.

"Absolutely. Who is it for this time?"

"Mostly Strategists, I believe. A lot of them are due for a refresher. I might ask Greer to come help wrangle her people, too. She can play fallen soldier for us to bandage."

I laugh. I love helping Mom teach first-aid classes. It allows me to socialize with people other than Healers and classmates at school. However, like Greer, Strategists are not known to be big talkers. When they do talk, it's mostly about weapons, fighting styles, missions, and attacks—all things I am not interested in discussing.

The Strategist classification consists of mental abilities that do not involve any level of manipulation of the mind to whom you are focused on. Abilities such as foresight, truth-detecting, mimicking, and more. They make up a large part of our fighters, along with Elementals.

"I think that's a great idea, but don't give her any speaking parts because then I'm sure she will decline to help," I say.

"Good thought." Mom laughs and we continue our way home.

As our numbers grow, so do our range of abilities. The elders have conceded to the people's request for a classification system to help identify and group individuals based on similarities in abilities.

These classifications will be used only as a label, not as a means to separate. Those seeking to separate the pack using the classifications will be punished, for we are one people, not groups of different people.

-History of the Original 142 Bloodlines

CHAPTER 4

THE WEEK PASSES WITHOUT incident or drama. Mom's first-aid class was easy and full of more laughter than learning. I also ended up volunteering at the daycare for the rest of the week, and the children did a great job keeping me busy. However, while I had hoped they would keep my mind off of Trey, they only made me think of him more than usual. I spent a lot of time wondering what our future would be like, how many kids we would have, and what it would feel like to hold a baby we made together for the first time.

We've actually had conversations about it before. It seems crazy to think about those things so young, but in our world, we marry and have kids young. Like Ms. Molly said, it wouldn't be surprising for us to be married by the end of next year. Trey would be nineteen, and I would be eighteen. The thought doesn't scare me. If anything, it excites me, and we would be fulfilling our duty to the Order to keep our bloodlines strong.

The Order believes that it is our blood that the Great Hawk imbued with our unique connection to nature, and it's that connection that gives us magic and our abilities. Meaning, the purer the Hawk bloodline, the stronger the connection, and vice versa. Over time, some bloodlines have been so diluted with regular human blood that those Hawk descendants assume that the emotions they can sense in other people is just good intuition and nothing more.

Despite the Order's efforts to stress the importance of having children with other Hawks, relationships with humans still happen, and there is not much that can be done about it. Marriage to a human is strongly frowned upon, though. If someone does marry a human, they are cut off from the Order and forced to live outside of the safety of the communities. This is for everyone else's safety and to keep the Brethren from trying to infiltrate us. There have been exceptions to this rule throughout our history, but there are a lot of tests a human has to undergo in order to be allowed residence and full access to our knowledge.

Greer's family was once one of the five purest bloodlines in the world. These families take blood purity to an extreme by arranging marriages for their children to other strong-blooded Hawks. There was no human blood in Greer's line until her father, Gavin, left his matched fiancé at the altar to run off with Greer's mother, Amalie, a human nature photographer he had fallen in love with.

Considering what was expected of Gavin, he left the Order without a word and married her in secret. They stayed in hiding successfully for five years, frequently moving to someplace new, until they died tragically in an accident. The three of them were on their way home, driving on mountain roads during a snowstorm, when Gavin lost control of the car and smashed into a tree. Greer survived the crash from the backseat, and our family took her in, raising her in the Order's way. It was a horrible accident that no child should have to experience, but Greer has told me before that she is grateful that they died from a normal human accident as opposed to being taken out by the Brethren like most of our people. I don't blame her at all for that point of view, and despite everything that happened, I like to believe that nature had a good reason for her ending up as my sister. I couldn't imagine my life without her.

"I promised I would be back before school started," Trey calls out to me, jolting me from my thoughts.

I leap from the carefully laid-out blanket under our tree and run to him. Hopping into his arms, I let him hold me. I missed him so much. Whatever this mission was for, it didn't allow him to text much or video chat at all while he was gone, which constantly threatened to put me in a bad mood despite my determination to stay positive.

He sets me back down, and I close my eyes, arms still encircling him, and allow my senses to check him for injuries. I know he would tell me if there was something wrong, but it makes me feel better to check him anyway. Finding nothing amiss, I look into his eyes, which seem to carry an echo of pain behind them, and ask, "How did the mission go?"

His smile is weak, but he answers, "It was successful. I'm just happy to be home."

Grabbing each side of his face with my hands, I pull his lips to mine. Soft and unhurried, like normal. I allow myself to relax, and slowly, I release my tight grip on him. Trey takes my hand gently, and we walk the few yards back to the blanket I laid out under our tree.

As we settle in, I ask, "I suppose there still isn't anything you can tell me about it?"

"No, but even if I could. I'd rather not talk about that stuff with you."

I frown at him, opening my mouth to protest, but he quickly adds, "I didn't mean it like that. What I meant to say is, I'd rather talk about happy things with you. Like what you did this week, or something that made you smile."

I blow out a breath. "Okay, I get it. My week wasn't all that interesting. I ended up helping out at the daycare all week, then it was the same old, same old. I really enjoyed being with the children, though. They always lift my spirits."

Trey's eyes lighten, the echo of pain disappearing. "I bet you're a natural with them."

"You would bet right. I love every single one of them, even when they are little monsters half of the time." I laugh, then continue, "They kept me busy, and I was exhausted every night, so it was good. It did make me miss you a bit more, though. I thought a lot about our future and what it could look like one day."

The corners of his lips turn into a soft smile, and he pulls me to him.

His lack of response makes me shift uncomfortably. Normally, he would jump on that opportunity to dream with me. Trey loves to dream and plans things out to the same extent as I do. He must be tired if he's not being very talkative tonight. I just can't shake the feeling that something is off, but I know I can't push him to talk about something if it is against his orders, so I decide to change the subject. "When do you have to get signed up for classes?"

Trey is starting college this year, while I still have one year left of high school. It's like being stuck in the kiddie pool while he gets to go swimming in the deep end. At least I have Greer and my best friend, Ash, to keep me company.

"I'm already signed up and ready to go," he answers.

"I know we have briefly talked about it, but what's the plan for us?" The college is only in the next town over, but the problem is that our community is so secluded that we still live forty-five minutes away. With all the classes he will be taking, study time, and the commute, our time together will be minimal until his first break.

"I'll be home every night. I might have to dedicate a few to studying, but I will still make time for you. Don't worry," he reassures me.

"Unless you find someone much prettier and more mature than me," I say lightly, but I can't deny the small amount of worry I have felt over such a thing happening. I'm not insecure—not in the least. I also don't doubt Trey's love for me. But I am aware of my shortcomings, even if a human girl wouldn't be a real option for him long-term.

Trey looks at me sharply and asks, "You aren't actually worried about that, are you?" He sees right through me, like always.

"No! I just know that humans can be alluring. They come with minimal attachments and thinner waistlines." I mumble the last bit.

Trey laughs. Not the response I expected, but it could be worse. He grabs my hands and, finding my eyes, says softly, "Talliana Hoffman, I have never known you to be the insecure or jealous type. Don't start now. Not on my account."

"I've never had a reason to feel insecure before now. Not that I think you would just leave me like that. I know you wouldn't. But it's college...and I guess...I'm just being stupid."

Trey swallows hard before saying, "You have no reason to feel insecure. I'm yours and will be until the day I take my last breath. Do you understand?"

I nod, feeling comforted but also like things are still off. I curl up in his arms, settling into our usual position. We stay like that for a while, while I mull over what to say or do next. Then, a thought strikes me, and I announce, "I want to go for a swim."

Trey laughs, but when I don't join him, his face takes on a look of bewilderment. "You're serious? The water is going to be cold."

"It's still summer, technically, so it can't be that cold," I reason.

"In case you forgot, we live in the northeast. The water is cold here most of the time."

I don't keep arguing with him. Instead, I stand up and lift my shirt over my head.

"Talli..." His tone is low, a warning that causes goosebumps to cover me from head to toe. I kick off my shoes and take off my shorts next. I stand there and allow him to get his fill of me in my bra and underwear. I seriously regret not putting in the care today to make sure they matched, but I'm not sure he cares if the look on his face is any indication.

I slowly walk backward and say, "I promise to keep you warm if you come in with me."

He groans, a guttural sound. I know Trey absolutely hates being cold; he detests the winters here, while I relish in them. I'm being cruel, I know it. But I can't think of a better way to get him out of whatever is going on in his head.

Just as my heels feel the chill of the water on the small rocky beach, he says, "I will get in if you admit which cheesy rom-com movie you got this idea from."

I laugh. "Guilty as charged. It may be cliché, but it's an effective mood-lightener. Come on Trey, you have been so serious lately. Be young with me for one night. Please."

I move further back in the water until it's up to my knees, and then I stop, knowing a drop-off is just behind me.

Trey reluctantly stands up and slowly removes his clothes until he is also in only his underwear. I stand frozen as he stalks toward me with his lightly sculpted abs on full display. I could stand here for the rest of the night and just look at him. He's perfect. The perfect height for me at six feet even, not too tall or short. The perfect balance of muscles, none look like they are worked harder than the others. The perfect way he looks at me, like I am his whole world.

Once he is only a step away from me, he says, "It should be a crime how much power you have over me."

"But I'm a Healer. I can't manipulate you into doing anything you don't want to do."

"You're wrong. You have just manipulated me into freezing my ass off, and all you had to do was give me that look. That look is more powerful than anything someone could do to my mind."

Before I can produce a response and ask him to elaborate, he picks me up and jumps off the ledge of the drop-off. I squeal at the shock of the freezing water, and he laughs. Encircling my arms around his neck, he moves us deeper into the lake. The water gets slightly colder, but my body is adjusting quickly now. Letting go of his neck, I swim off in a different direction.

"What happened to keeping me warm?" he calls out.

"I meant by forcing you to swim around. What did you think I meant?" I give him a wicked grin, and to my delight, he falls for my trap and immediately starts swimming after me. I am a strong swimmer, but I am no match for his long arms. He catches me quickly, and without too much of a fight, I wrap myself around him, pressing our cold, wet bodies together. Then, we float under the moonlight, simply enjoying the peacefulness of the moment.

Eventually, Trey convinces me—well, more like drags me—out of the water. We lie back down on our blanket, dripping water all the way, and I don't even have a moment to settle before he is on me, kissing me, savoring me. The cool breeze in the air threatens to freeze me in my soaked scraps of fabric, but Trey's body covers mine, and he blocks the worst of it.

We've swum together plenty of times this summer, but doing it tonight, like this, feels so much better. So much more intimate. I melt underneath him as the heat of his kiss intensifies, and it is more than I have ever felt before. I am not the only one with power here. He consumes all that I am.

Trey pulls away once I feel like a puddle on the ground, ready to give him everything. If he asked, I would right now. But, to my annoyance, he climbs off of me like the gentleman he is and hands me my clothes. We get dressed and pack up the blanket, and then he walks me to my door. Before I reach the back porch steps, he pulls me to his chest.

"Promise me something," Trey whispers into my hair.

"Anything."

"That no matter what happens, you'll always remember how much I love you."

The warmth and happiness that fills my chest rushes out, and I'm flooded with concern instead. I pull back to look at him. "What's going to happen?"

He smiles sadly, brushing my hair behind my ear. "Nothing. It's just been a long week without you."

"There are still two more weeks before you start classes and so help me, if they send you out again before then, there will be hell to pay."

Trey pulls me to his chest once more. "If only I could freeze time. I would live right here with you."

I squeeze him tighter, then say into his chest, "I think that sounds like a wonderful plan."

"But, you need to get some rest for school tomorrow. It's your last first day. I want you to enjoy it."

I smile at him, warmth returning to me once again. He leans down and presses his lips to mine for another moment before he breathes, "Goodnight, Talliana."

"Goodnight. I'll see you after school," I say in return.

Trey kisses my forehead in farewell, and I reluctantly step out of his arms and go inside, feeling light and wonderful and not the least bit cold.

CHAPTER 5

TODAY IS THE FIRST day of my senior year of high school. The thought jolts me upright in bed, and I spring to my feet before reaching over to turn off my alarm. This year is going to be the best one yet, and I am ready to get started.

"Senior year! Can you believe it, Greer?

"Yes, I can believe it, and it couldn't have come fast enough." She groans as she turns over in her bed and stretches.

"Are you really that ready to be done?" I ask her in surprise.

"Yeah, I am. If this summer has taught me anything, it's that I can contribute more to this community than sitting on my ass learning algebra half the day."

I swallow, thinking about how different everything will be after school, but I can't stress about that right now. I want to enjoy this year. I turn and go about my regular morning routine, getting ready for school.

Greer walks out of our bathroom in black skinny jeans and a purple t-shirt. Her alabaster skin is still shiny from the steam, and her long hair is wrapped in a towel. I'm standing in front of my floor-length mirror, almost done with my signature makeup look—concealer, foundation, mascara, and a little bit of sparkle on my eyelids—when I feel her eyes on me.

"Yes?" I ask.

"Something is going to happen."

I turn to her, my eyeshadow brush in mid-air, searching her face. When Greer says something like this, it is not to be taken lightly. I feel the fear roll off her and right into me. It must be enough of a feeling that her mental shield has slipped, exposing her emotions to me.

"Any particular person or situation this feeling might be related to?"

She tenses and meets my gaze, locking her eyes with mine when she responds, "You."

My pulse quickens and my shoulders tense. "Seriously? On the first day of school? Couldn't you have waited until the second or the third?"

"You know I can't control it," she points out. She's right, I do know. It doesn't mean I am not annoyed just the same. Greer has foresight. For her particular ability, she can sense emotions before they happen. While it can often be extremely helpful, it can also be extremely inconvenient. Yes, I appreciate the heads up on the negative emotions, but it also makes me a nervous wreck leading up to the emotion I am supposed to feel.

"What am I going to feel?" I ask.

"It was too muddy to discern. It just feels bad."

Swallowing hard, I finish getting ready. When it's painfully clear to her that she has put me on edge, she adds, "I'm sure everything will be okay. Just be on high alert. Don't let thoughts of Trey distract you too much." She grins at me, and her teasing helps to lift me back up—a bit.

Greer and I are sitting at our usual table in the cafeteria, half of our last first day of high school already almost over. We attend Lakeside School, but no one actually refers to it by name. We all just call it "The School" because it is the only one in our community and serves kindergarten through grade twelve. Nestled snuggly between state forests and natural preserves in the northwest corner of Massachusetts, the community itself isn't all that big. There are 450 residents, but enough kids to make us all feel like sardines packed into each classroom.

I've continued to be on edge all morning, waiting for Greer's warning to come to fruition, but nothing terrible has happened yet. I'm only slightly annoyed that Trey hasn't replied to any of my texts. He is probably busy today debriefing the elders on his mission, so I am choosing not to worry about it. Maybe my annoyance is what Greer sensed? Doubtful. Her ability is not precise, but it is more accurate than that.

Greer and I are casually chatting about gossip we heard today over our lunch when the last member of our trio arrives, looking disheveled as usual.

Asher.

His curly umber hair is unkempt and getting way too long. It's evident by the way he keeps trying to shove it out of his eyes. He usually wears thick, black-rimmed glasses that help keep his hair back, but he decided to try contacts this year. I have no doubt he will reexamine that choice by the end of the week, if not by the end of the day. His blue eyes shine bright, though, without his glasses dulling their light sea-glass hue. It's a color of blue I have always been jealous of, considering my own eyes are so dark.

If the looks he is getting right now are any indication, many of our female classmates seem to appreciate his lack of glasses. Not only do his eyes shine brighter, but his olive skin tone seems to be more obvious as well. As his best friend, I can easily say that he is handsome. I've always believed that, but I've also always considered him a cute kind of handsome, like he would look perfect in a boy band. But he is way too book-wormy for that path in life.

Ash drops first his lunch box and then himself on the bench seat at our table.

"Hey," he says quickly.

Neither Greer nor I respond. We only watch him for a minute for very different reasons. My reason being born from concern, I ask, "Ash, it's the first day of school. Why do you look like it's finals week?"

He laughs softly and responds, "I think I signed up for too many elective classes."

Greer says pointedly, "In case no one told you, you are supposed to slack off as much as possible your last year."

Ash startles at her response, clearly not believing her. "If that's the case, then I am sure you'll have no problem, Greer Solandis Meyer."

Ash pops a potato chip in his mouth like he just dished out a good burn. He always uses her full name when he tries to pick on her. It's equally adorable and disgusting. My parents never changed Greer's last name to our own, not because they don't consider her their daughter but out of respect for her family's legacy.

Greer's eyes sparkle with mischief, but she keeps eating her chicken tenders instead of responding.

Greer, Ash, and I have been friends since Greer came into our lives. We are all the same age and have spent almost every day together since. Inseparable is a word many would use for our little group. However, I have been trying to give the two of them more space recently, hoping that this agonizing tension between them finally goes somewhere. They are in love with each other, but both are complete babies when it comes to speaking it out loud. It's been like this for as long as I can remember. It seems I am the only one of us who is adult enough to admit my feelings to the person I want. I sit straighter in my seat and smile a little to myself at that thought, smugness settling in.

Greer clearly feels my shift in emotions and asks Ash, "So when did Trey get home last night?"

Ash looks over at me and smiles widely. "Hmmm...I heard him at two, maybe three a.m." He takes a bite of his ham sandwich and continues, "I think he was meeting some ditzy blonde. Oh no! It was a feisty redhead. The blonde was last week."

I throw my packaged cookie at him. "I hate you both," I mutter.

"Come on, Talli. You two are perfect for each other. He doesn't stop talking about you. He often tells me about something you do, forgetting I am already your best friend and know everything," Ash tells me.

My cheeks warm, and I recall the way he looked at me last night. God, I miss him already, and it's only day one of the school year.

Ash notices my now sad expression and says, "He was a bit off this morning. I think it's weird for him not starting school today with us."

"Probably," I give Ash a weak smile and continue eating my salad. It needs more shredded cheese. The dairy-to-healthy-stuff ratio is off.

Dairy and carbs, my favorite forms of comfort. Sighing, I put more ranch on top and keep eating.

Ash was adopted by Trey's parents like Greer was adopted by mine. Unfortunately, that is a common occurrence among our people. Ash's parents were close friends with both Trey's parents and my own, so we all grew up together. Four years ago, Ash's parents died during an attack by the Brethren. It was before midnight, which is a lot earlier than when they normally attack, and Ash was at my house watching a movie with Greer and me. We smelled the smoke right before Mom ran into the house to grab her phone to call the community's emergency defense team. Ash heard the house number she gave and ran out the door. He rushed into the engulfed house to look for his parents. When we reached the house, we thought we had lost him too, but once the emergency defense team put out the fire shortly after, they carried him out of the house unconscious. A fallen ceiling beam hit him on the head and pinned him, resulting in retrograde amnesia.

Greer and I visited Ash daily in the medical center to keep him company and try to jog his memory, but nothing worked. He retained basic skills but lost everything else. His name, memories, and identity were gone. His parents were gone. His home and everything he owned were all gone. It was almost like he woke up a different person entirely. Before the incident, he used to be more serious, and he struggled with anxiety. When he woke up, he was lighter and goofy. Undoubtedly, many of us would change similarly if all our problems and worries suddenly disappeared.

Regardless of what happened to Ash, our friendship didn't take long to knit back together as if nothing had happened. Trey's parents took him in, and Trey treated him like the little brother he never got to have but always wanted. I think Ash has a stronger bond with Greer, though, out of all of us, because they both suffered the loss of their parents.

I pull my focus back to what's in front of me to find them chatting about the astronomy class they shared at the beginning of the day.

"What part did you not understand?" Ash asks patiently.

"I think the better question is what part did I understand," Greer replies.

Ash gives a look, indicating that he is waiting for her to answer her own proposed question. She promptly obliges him by answering, "None, Ash. Absolutely none of it."

"What I don't understand is why out of all the electives you decided to take, you chose a science-based class. You hate science," I interject, even though I know why. She didn't like any of the options, so she chose the one that put her with Ash.

Greer narrows her eyes at me. "Because I think space is cool." Her defense is hilariously weak. I do in fact laugh, and Ash's lips curl upright in the corners.

"Don't worry, I'll help you whenever you need it. If you want to learn about space, I'll make sure you learn about it," Ash offers.

"Thank you, Ash. At least someone at this table is truly helpful." Greer says to him with a smile, then she sticks her tongue out at me.

I stick my tongue out right back at her and finish my lunch half-listening to their conversation about Jovian planets.

Greer's warning has been entirely forgotten by the time we walk through the front door of our house after school. That is until I see

Dad sitting with Trey's parents at the dining room table. My parents often have the Waterstones over, but not at this time of day when Dad should still be at his office. Not to mention that the air in the room feels thick with tension.

Something is wrong.

I look around the table and see Mrs. Waterstone's cheeks are wet with tears, while Mr. Waterstone's face looks grim, and the wrinkles between Dad's eyebrows tell me he is in deep-thinking mode. A chill creeps over my skin, and I hold my breath.

"Hey, girls. Come sit," Dad tells us. Greer and I swap concerned looks, then take seats at the table, bracing for what is about to happen. "Go ahead, Orsen."

Mr. Waterstone turns to me and asks, "Talliana, you were with Treyton last night, right?"

My heartbeat quickens as my worst fear is confirmed. This is about Trey.

A hundred horrible scenarios run through my head as I answer, "Yes."

Mr. Waterstone nods, then asks, "Was he acting normal? Was anything different? I know Treyton's shields are impeccable, but did you happen to sense anything from him?" His light-brown eyes are soft and kind as always as he tries to search mine. The once jet-black hair at his temples appears to be grayer than it was the last time I saw him—only a few days ago—and his face is drained of most of its color, making him look even paler than usual.

I think back, searching through all my memories from last night. He was definitely different at certain points of the night, but he was tired. At least, that is what I told myself so I wouldn't worry all night long.

"He seemed tired," I answer. "As if the mission had taken a lot out of him. But we mostly talked about him leaving for college and still finding time to see each other."

"Did he tell you anything about his mission?" Dad asks.

"No. He said it was classified. What is going on? Is Trey okay?"

Mr. Waterstone gently turns to his wife and says her name, "Angeline," prompting her attention. Mrs. Waterstone is not crying as hard as she was a moment ago, but tears still roll down her bronzed cheeks. Her bonded mouse, Pebble, is sitting on her shoulder, looking just as distressed. Its sand-colored coat and whiskers are twitching in a nervous rhythm. She blows her nose with a tissue and hands me a piece of paper.

I recognize Trey's handwriting immediately.

Mom. Dad.

This will be hard to understand, but I am leaving home, and I'm leaving the Order. I don't want to be a part of this any-more—the fear, the fighting, the death. I want the chance to live a normal life. Don't try to find me.

I'm sorry.

-Treyton

I feel like a brick wall has fallen onto my chest and has me pinned in place. My ears are ringing. I can't move. I can't breathe. I can't think.

"Talliana, have you spoken to Treyton at all today?" Mr. Waterstone asks. I shake my head no. In fact, I've texted him several times but never got a response.

"We tried calling him, tracking his phone, and we searched all over the community, but there is no sign of him. We don't even have footage of him leaving. Though, one of the front gate officers thought they saw him. Melisandre and Lemon are out now, trying to see if they can pick up his scent," he adds. That explains the absence of both Dad's and Mr. Waterstone's bonded creatures.

Mom breezes into the room, bearing a tray of cups. "I have tea. Something to help the nerves."

Mr. Waterstone takes two cups, placing one in front of himself and one in front of his wife.

"Thank you, Rose," Mrs. Waterstone says before taking a big sip.

Thinking of the one place his parents wouldn't know to look, I am suddenly out of my chair and running out the back door. I hear Greer calling out from behind me. I ignore her and keep running up the path through the forest. I don't slow until I see the lake.

I cautiously approach our tree, scanning for...well, anything. I'm desperate to find something that will explain this. White catches my eye, and I rush toward it, finding a note underneath one of the large roots that jut out from the dirt. Dropping to my knees, I grab it from where it is tucked away safely. I expect some kind of explanation or a love note, but all it says is, "*I'm sorry.*"

NO.

I pull out my phone from the back pocket of my jeans and try to call him. It rings endlessly with no answer. My eyes burn. I try again and get the same result. After the third attempt, I drop my phone on the ground next to me and allow the tears to flow freely from my eyes. How could he leave? How could he hold me last night and not say anything to me?

I realize with sudden clarity, he didn't respond after I said that I would see him today. Sobs start to rack my body, and I curl into a ball on the cold ground. I feel the press of Greer's hand on my back, rubbing small circles, trying to coax my breathing to calm and my heartbeat to slow. But as my chest finally begins to move in a steadier rhythm, my stomach feels wrong, as if there is something inside that it doesn't agree with. I sit up and straighten my back, then breathe through the unusual sensation. Slowly, it fades.

Greer moves with me as I scoot back to rest against the tree. I continue to cry quietly, both of us staring out at the lake until the sun begins its descent, and I find the strength to move again and go back inside.

To abandon the Order is to turn one's back on oneself. We are Hawks. No matter how far away you go or how much you try to pretend it's not there, the magic and its purpose will continue to thrum in your veins. It runs deep in our bloodline, whether we wish it to or not. There is never an escape from our blood.

- The Laws of Magic

CHAPTER 6

THE NEXT MORNING, I race down the stairs to catch Dad before he leaves to start his day. The front door is just about shut, so I holler, "Dad! Wait!"

The door swings open again, and Dad's eyes find me. "What is it, Talli?"

"I want to help look for Trey," I say quickly.

He walks back through the door, slowly shuts it behind him, and replies, "I appreciate you wanting to help, but there is nothing you can do right now. There's not much many of us can do. Chief Lu has her best people on it, and the rest of us need to let them do their job."

My face falls, then I ask, "I know where he will go if he comes back. Can I wait there just in case?"

Dad rests a hand on my shoulder and says, "Talli, please go to school. I'll feel much better knowing you are there and safe. I promise, you will know as soon as we find him."

He turns toward the door again, but before he can open it, I ask quietly, "What happens once you find him?"

Dad looks back at me, "Our people are not prisoners here. So, we will talk to him and make sure this is truly what he wants. Then, if he still wants to leave, he is an adult and can choose that for himself. We'll let him go."

"I want to talk to him."

Dad places a hand over his heart. "You have my word as elder, you will be given the chance to talk to him before we let him go. If anyone could sway a person, it would be you."

His smile is soft, and I return it with a half-hearted one before he leaves, shutting the door behind him.

I plop down on the bottom step of the stairs and try to process everything. I was up all night going through every conversation I had with Trey since we officially started dating three months ago, looking for any possible explanation for him running off. There is none. Trey never liked the fight we were born into, always wishing for another way, but he accepted our fate, and we had plans to get through it together. He was going to be an elder one day, and I his wife. He wouldn't have left me.

Being an elder means being a community leader in some capacity. Dad and Mr. Waterstone are elders in our Massachusetts community of the Order. There are branches scattered all around the world, but in the United States, each state has one community, with the exception of California and Texas, which have two due to their size. Each community consists of three elders to lead and defend the local area. One elder acts as mayor, the second acts as chief of police, and the third can either be head of education or chief of staff at the medical center, depending on their abilities.

Elders are elected by the community to serve until their retirement, death, or if the community collectively votes for them to step down. Even though anyone can run in an election, when it is time for a new elder, children of past elders are often groomed to take over the position, as is the case with Trey. This, however, is not the case with me. Dad knows that I have no desire to become an elder, but Greer hasn't completely turned down the idea, so she is involved in a lot more than I am. I wouldn't say she is being groomed yet, but I have no doubt it will start after she graduates high school.

"Talli, are you ready for school?" Mom pulls me out of my thoughts, and I look up at her, finding her eyes studying me.

"I just need to go grab my backpack." I stand up and almost jump from Greer being suddenly behind me on the stairs.

"I have it," she says, holding it out to me.

I take the offered bag, and Mom says, "Good. Now, I feel like this goes without saying, but remember what your dad said last night about what's going on."

My pulse quickens, and Greer replies for the both of us, "Trey decided to transfer to a college in Virginia. He left early to get settled."

Mom smiles and hugs us both. "Try to have a good day at school, girls. And Talli, trust that everything is being done to find him."

The last place I want to be is at school, and the last thing I want to do right now is lie to Ash about where his brother is.

"Seriously, who just runs off without saying goodbye?" Ash complains.

"I guess he had to leave quickly to set up his classes since it's so late," Greer offers.

"Most colleges let you register online or over the phone," Ash argues.

Greer looks to me for help, and I weakly offer, "He texted and said something about all the classes being full online, so they needed him to go in to ask for exceptions from the professors."

"Well, that makes a little more sense. But I didn't even know he was considering a different college."

"I didn't either." I press my lips together, not wanting to continue this discussion.

The bell rings, and I let out a sigh of relief. Lunch and this conversation are over. I quickly leave my seat at our lunch table and head to class, leaving Ash and Greer in the dust behind me.

Ash is a full-blooded human, not a Hawk like the rest of us. His parents were a rare exception to the "humans don't live in the communities" rule because Dad recruited them to aid the Order with their non-magical talents. Ash's mom was a biologist dedicating her life to natural sciences, and his dad was a mechanical engineer. Together, they designed and built the most amazing things, from armor and weapons to communication tools and elixirs. Their loss was devastating to the community, not only personally, but also because of their skills and everything they did to give us an edge over the Brethren.

When Ash lost his memory, the elders decided to keep the truth about the community from him. They thought it was best to let him have a somewhat normal childhood for as long as possible. I'd argue that decision was the hardest thing that could be asked of Greer and me, but we are careful to keep our true selves hidden and make sure that everyone else around us does too.

Even though our community is secluded, we still operate like a normal human town for the most part. We have curious humans and government officials visit every now and then as they would anywhere else, but they seem to just view us as paranoid rich people. So, hiding everything magical from Ash is challenging, but not impossible. It helps that he has always lived here and rarely leaves, so his perception of normal is a bit skewed.

Walking through the hallways, everyone's face is a blur as I weave through the groups of students using their last few minutes before class to chat. Some Strategists push each other around in good fun. Intelligence students raise their noses and sneer at other classifications if they dare to get too close. A few Elementals loudly laugh over something, likely an inappropriate joke only they would understand. A group of Healers trade small cloth baggies of ingredients that can be used in more questionable elixirs. I feel a baggy being pressed into my hand as I pass them. I lift the green drawstring bag and carefully open it. Peering in as I keep walking, I recognize the light root. Ginseng. Next to it is a small white folded paper. No doubt someone has some great new idea for an elixir that will boost focus, and that's why it is going around to members of my classification. Many will brew it and sell it to classmates in other classifications.

I stash it in my pocket to look at later. It's rare that I actually brew any of the recipes that come to me in this fashion unless I think the creator is onto something that could benefit others, not just their own monetary gain. This is unlikely anything I will want to brew, but having ginseng on hand doesn't hurt.

Normally, I would have taken the time to stop and talk to the other Healers and find out more about it, but I'm too busy spiraling over Trey. He's gone. But the world and everyone in it still goes on like nothing happened. Like the smartest and most selfless man didn't just abandon us, his people. His friends. Me. Like my heart didn't fall apart less than twenty-four hours ago.

I take a seat in my Algebra II classroom. After settling in, I look up to find Mr. Simon giving me a sympathetic look before starting his lesson. He is one person that I'm confident knows something about what's going on.

Mr. Simon is not only a math teacher, but also Greer's and my trainer. A six-foot-four giant of a man who served in the military for a long time before settling down in our community. He told us once that he was an investigation officer for the U. S. Army for the last ten years of his service. Tattoos and scars cover his tanned skin. Which he has more of, I don't know. Greer and I were unsuccessful the one time we tried to count. Despite his pristine physical condition, his gray hair and shortly trimmed gray beard are quick reminders that he is older than our parents.

There are other trainers in the community, usually a few for each classification. However, when Mr. Simon arrived seven years ago, the elders collectively convinced him to personally train their children. Children of elders don't often get special treatment, but we are held to an unspoken higher standard, so the extra attention that Mr. Simon gives us helps. We train with him four days a week, and even though he might not have been told exactly what it is, he has to know something is going on since Greer, Trey, and I all missed our lesson last night.

Class drags on longer than I ever thought possible, the equations on the chalkboard looking like gibberish by the halfway point. Considering I actually like math, I'm disappointed in myself for not being able to focus better.

The bell rings overhead, and everyone in class practically jumps out of their seats. I'm moving a bit slower today. The usual pep in my step is nowhere to be found.

"Talli, can I talk to you for a second?" Mr. Simon asks.

Halfway to the door, I turn on my heel and walk over to the front of his desk where he is leaning against it. Seth, a large German Shepherd and Mr. Simon's bonded creature, sits next to him. His fluffy tail is sweeping up all the dust bunnies under the desk as I approach. I reach down and scratch behind his ear, knowing exactly how he likes to be pet.

"I'm sorry about what happened with Trey," he offers softly.

"You know, then? Everything?" I ask, unsurprised.

"I was told this morning."

I nod. I'm glad there is at least one more person that I can talk to about this.

"That is the question, though, isn't it? You apologize for what happened with Trey, but we don't *know* what happened to him," I say, hoping that he may know something more. Mr. Simon is always the first adult to tell us things, even when we aren't supposed to know. He trusts us kids, because I think more than most, he knows what we face.

"I was told he left a note," Mr. Simon responds.

"He did. I read it, but you and I both know he wouldn't have just left. Trey is better than that. He isn't a coward and he isn't selfish."

"I'm not saying he is either of those things, but he is a smart young man who could do anything he wants in this world. He could have wanted a better life outside this community."

I cross my arms over my chest and give him a glare that says I think he is full of shit. Mr. Simon is like an uncle to me. One I'm incredibly close to and can trust with anything.

After a moment, he lets out an enormous sigh. "Alright, I agree with you. I don't think he just left, either. For so many reasons, but especially because I know how much he cares for you. If he had truly decided to leave, I know he would have taken you with him."

My chest warms at his comments. Only for a moment, though, until it sinks in that he agrees with me. The Brethren might have taken Trey or...My eyes start to burn, and a lump forms in my throat. I stop the thought before it fully forms. No, I will not believe he is dead. I know that the Brethren do not keep prisoners. They just kill and burn the bodies, but he has to be alive. I'd feel it if he was gone, wouldn't I?

Mr. Simon follows my train of thought. He says carefully, "We assume nothing, okay? I'm sure the elders are doing everything they can, but I'll see what I can find out."

"Thank you." I turn to walk out of the classroom once more, but Mr. Simon stops me again by adding, "Oh, and Talli, work on those shields. Your grip on them should never waiver, especially when you're upset."

From a young age, Hawks learn to build a mental wall around their minds to protect themselves from other members sensing their emotions. Even though we have the ability to turn the sensing on and off for the most part, people being people, some have no sense of respect for others' privacy.

Dad used to explain to us that it's like an old radio. Each person's mind has its own frequency or station, if you will. You can't hear everyone's station at once. Instead, you must deliberately change the channel to hear a certain person's station. When someone isn't shielding, whether they are a Hawk wanting you to hear them or a normal human, you can feel their emotions coming down the frequency you are tuned into. If someone is shielding, it's like hearing static or nothing at all, depending on the method they are using to shield.

Now, some humans are naturally quiet with their thoughts, so you may simply hear that sound is there, but the volume is too low to understand any of it. Then, of course, some humans practically scream their emotions at you, their frequency easy to pick up on and hard to lose.

"Yes, sir," I respond, embarrassed I had let them slip. Then I walk out the door, ready for the day to be over.

CHAPTER 7

"IF YOU WERE TO use basil leaves instead of mint in this mixture, what would you have?" Mom quizzes me as I stir the boiling pot on the stove.

I search my memory for a minute, then answer, "An elixir for pimples rather than cysts."

"Very good, sweetheart. Both I have to brew often for your dad's back." She waggles her eyebrows at me, and I laugh despite being mildly disgusted.

When Dad is stressed, he sweats, and he is typically stressed for good reasons. Being an elder and the mayor of the founding community in the country is a never-ending job. It's not one you can leave at the door when you get home. It's something that becomes who you are as an individual. And the elders of our community, specifically, are in a unique position where, even though there is no rule that officially deems it this way, many other states look to us for guidance. If we decide on something or make a change, most of the East Coast, at the very least, follow suit from our example without question.

Dad found the perfect match in Mom, though, I have no doubt. She is the level-headed one who always keeps a clear mind and does her best to keep him calm with her elixirs and abilities.

Mom's ability is hard to explain since there is no blanket term for it, but it's almost like nurturing to the extreme. She could meet a stranger and, without them saying a word to her, know what would make them feel better instantly. Like now, staying busy makes me feel better, so she has asked me to help her stock up on household elixirs.

Healers can have many different abilities, including ones that aid in human healing, animal healing, and mental health. Some have abilities that make them better with the ingredients, like inventing new elixir recipes or improving on old ones.

"Stir for thirty more seconds, then take it off the heat," she directs me, and I obey.

I pull the pot off the heat and then pour the green liquid into our awaiting cauldron with the rest of the ingredients. Mom mixes everything together with her large wooden spoon while I get the funnel ready on top of the first small glass vial.

Once she is finished, she pulls the spoon to her nose and takes a good whiff. Her nose crinkles in disgust and then nods. Together, we bottle the elixir into the vials, and it takes everything I have in me not to pinch my nose with my free hand. This elixir is one of our old recipes, and the older the recipe, the worse the smell is likely to be.

Despite our goals always being aligned, Healers can be divided because of our opinions, not unlike the doctors and other professionals in the human medical field. Many Healers believe healing should be based only on our old texts and rely solely on magic, while others believe in using the science behind modern medicine in conjunction with our magic. Mom and I fall into the latter category. As Mom often says to people, change is necessary to grow.

When the last of the elixir is gone and we have a neat row of ten full vials, I take a long, much needed deep breath and ask, "What's next?"

Mom chuckles softly. "Anything in particular you need to make?"

"Got anything to cure my worry?"

"If I had a recipe for that, our doorbell would never stop ringing." Her tone is meant to be light, but it comes across as sad because she is right. All our people do is worry and look over their shoulders. Our community, like all others in the Order, is gated and has a security team that constantly patrols, looking out for signs of the Brethren. Still, even they can only do so much against people hell-bent on burning us all into ash day and night.

"I try my best to stay out of the inner workings of everything around here." She gestures wildly around her, meaning she stays out of Dad's job and what it entails. "But I do know they are doing everything possible to find him."

"I know." I try to force hopefulness in my voice, but it's no use. It's been four days since Trey left, and there has been no more information on what happened. I have been sick to my stomach with worry, and the purple circles under my eyes have deepened significantly from lack of sleep.

I do think to ask, though, "Do you know if there have been any sightings of Theora?"

"There hasn't been. Which means she is with him, wherever that is." That is a good sign.

Theora is Trey's bonded creature, an eastern barn owl. If a bonded Hawk dies away from the community they belong to, their bonded creature will return to the community to mourn. The only exception to this practice is if they die, too. I push away that thought quickly before it has time to settle.

A bonded is a creature that chooses one of us to be bound to for as long as we live. Once a bond is formed, it enhances a Hawk's unique individual ability or may even give them a new one, depending on the strength of both the Hawk and the creature. The bond also allows the bonded and Hawk to speak mind-to-mind and enables the bonded to share the Hawk's life force, pausing the creature's aging once it passes maturity. When the Hawk dies, the creature will resume its natural aging process until or if it bonds again.

Decades—or maybe even centuries—ago, almost every Hawk had a bonded creature, but now it has become less common. Some would say it's because magic is fading in the world, but others would argue that fewer of us are worthy of a bond. In today's world, only the stronger members have them. Many of the ones with weaker blood-lines don't. In our family, Dad has a bonded, but Mom hasn't been blessed with one.

"Where did you go?" Mom asks softly.

I pull myself out of my thoughts, realizing I am staring at the counter intently. "I'm sorry. Spaced out for a minute, I guess."

Mom's look is concerned, but she says after a moment, "Let's make some bath bombs next."

The tension between my creased brows eases, and I grin at her. That is a perfect idea, but I add, "Then brownies. That way, I can enjoy them while I'm in the bath."

She laughs. "My brilliant daughter. I take all the credit for that mind."

"I'm sure you do," I reply, my mood lightening at the idea of temporarily soaking my worries away.

I ease myself into the hot water, up to my shoulders, and lean my back against the side of the tub. I close my eyes and take several deep breaths, in and out, until my heartbeat slows to a stable rate. There is something about the water that always calms me. I let my mind drift, and even though it starts with a funny story I heard in school today, it inevitably falls to the one place I don't want it to go.

Blistered hands rested in my lap, palms up, while I worked ointment into them and wrapped them with clean bandages. I kept looking up from my work to find him smiling at me.

"I'm starting to think you're getting hurt on purpose," I said to him, lashes lowered.

He hummed as if thinking it over, then replied, "That would be reckless of me."

"Yes, it would be."

"Good thing I have a very talented Healer to patch me up."

I still didn't meet his eyes, but I smiled as I said, "You don't have to hurt yourself to gain my time or attention."

"I know, but I love watching you fuss over me."

I did look up then and scowled at him. He laughed, and, using one of his newly wrapped hands, he pulled me onto his lap. Grabbing my face, he tucked a strand of my hair behind my ear and kissed me.

My heart rate kicks back up, and I try to dispel the memory. I sit up in the bath, causing the water to slosh, and scrub my face with my wet hands.

I can't think about this right now.

I can't think about *him* right now.

I have to trust the process. The elders will find him, wherever he is, and fix this.

I lean back against the tub again and start listing ingredients for different elixirs. Then, I move on to their uses and how long each one lasts until they expire, but my mind drifts again to the scent of vanilla and leather.

"I love you," he stated out of nowhere.

Looking up from my book, my eyes locked with his, surprised. "What did you say?"

"I know we have only been together officially for a month, but I do. I love you."

My heart felt as if it would flutter right out of my chest, "I love you too."

"You're not just saying that to spare my feelings?" he asked, his tone light considering the question.

"Of course not!" I practically yell, crossing my arms, my book discarded on the table beside me.

He suppressed a full teasing smile at my movement, but I didn't miss the lift in the corner of his mouth. He stood from his seat across from mine and then kneeled in front of me. Grabbing my neck, he pulled my face toward his, kissing me until I slid right out of my seat. I fell into his arms, and we tumbled to the floor together, laughing and kissing until we heard my dad making an obvious effort to stomp his feet loud enough to make his presence known.

Trey helped me right myself, and then he said, "I want to show you a special place I found."

I fully submerge myself under the water and hold my breath until the ringing in my ears subsides and my lungs burn. I reemerge and gasp for air. After a moment, when I can breathe normally again, I exit the tub and get dried off.

It's no use. Even the one place where I feel the most at ease can't quell my thoughts of Trey.

If he had just told me he was leaving or had said goodbye, I wouldn't have understood or agreed, but at least I wouldn't be going through this nightmare right now. He could have done at least that for the woman he claimed to love.

But did he have a choice?

That is the question that I cannot get out of my head. Because he did love me. He *does* love me. I can't explain how, but I know it deep in my bones, despite his actions right now saying otherwise.

The last time I saw him, he told me, "Always remember how much I love you." I can't forget, and I won't forget.

I finish drying my wet hair, get dressed in my pajamas, and go to bed, knowing it will be another restless night.

CHAPTER 8

September

A WEEK PASSES, AND still, no one has found Trey.

Chief Lu, the chief of police and the third elder of our community, found a surveillance video from a gas station showing Trey leaving the state in his own truck with no sign of distress or injury. Mr. Waterstone even called the college he was going to attend and they informed him that Trey withdrew from all his classes. All other communities have been put on alert to watch for him, but once he left the state, it is almost as if he disappeared without a trace.

A light breeze gently rustles my hair as I close my eyes and try to breathe deeply. I am walking home from school today. Mom usually offers to drive me home on afternoons when Greer has Strategist class, but I declined, hoping the quiet walk and fresh air would help clear my head a bit.

I'm almost home now, but as I pass by Trey and Ash's house, I see Mrs. Waterstone in the front tending to some of her flowers. She is an Earth Elemental. Her specific ability aids her in growing the plants that are used in all our healing elixirs.

Elementals are divided into four types: water, fire, earth, and air. Their abilities can range from controlling the element itself in its simplest form to having a specific attunement to something within the element. For instance, some Water Elementals can manipulate and shape water, while others can create ice or extract moisture from the atmosphere to generate rain. Since Elementals have four subcategories with many abilities under each one, they are the largest classification within the Order.

I look back to Mrs. Waterstone, and there is a tug in my gut to go talk to her, like an invisible cord pulling me toward her. I can wallow in self-pity as much as I want, but I can't imagine how she feels right now.

Her intricately braided hair is swept over her shoulders with a large-rimmed, bright pink hat keeping the worst of the sun's rays off of her skin. Mrs. Waterstone loves bright colors. She is always either wearing them or decorating her house with them. Apart from the hat, she looks so natural and at peace as she kneels in the dirt, pulling out weeds and trimming where the plants are slightly overgrown.

She turns and spots me, giving me a small smile. "Ah, Talli. Come here, child, and help me pull some of these weeds."

I go and kneel next to her, feeling completely lost. "I'm afraid I know nothing about tending plants."

A small chuckle leaves her, and she gently grabs one of the flower stems in front of her. "See this? This is what the flower stem looks like. These need to stay put. But these," she pulls out the green stem that doesn't have any flower buds, "are weeds and need to be pulled out. If I ignored them, they would choke out the flowers until they die." She looks at me then, lifting an eyebrow at me, daring me to read into her last statement. I want to, but I push it aside.

"Weeds mean flowers die, and that is bad. Got it." I smile at her and get to work, noticing that Pebble is in the flower box, too, moving small rocks that are scattered about into a small pile.

We work in silence for a moment until she asks, "How are you doing?"

"I actually came over intending to ask you the same thing." Neither of us taking our eyes off our task, I continue, "Honestly, I'm not well. I...I don't understand what happened. I know we have the evidence showing he left, but it doesn't feel right."

She makes a small humming noise in her throat as if to say she understands, then says, "When all of you were little, and it would rain, you and all the other kids would run right out the door afterward to jump in all those dirty puddles, not a care in the world. But not my Treyton." A warm smile spreads across her face. "He would gather all the clean towels around the house and bring them outside, carefully placing them on the dry porch before he went to have fun himself."

The image of little Trey struggling with a big stack of towels makes me grin. "Why did he do that?"

"So that once everyone finished playing, they could clean up before going home. He told me he didn't want the other kids to get in trouble for tracking mud into their houses."

I laugh. That is totally a Trey thing to do. Being so concerned over something that no one else is worried about.

Mrs. Waterstone continues, "Problem is, his action had the consequence of having to help me wash them all after. My son's greatest flaw is acting without thinking through the consequences."

I think on that one for a second. When I don't reply, she presses on, "He cares for everyone around him so much and would do anything for them, despite what it means for himself. He can be impulsive because of it."

"So, you don't think he just left, either?"

"I believe he did make the choice to leave, but for a good reason." I've thought about that too, but could never think of a good enough reason to justify leaving without saying anything. If it was a threat to the community, we are strong enough to deal with it. Trey isn't stupid enough to trust the Brethren if they promised to never attack our community again.

Mrs. Waterstone turns and locks eyes with me. "Talli, did you know Healers have the strongest intuition out of all the Order's classifications?"

I startle at that. "I always thought Strategists had the strongest intuition."

She shakes her head. "When you're assessing someone's injuries, where do you feel it? Your head or your gut?"

"My gut."

"Exactly. A Strategist with an ability like your sister's knows someone's next move because they can read their body language. It's in their head, whereas Healers are led by intuition—a knowing in your gut. In the case of your ability, if your patient is unconscious or feeling pain all over, you wouldn't be able to get a read on them. So, you must rely on your intuition to guide you," she explains.

"I never thought of it that way."

"Sadly, most don't. Most squander that extra gift, but don't be like everyone else. That intuition will guide you through everything. Trust it," she urges me fiercely.

Before I can reply, she asks, "Now, what is your intuition telling you about Treyton?"

I close my eyes and concentrate. I turn off my thoughts and try to focus on the unexplained knowing in my gut. I say the answer as I see it there inside of me, "He is alive."

I open my eyes, and she visibly releases a breath. Her shoulders seem to relax a little as she says, "Good."

I didn't realize how afraid I was that he could be dead until this moment. Now, I feel like I have some level of confirmation that he isn't. Not that I would normally believe my gut was confirmation of anything factual, but Mrs. Waterstone seems to believe that it is, and her confidence in me boosts my own.

She stands up then and brushes herself off. "Thank you, Talliana, for your help. Trust your intuition always. When all seems lost, look inside yourself. You'll find everything you need there." With that, she extends a hand to Pebble, who quickly scurries up her arm, and goes into the house, leaving me there with dirt under my nails and a lightness I haven't felt since Trey left.

I brush myself off and turn to leave when I hear the front door open. I turn around and see Ash standing on the front porch, quietly studying me, a book clenched up against his chest.

"Hey, Ash." I saw him at school no more than thirty minutes ago. His face was light then, but now? It looks confused. I tune into him for a moment and sense confusion and pain. Mental pain, not physical. I sever the connection and ask him, "What's wrong?"

"What were you two talking about? You and my mom."

"We were talking about how much we miss Trey." Not a lie, I decide.

"Yeah. He is really busy, I guess. He's not answering my texts much," he says cautiously.

Does he suspect something? We have all been careful, but he is logical and extremely resourceful. An Intelligence Officer who works for Dad in the Mayor's Office set up a message routing system for Trey's phone number, so any messages his phone receives, they can see and respond back if needed. Apparently, Ash keeps them busy.

"I'm sorry. He hasn't been answering mine much either." I don't have to work to force the sadness into my tone.

Ash leans on the white railing of the front porch and eyes me again, his assessment making my skin itch. Eventually, he sighs and says, "I'm sure once things settle for him, it will be better."

"Yes, I'm sure it will be. Why don't you come over after dinner for a movie? We can wallow together."

"It's a school night," he points out, but I see him relax.

"It's the second week, and there isn't any homework yet. Plus, I'm lonely and need some company."

"What about Greer?"

"You are better company than Greer." A half-joke, which he recognizes. I love spending time with my sister, but she isn't always the best for light conversation. Ash is better at having a brighter outlook on things, and he is a more effective distraction. With Greer, I would just feel the need to obsess over my theories of what happened to Trey, but I can't do that with Ash.

He smiles and relents. "Alright, but I'm picking out the movie."

"Deal."

The Elements were the first abilities to present themselves after the Order was given. The magic within them has the most profound connection to nature itself.

Elementals are made up of four houses: water, earth, air, and fire. Water heals and restores. Earth builds and grows. Air carries and supports. Fire attacks and protects. All four houses require the others for balance within nature.

- Elementals: The Four Houses

CHAPTER 9

"You know what I thought about today?" Trey's hand gently stroked my cheek, and I turned to look at him from where I was lying next to him.

"What?" I asked.

"Our kids. If they will have your hair and freckles, but have my eyes. What their abilities will be. Which grandparent would spoil them the most." The corners of his lips turned up, and I turned to lie on my side and face him. We were under our tree by the lake, lying on an open sleeping bag.

"Definitely my dad," I said, laughing.

He laughed, too, and agreed, "Yeah, I think you're right."

"I want that with you. I want all of it. Things are getting worse out there, though, and I'm scared, Trey. Our training is getting harder, and soon, Dad might start asking Greer to go on real missions. You're already going on dangerous ones. What if he asks me to start going as a Healer? I know it's uncommon, but it could happen."

Panic rose in my chest. Trey pulled me to him and ran his fingers through my hair, his chin resting on top of my head, trying to calm my rapid heart.

"I'm not going to let anything happen to you. I would sell my soul to keep you safe," Trey said soothingly into my hair.

I pulled back, though, and gave him a serious look, "I don't want you selling any part of yourself for me. I want you to stay safe."

"I can't promise that I will always be safe, but I will always do everything I can to get back to you."

"Promise me forever, Trey. Please." My plea sounded pathetic, but I needed to hear it from him because I was so scared to lose him.

"I promise you every breath I take."

He pressed his lips to mine, and I let him erase the worry that threatened to overtake me. Trey and I will do it. We will make it through this together. We have to.

I startle awake and look around. I'm in my bed. Alone. Trey is still somewhere, and me? I'm here. We aren't getting through it together. I wish more than anything that I could close my eyes and emerge back in Trey's arms, back to his memory. I stifle a sob by pressing my face into my pillow.

"Talli?" Greer's groggy voice is soft and comes from the other side of the room.

"I'm okay," I answer weakly.

Her blankets rustle, and I look up to see her standing by the bed. "Move your ass over." Without protest, I do as she says, and she climbs into my bed and gets under the covers.

"We'll figure this out, and I swear, if we find him safe somewhere, I'll kill him," she vows, back facing me.

"No, you won't."

"You're right. I'll hand you my sword so that you can kill him." Her voice is serious, and I don't doubt that she would try.

"That's my sister. Always with my best interest at heart," I say, my tone dripping with sarcasm.

"Goodnight, ungrateful."

"Goodnight, dramatic." With my heart lightened from the bickering and my body a little warmer from her being close, it is enough to fall back asleep.

"Talli, pick up the speed. You're not going to outrun a man coming after you with fire by lightly jogging," Mr. Simon barks at me from where he is sparring with both Greer and Mei-Lien, blocking both of their attacks with ease. How he can pay attention to me and them simultaneously will always be a mystery to me.

I groan as I glance down at the treadmill I am apparently only lightly jogging on and hit the button twice to pick up my speed, appeasing him for the time being.

Today in training, we are focusing on working together when going up against someone. Greer and Mei-Lien are on attack duty while Mr. Simon defends.

Out of the three of us girls, Greer is the strongest fighter; her every move is graceful and fluid. Along with Greer's ability to occasionally sense someone's emotions before they have them, she can also sense someone's movements before they make them. The combination of this ability and her physical deftness makes her lethal and usually unbeatable. The only exception is when her opponent is fighting on muscle memory alone with no thoughts. Mr. Simon being one such opponent.

On the other hand, Mei-Lien Lu is still a strong fighter, better than me, but her movements are precise and methodical. It doesn't take a practiced eye to know that she fights with certain positions and attacks that she knows well, and that's about it.

Mei-Lien is petite, almost a foot shorter than Greer, but what she lacks in height, she makes up for in personality. She is wearing a purple crop top and running shorts to train in today, and I can see from here—on the other side of the large training gym—that the fabric is a shiny spandex that threatens to blind me every time the light hits it just right. Her black hair is pulled up into a tight ponytail, but at the base, it turns into a colorful art exhibit of hair dye. It almost looks like a rainbow pouring out of her head.

I giggle at the thought but quickly stifle it as I almost trip on my own feet in distraction.

My task during training is to practice skills that keep me out of the fight as much as possible during a Brethren attack, such as running or incapacitating an opponent enough so that I *can* run.

Being a Healer, my job is to stay safe so that I can help treat injured people after the battle. It's a job that I am content with, considering I have little hand-eye coordination when it comes to fighting, coupled with impaired balance.

When Mr. Simon first got here, he dragged in one of the balance beams from the elementary school's training gym, which is located at the school instead of the community building where we train. He made me walk back and forth on it for a month straight until I could learn to run without risking a fall.

For Greer and Mei-Lien, they train to fight in an attack and for missions.

All the communities in the country serve a specific purpose that benefits the entire Order. For example, many of the midwestern communities have the primary purpose of growing plants needed for elixirs. Ones that you can't grow in less ideal climates, regardless of magic. Communities closer to cities, like Connecticut and Virginia, have the role of trying to fulfill our given order to influence humans toward the light and weed out the ones with dark intent. They are the only two communities that work predominantly outside their communities, instead holding several positions in the government and in large corporations that allow them to influence decisions that could harm us or nature. The bonus is that their large salaries also help to finance the Order's pricier needs. Texas, Maine, and Oregon all have the purpose of weapons sourcing. They make or obtain weapons we need to protect ourselves. There are numerous purposes, but our system relies on each community for it to work. If one fails, then the rest might fail, too. It is a precarious balance that requires everyone to work together.

Massachusetts has two primary purposes: defensive technology and missions. We used to be the leading community in developing new technology—things like shields, alarms, communication devices, and more—to aid in the Order's defense system. However, recent developments have been lacking since we lost Ash's parents, the Hansens. They were the brains of our operation, without a doubt. California, the other defensive technology community, has been showing us up ever since. Missions, however, are our other purpose. There are four other mission communities—Colorado, Michigan, South Carolina, and Montana—and it is our responsibility to engage in reconnaissance, attack Brethren bases, and provide backup where needed. Essentially, we do the dirty work.

Mr. Simon, Mei-Lien, and Greer stop the exercise long enough for the girls to get some water while Mr. Simon tells them what to fix.

"Mei-Lien, I don't want you to rely on your ability to carry you through a fight, but you need to be better about trying to integrate it."

"I can't use it unless I can touch you, and you're not letting me touch you," she says, her tone dry and bored.

"That's the point. Find ways to touch me and be ready to compel me before I can move again."

Mei-Lien is in the Intelligence classification. Intelligence Officers have abilities that involve mind-manipulation. These abilities can include compelling, memory-seeing, dream-walking, thought-reading, and image-shifting. Intelligence is the smallest classification with the rarest and most sought-after abilities. Memory-seeing, in particular, doesn't even exist anymore and hasn't in a very long time.

Mei-Lien's ability is compelling. She can make someone say or do anything with just a touch. Once she lets go, her control over someone's actions wears off in a few seconds, if not immediately. However, in the last fifty years, the Order learned that the ability can be used to alter memories, and the effects can be permanent if the Hawk is powerful enough. It's been a game-changer for our side of the war.

Her eyes roll, and to my horror, Mr. Simon beckons me over to them. I reluctantly slow my run and turn off the treadmill. Another task of mine, aside from running, is occasionally being a target for Greer and Mei-Lien to utilize when Mr. Simon needs to teach them a lesson. I used to also be a target for Trey, but he had a way of always getting me to come out on top or doing something to embarrass himself instead of me—my true hero. A pang of hurt hits my chest, and I bury it deep down. Not now.

"Talli, would you be so kind as to spar with Mei-Lien? Do your best to avoid letting her touch you," Mr. Simon directs me.

I groan loudly, and Mei-Lien smirks, her angular brown eyes expressing all the things she is going to do to me. She and I both know she will touch me far more than I would ever want or allow her to under normal circumstances.

I nod, though, and take up position on the mat, waiting for Mei-Lien to take up her spot across from me. It's not like I never get any fighting training. It's just that I am not good at it in the least bit. But I grit my teeth and try to be quick when Mr. Simon calls, "Go!"

I leap away from Mei-Lien's lunge and sidestep her, letting her hurtle past me. I spin around to face her and see a wild smile on her face.

"She's trying to scare you, Talli. Focus on your steps," Greer calls out from the bench.

I take a deep breath and throw my arm out to block her from grabbing at my shoulder, but in doing so, I unintentionally give her access to my forearm. She catches it in a vice grip, and immediately my mouth spits out, "I'm a baby chicken that runs from fights." I throw my free hand over my mouth and wrench my captured arm away from her.

"Good. But focus on things that will stop Talli from fighting. Making her insult herself won't get you that far," Mr. Simon reprimands.

We line up and go again. This time, Mei-Lien grabs my side when I try to turn away and she compels me to drop to the ground, which, to my amusement, causes her to tumble down with me. I swiftly regain my footing and scramble away from her, putting the mat between us as she gets back up. Without pause, she runs for me again and switches to a slide at the last second, grabbing my foot, and before I realize what's happening, she's sitting on my back with one finger pressed to the side of my neck. Without control, I blurt out, "I miss my boyfriend who always came to my rescue, but he left me, and now I'm alone and sad."

Rage boils through me, though I'm not surprised that she knows the truth about Trey. Her mom tells her everything. I jerk backward, throwing her off my back. Her shriek of surprise is music to my ears as I spin on my knees and go right for her throat. As soon as I have one hand on her neck and the other on her wrist under me, the urge to squeeze overwhelms me. She needs to learn her lesson. I need to show her that she can't mess with me. I won't tolerate her bullying anymore.

Her heartbeat thrums underneath my thumb, and it's like an electric shock to my system. *God, what am I doing?*

I quickly remove my hand from her neck, but before I can climb off of her, she compels me to let go and run right for the brick wall ten feet behind us. Halfway there, her command in my brain wears off, and I stop before I can face plant into it.

My face feels like it's on fire, and my brain itches from being compelled so many times, but anger still has a hold on me as I turn back to where she is sitting up on the mat.

"Enough." A strong voice booms over the room.

I look over to see Chief Lu standing by the double doors to the training room. Her plain black suit and white shirt are pristinely pressed. Her black hair is chopped into a short bob, making her face appear more narrow. Her bonded Siamese Peninsular Pit Viper, Midori, is wrapped around her right arm, taking up its entire length. His green skin and yellow eyes are an alarming contrast to the muted attire the Chief is wearing. Midori is not often with her. Usually, he spends his time in the forest hunting for meals, but on top of that, seeing a creature such as that might send Ash into hysterics if he became unlucky enough to meet it. Many of the not-commonly-a-house-pet bonded creatures keep their distance during the day to keep up the "average human community" appearance.

Chief Lu looks like she's had a hard day, her usually unrevealing face seeming worn. I turn to Mr. Simon, who also looks tired, and I blow out a long breath, letting the anger go out with it.

Mei-Lien is on her feet and walking over to her bag, which is set down next to the bench opposite the one Greer is still sitting on. She collects the bag and clicks her tongue twice until her bonded fuzzy black cat, Onyx, comes out from behind the racks of weights. The long-haired creature winds herself between Mei-Lien's legs until she bends down and picks her up. Onyx climbs up onto her shoulders and lies down around her neck like a scarf. Her orange-yellow eyes watch me closely as she, Mei-Lien, Chief Lu, and Midori all leave the room.

Something else that makes Mei-Lien completely insufferable is that she bonded with Onyx when she was just three years old, the youngest anyone has bonded in a long time. She is one of the few in school who has one, and she ensures that no one forgets it. Bonds usually happen any time after a Hawk goes through puberty, whether it's at the age of fourteen or forty. Dad really thought Greer or I would have one by now, considering our bloodlines, but we still haven't been fortunate enough.

Greer slaps her hands down on her knees, jolting both Mr. Simon and me out of being mutually frozen by the situation. "That was entertaining," she announces a little too loudly.

"My brain itches," I complain out loud and drop myself next to her on the bench. Mr. Simon looks like he doesn't know what to say.

After a long awkward moment, he finally says, "Let's call it a night."

"I agree. I have a date with some pizza and garlic bread I'm eager to get to," Dad says, his light tone coming from where Chief Lu was standing only moments before. Melisandre, his bonded panther, stands at his side looking at us all, an amused gleam in her eyes. Just like that, everyone relaxes. I guess tonight is the night for all the bonded creatures to be out.

Greer and I start collecting our stuff.

"Simon, care to join us tonight? Plenty of bread to go around," Dad offers.

"Thanks, Aaron, but I have some plans tonight," Mr. Simon responds, his tired demeanor lightening almost instantly. Seth trots over from his sleeping spot, giving Melisandre a show of his teeth as he stands next to Mr. Simon. Melisandre lifts one paw to her mouth and starts cleaning it. Their coats are nearly the same shade of tan, which seems almost wrong considering how opposite they are from one another.

"Plans? That sounds mysterious," Dad jokes.

"Ms. Trisha is coming this weekend," I answer conspiratorially, and the tip of Mr. Simon's nose turns pink. Ms. Trisha is a Healer from the New Hampshire community and is a close friend of Mr. Simon's. Very close friend.

"Trisha Garner? You two back at it again?" Dad prods, a large grin spreading across his face.

"Well, yes...Well, no...Well, I'm not sure." Mr. Simon is rarely nervous about anything, so to see him worked up over a lady friend lightens my own heavy heart.

Dad puts a hand on his shoulder and says, "Life's too short, and war is too long, my friend." Mr. Simon nods back at him, and with that, we head home.

CHAPTER 10

PIZZA AND GARLIC BREAD sufficiently consumed, Greer and I are both at our desks in our bedroom. She is painting, and I am doing what we both should be doing: homework.

My stomach feels so full that it's an effort to move, but I am grateful for the carbs filling up the pit I was feeling in my stomach after the fight with Mei-Lien.

Our community has one small pizza shop, *Elemental Pizza*. It's owned by Mr. and Mrs. Korpela, who are both Elementals, fire and air, respectively. Together, they make a great team, creating the best wood-fired pizza.

As casually as asking me to pass her some water, Greer says, "She beat you tonight."

I scoff at the unnecessary observation. "In case you haven't noticed, she always beats me on the sparring mat."

"I mean, she knows how to strike a nerve in people, but she really got to you tonight. I've never seen you go rage-monster before." She looks up from her painting notebook and pins me with a look. One that I am very uncomfortable receiving.

"She was being a bitch." My excuse is weak, but I use it anyway.

"She is always being a bitch. That's her nature. Just like it's your nature to brush her off. I'm usually the one you have to bring down from rage-monster mode," Greer points out.

Greer and I have never been able to truly figure out exactly why we are always Mei-Lien's primary targets. She bullies half the school with an "I'm better than you" mentality, but when it comes to Greer and me, it's like we are her sworn rivals. We can only assume it's because Greer is better on the mat, and I'm always chosen for leadership roles over her at school. I can't help it if people like me better. Well, actually, I can. I am a hell of a lot nicer to everyone than she is. Mom always told me that the simple act of being kind gets you a lot further with people than anything else ever could.

I hunch my shoulders over my desk, feeling very defensive at the moment. "I'm allowed to have bad days, too. Even if it's not in my nature to have them. She also seems to be targeting me more than you recently, so give me a break."

"Now that you mention it, she is shifting more focus on you. Maybe you're just becoming an easier target." I scowl at her, and she quickly continues, "But! I'm not saying you're not allowed to have bad days. I'm saying that I didn't recognize you today. You went dark, and it scared me a little." She pauses and waits for me to process.

Dark? That's being dramatic. I was upset, and Mei-Lien was pushing me. I wouldn't have actually strangled her or hurt her beyond easy repair, anyway.

When I choose not to respond, Greer adds with a hint of her bland humor, "The rage seemed to focus you. I thought you might make a decent fighter for a minute there. If you learned to use it to your advantage."

"Know of any good classes for that? How to Use Your Rage-Monster 101, perhaps?"

The corner of her mouth kicks up. "I'll let you know if I hear of one."

I nod and go back to staring at my English homework.

After a handful of heartbeats, I say, "It would be nice, though." She raises one thin black eyebrow at me in question. "To not have to run. To be able to fight. To not be useless where it counts."

"You are Talliana Hoffman. There is absolutely nothing useless about you. You are the one person I would want to bring into a fight with me because you are the one person who could patch me up better than anyone else. You are a badass at healing, and if it came down to skill at using your ability, you would wipe Mei-Lien off the mat."

"Thanks, Greer." My voice is softer now. I do start to feel a little better with my sister's reassurance, but I am anxious to turn the attention away from me. Greer's and my desks are not side-by-side, but on different sides of the same wall with the closet in between. I stretch my neck up, trying to peek at what she's painting. I wrinkle my nose in confusion at all the gray I see on the page. "Whatcha painting?"

"I'm not sure," she says, eyeing the paper in front of her like a puzzle.

I stand up from my chair and walk over to her desk, peering over her shoulder at the gray blobs. "I'm not sure either," I say, and she laughs, the loosely tied bun on her head bobbing with it.

"Anything inspire it?" I ask.

"I don't know. It feels like something I've seen or am going to see." She picks up the notebook and turns it on its side, looking at it with a tilted head. "Maybe it's something I feel or will feel. Maybe it's an emotion?"

Greer's confusion at her painting has goosebumps running down my back. This isn't the first time Greer has painted something with no explanation as to what it is or what it's for. Usually, the images are a lot clearer, though, and easier to figure out.

She's been drawing and painting since she came here and it seems to be another way her foresight abilities manifest, painting future images or feelings. Outside of Elementals who can manipulate their element in many ways, Hawks from the other three classifications can rarely use their ability in different ways like Greer can. But foresight is so strong in her bloodline that most of them are born with it, and when they are, it is unmatched compared to anyone else with that same ability.

I squint my eyes a little at the image and decide, "It almost looks like smoke."

"You're right!"

I watch as she adds more gray paint with long, precise strokes, and then she holds it up again for both of us to examine. "They are shadows blocking out the moon." Her tone is certain now and I am relieved that we figured it out quickly, but I am also concerned about what it could mean.

"That sounds...umm...not like a good thing," I stumble through my thoughts out loud.

"No, it's not meant to be bad. It feels good to me. Like they are helping in a way."

"Helping what?"

"I don't know."

A wall made of shadow erects before me, blocking out my access to the lake.

To water.

To safety.

I spin around to face the fire at my back—fire that is consuming the forest. I feel the heat of it on my cheeks, threatening to burn me. I cry out for help, but the roar of the fire drowns out my voice.

"Someone, please!" I cry again, and the shadow shifts behind me.

Turning around, I see a small hole in the middle of its massive wall, which gives me a tiny glimpse of the water beyond. I race toward it, and without hesitation, I claw at the hole, trying to make it bigger. It eventually gives way, crumbling away like dirt and then evaporating like smoke as it falls. I scramble through it. Falling out on the other side and right into the lake, water closes over my head and fills up my lungs. I start to choke and convulse until something grabs me and pulls me above the water. I cough and spit out the water in my lungs, then splash around trying to find what grabbed me, but nothing is there.

"Talli!" I hear a scream. One I can't place. I turn back toward the shadow-wall and see through the now much wider hole Trey, Greer, Ash, Mom, and Dad on the other side with the fire raging behind them.

"Come through the hole!" I cry out to them, but no one hears me. No one is doing anything. I fight the current, trying to get to them, but there isn't enough time. The fire will get to them first.

"Someone save them!" I scream.

The shadow moves, changes shape, and then it encircles them. Fear grips my heart. The shadow is going to hurt them. I work harder to push through the water, but I make no progress to reach them.

The shadow lifts them into the air and takes them away from the danger.

"They are helping in a way." The words echo around me—Greer's words.

The shadow is saving them from the fire. The relief is short-lived, though, as I watch the fire move closer to me. It is impossible, but it dances over the water. Taking a deep breath, I smell gasoline and look down. I'm not in water anymore, but in an inky-black liquid. Changing directions, I try to swim through it, but it's like trying to move through thick mud. My efforts are futile. There is no escape. The shadow that was trying to save me saved everyone I love instead when I asked it to.

I stop fighting. It's either drown in whatever this is or let the fire take me. I fully relax my body. Without a doubt, I know my choice. I won't let the fire have the last laugh. At least I can die knowing everyone is safe.

I take one last breath, and as I exhale, my body sinks, and everything goes dark.

WE HAVE STARTED INSTRUCTION TO TEACH THOSE IN OUR COMMUNITY HOW TO BUILD A SHIELD IN THEIR MINDS FROM ONE ANOTHER. IT HAS BECOME APPARENT HOW MANY ARE MISUSING THEIR ABILITIES, TREATING NEIGHBORS LIKE ENEMIES BY INVADING THE PRIVACY OF THEIR THOUGHTS AND FEELINGS. THIS CANNOT CONTINUE.

- JOURNAL OF BERTRAM MEYER

CHAPTER 11

"TALLI, DO YOU KNOW why you are here?" Ms. Horn asks.

"If I had to guess, I would say it's because Mr. Simon is a snitch."

She scoffs. "He's your teacher, your trainer, and someone who cares very much about you."

I know it's all true. I am here because Mr. Simon is concerned about my control and mental shielding. Valid concerns, really; it's just embarrassing nevertheless.

After school today, he quietly asked me to come with him and brought me to Ms. Horn's classroom. I'll give him credit, though, he did it so quietly that no one else in the school should ever know I was here except for Greer when I tell her later.

Ms. Horn is a young Hawk with a self-chosen Intelligence classification and is our community expert on shielding. She may not have a unique ability or a bonded creature, but I have heard about how good she is at shielding.

She mostly works with our elementary school-aged kids, posing as a language arts teacher as she teaches them how to control their emotions and build mental shields. Something vital before they come into any real abilities. That being said, someone should not be brought back to her after they pass her class as a small child. I've heard of the occasional kid coming back to see her while going through puberty—which I think is reasonable, all things considered—but never at my age. Especially not the child of an elder. I never actually had her as my teacher since she is only in her late twenties, but I feel the same sentiment, considering this is still the same classroom I learned how to shield in from her predecessor.

"There is nothing to be embarrassed about. I think all you need is some reminders, and you'll never have to see this classroom again," Ms. Horn reassures me as she swiftly pulls her golden-blonde hair into a loose bun. That act alone of her putting her hair up makes me want to run for the hills. If she's getting prepared for hard work, I might as well settle in because it's about to be a long afternoon.

"Now, let's talk about the situations where you felt a little emotionally charged. Tell me, what happened to make you feel that way?"

"Well, Mei-Lien was intentionally pushing my buttons, and that pissed me off."

"Ah." She plops down on the rug across from me. It is bright and colorful with lots of different animals depicted on it. I am currently sitting on top of a lion and she just sat down on a polar bear.

"I went to high school with her older brother, Jasper. He was...I don't like the word because I know it's not technically accurate, but he was perfect. He was always the best at everything. Fighting, school, missions. Everyone loved him and from what I hear, nothing has changed. He is still the super-popular guy who is well on his way to becoming an elder for the Maryland community one day."

My face must indicate how hard I am trying to see her point, so she continues, "My point is, could you imagine growing up in that kind of shadow? She must feel like she has a lot to prove and you and Greer do have a tendency to excel more than most." Her use of the word "shadow" makes the hair on my arms stand up, but I quickly rub them to rid myself of the sensation.

I guess Greer and I were right, though, about Mei-Lien. She is threatened by us and is cruel to us to try to bring us down a level or two—classic mean girl behavior. I've seen it in a hundred movies and read it in some books, too.

"Just some food for thought. Now, back to our lesson. Anything else making you feel emotional?" she asks.

"Besides our entire existence? The war? Constantly worrying about the roof over my head burning down?"

Her lips curve in the corner. "Yes, besides all of that."

Sighing, I answer, "I don't know. Everything was fine, but then Trey left, and nothing feels right anymore."

"Right, I heard about his transfer to the Virginia community. That has to be hard, losing your first love like that." Her words jar me a bit and then I remember that she doesn't know the truth. Only a few do.

"Yes," I say between clenched teeth. "He was supposed to stay here but changed his mind at the last minute and just...left," I explain.

"Are you two..."

"Let's talk about shielding, please," I beg her. I really don't want to talk to her about Trey. She won't understand, and I don't know her all that well, either. I just want to get whatever this is over with.

"Yes, of course. I didn't mean to make you feel uncomfortable, I was only trying to get a sense of where you are emotionally so that we could get to the root of why you're having trouble shielding." She straightens her back and starts her lesson, "What kind of method do you use for your shield?"

"Static," I answer.

"What? Oh, the Hoffman analogy." She laughs. "I have heard your dad explain it that way before. Really, we call it the paper bag method because you're essentially throwing a paper bag over your emotions. It's an easy method that most people adopt, and it also doesn't take much concentration to maintain. However, as easily as you can throw it on, it can be blown away. The paper bag muffles your emotions well enough, but if you become too focused on a certain emotion, it can still filter through. That's why when you were feeling really angry or sad, Simon could still sense your emotions."

"Okay, all that I understand, but how do I keep it from faltering even if I become focused?" I ask.

"The only thing you can do is try not to focus on specific emotions when you are around others. Only allow yourself that kind of thing when you are alone."

My brows crease, trying to think through how to be more conscious of when I start to focus.

Ms. Horn then offers, "I can teach you how to be more self-aware, or I can teach you the brick method."

"Healers don't normally learn that method," I argue, even though the idea of it is appealing.

"There are no actual rules for who learns what. There are only norms based on what a Hawk does for the community. If you want to learn something new, you can be taught."

"What would it take if I wanted to learn?"

"Not as much as you would think. I'll teach you how to build your foundation, and from there, you have to put in the effort to lay the bricks down until you have a beautifully built wall. Then you'd return, and I'd test it for weak spots. Or I'm sure Greer could even help if you're more comfortable with that."

It'll be hard work. I know it will be, but the benefits could be worth it. Worst case, I am terrible at it, and nothing but time is lost.

"Alright, where do we start?" I ask.

Ms. Horn beams, jumps to her feet, and goes to her chalkboard. She literally makes a drawing of bricks lined up in a row and says, "We start by learning how to visualize your first brick."

Feeling mentally dead, I leave Ms. Horn's classroom. After we finished practicing building my shield, she mentioned teaching me how to use my "inner eye" to see shields as well as emotions inside a person's mind, instead of just relying on feeling alone. I have no idea what any of that means, but I nodded nonetheless, not wanting to ask for an explanation and be stuck there any longer.

Walking out of the entrance of the school, I see Mr. Simon and Seth waiting for me on the steps. "Have you been waiting all this time to say you're sorry for putting me through that?" I ask.

He stands and slowly turns around to face me, "You look un-harmed, so I believe no apology is necessary."

"Get an MRI scan of my brain, and then you would believe otherwise," I reply dryly.

Mr. Simon chuckles. "I'm sure I would, but it's good for you. Stronger shields will serve you well."

I nod. He is right, and I am grateful, but I don't feel like admitting that to him at the moment. All the positivity, grace, and kindness Mom has taught me to approach life with feel like distant characteristics of myself that I can't reach right now.

"Why are you waiting for me?"

"I wanted to see you home safe after dark, and I also wanted to talk to you about something," he explains.

Reluctantly, I fall into step beside him as we head toward my house. The street lights illuminate our path well enough, and there are still a few people out and about, but it feels like we are alone on the streets. I always feel safe being out by the lake in the dark, but being out on the street walking at night has never been comfortable for me. I can never stop my brain from conjuring up all the different places the Brethren could be hiding out here.

Mr. Simon doesn't wait long before he says, "I want you to prepare yourself for the possibility that we don't find him."

I stop mid-step and look at him. Mr. Simon wouldn't be saying this unless he was almost certain we wouldn't find him. My pulse thrums loudly in my ears.

"Why?" I ask slowly.

Mr. Simon stops as well. "The elders have had the Order's best trackers out looking for him, and no one can pick up his scent anywhere. It's been just over a month since he left, and we should have something by now."

"What are you not saying?"

He sighs. "They called off the search tonight."

"What?!" My heart goes from a rapid beat to not beating at all.

"There is still an alert out at all the communities to watch for him, but they can't keep using essential resources to turn over every single stone for someone who left a note saying they left of their own accord."

My body goes rigid in defense. "There has to be more to it than that!" I shout at him. "How does someone go from actively trying to build a future here one moment to just abandoning it the next? How can he talk to me the night before about *our* future and then leave me like that? With no explanation or more than a worthless note saying he was sorry for ripping my heart out?"

A sob escapes my lips, and I press my hand to my mouth. Mr. Simon grabs my shoulders, and I feel Seth brush against my leg.

"I'm not telling you to give up hope altogether, okay? But you know that I am just trying to be realistic with you. He could still turn up, and I pray to the Great Hawk that he will, but you need to know what's going on. I fear that not everyone here gives you enough credit for how strong you are."

I look up at Mr. Simon, tears still brimming my eyes. I know he is here saying all of this out of love and concern for my well-being, but it hurts. The truth hurts, and I'm afraid it will never not hurt. That's his specialty, though. As a walking, talking lie detector, Mr. Simon knows the cost of a lie more than most. But despite his truth, I also know my truth—that what I feel inside is real, that Trey is out there, and that I will see him again.

Calming myself the best I can, I say, "I appreciate you telling me, but I know we'll find him again. There isn't any other option. I simply won't accept it."

Mr. Simon releases my shoulders and replies, "I hope you're right."

He offers a sad smile, and we continue our walk in silence.

CHAPTER 12

October

I CAN'T BREATHE. I can't breathe.

I quietly but quickly get out of bed and pull on my red sweatpants and sweatshirt. My boots go on next, and I tiptoe out of the bedroom to not wake Greer. I climb down the stairs and go out the backdoor. The chill of the night slams into me, and suddenly, I can breathe again. I take two deep breaths, but my heart is still racing. It was that dream again with the shadow, the fire, and the black liquid that took me in the end. It keeps plaguing me, and I feel like no matter what I do, I can't change the ending.

I follow the pull of my intuition and run to the lake. Run to our tree. I should have put on a heavier coat. It's only late October, but it feels below-freezing right now. That's unusual.

I push the thought away—such a pointless concern. I don't stop or slow my pace until I'm face-to-face with the lake, our tree at my back. I squint in the light fog, looking for a sign of something, anything. After ten heartbeats of nothing but still water, I slump to my knees on the small bank that rises about a foot away from the shallow part of the lake below.

Falling forward, I place my hands into the dirt. It's hard and cold from the temperature. I try to dig in with my nails, but it doesn't budge. I lean forward so that my face hovers over the water and search for my reflection, but there is a small layer of ice there. I reach out my hand to touch it, and the instant my pointer finger touches the ice, it disappears, and the water ripples.

Looking up in shock, I see the ripple running down the lake in a big semi-circle, the ice melting where it hits. As soon as the ripple is out of sight, I'm knocked over by a pain in my head. It is like being struck by a blinding light, the sting radiating from behind my eyes. The wind that was still only a moment ago blows viciously, catching my hair and throwing it into my face.

A scream echoes in the distance, one full of pain.

A sharp sting hits my leg. I brush the hair out of my face and examine it, but nothing is there. My leg is fine and doesn't hurt anymore. Neither does my head.

I sit up from where I was sprawled on my back, and the scream rings out again. I focus on it, biting back the tears as I take an invisible blow to my stomach. The scream is from a deeper voice, a man's voice. "Go on! Hit me again!" the voice says, and everything inside of me halts at the sound.

It's Trey's voice. I know, without a doubt. I look around fruitlessly, knowing he isn't here. He isn't anywhere near here. How am I hearing him right now? How am I feeling what must be his pain?

Icy fear and sorrow builds within me. I don't understand. I don't understand at all.

"Trey," I lightly breathe his name, letting the wind carry it. Drawing my knees up to my chest, I start to cry. Something cold touches my nose, and I realize snow is gently falling around me. This is hopeless. I will never see him again. He is out there hurt, and I'm here, doing nothing.

"I'm so sorry. Please hold on. I'll find you," I whisper and let the wind take those words, too. If I can hear him, maybe he can hear me.

I look out at the lake again when the next scream sounds. My eyes catch something on the ground about a yard away from me. A lizard staring at me.

The color of its scales is so unusual. They are a blue-purple color. A bright shade of indigo, if I had to guess. Its head is tilted to the side like it is studying me. I search my memory to see if I know of any blue lizards, but I come up empty. I'm sure some exist, just not in Massachusetts. It has to be about ten inches long from the tip of its nose to the end of its tail.

Another scream startles me out of concentration. The lizard moves its head out toward the lake at the sound.

"Do you hear it too?" I ask the little thing.

It blinks at me in response. I take that to mean yes.

"Where do you think it's coming from? I know who owns the voice, but I know he is not here."

It blinks at me again and runs its leg over its head, like a cat trying to clean itself. I gape at it, and it does it again. I realize now what it's saying, "My head? The sound is coming from my head?"

It blinks again. Yes.

"So, either my ability is changing to something that's not possible, or I'm going crazy."

It blinks again. Well, that's unhelpful. I sigh right before another scream sounds, and pain runs up my arm.

I clench my teeth at the brief throb and ask the lizard, "Will you keep me company for a while? Unless you have somewhere else to be, of course."

The lizard comes closer and lies down next to me.

"Thank you," I say, my gratitude barely a whisper as I close my eyes.

I stay sitting in the snow with my lizard friend and don't move until Trey's screams no longer echo in my head.

When I get up the next morning, it's no surprise that I am sick. I don't know how long I was outside last night, but long enough that my immune system couldn't handle it. I had closed my eyes for a while, and when I opened them, the lizard was gone. Probably to find a warmer spot.

I stumble downstairs and start rifling through our cabinet full of elixirs. It's barely a minute before I hear Mom behind me ask, "What's wrong?" with worry lacing her tone.

Not stopping my search, I answer over my shoulder, "It's just a cold."

"Let me look." I step out of the way, and Mom reaches in and immediately finds the vial I was looking for labeled "Common Cold." She gives me a critical eye, then nods after a moment and hands it to me to drink.

I down it in two quick gulps and hand it back to her. Before I can move, "Back into bed," Mom announces. "You're taking the day off."

"I'll be fine." I try to move past her, but her glare stops me.

"Just because your cold will be gone in a few moments doesn't mean you can't take a day to lie in bed and rest."

I open my mouth to argue but smartly shut it. Resting isn't a bad idea, especially when I feel I have no mental capacity for school anyway. "Alright."

"I think I'll call into work and play hooky, too. Get into bed, and I'll bring up some cinnamon rolls in a few minutes."

I give her a big smile, then head back up the stairs. Cinnamon rolls are my favorite. Mom's ability to know precisely what would make me feel better makes me the luckiest daughter in the world.

I climb back into bed and focus on the feel of the elixir working its way through my veins, the magic clearing out the virus and boosting my white blood cells to help them expel the sickness from my body almost immediately. The elixirs we make aren't all that different from normal pharmaceuticals, but the magic we infuse into our ingredients boosts them so that they work way faster and more efficiently.

When my body feels better, Mom comes into the room with a tray of cinnamon rolls, orange juice, and a tablet.

Sitting up, I accept the food tray, holding it up so Mom can climb in bed next to me. She grabs the tablet and turns on a true crime show, propping it up so we can watch it while we eat in my bed. I crinkle my nose. Greer likes these shows better than I do, but my usual romantic comedy pick makes my stomach turn at the thought. So, I don't argue.

I let about half an hour of an episode go by in silence, enjoying Mom's comfort, until I finally break it. "Mom?"

"Yes?"

"Have you ever heard of someone being able to hear another person from far away? Like really far away?"

"Hmm...Someone can get heightened hearing from their bonded if they are a creature that has that ability already. I think a mile is the farthest recorded, though."

"Do you think lizards can hear well?"

Mom laughs and replies, "Talli, I am a people nurse, not a reptile nurse. If I had to guess, I would say no, since they don't have any outer ears like dogs, but I honestly have no clue. What is this all about?"

Her eyes are soft, but I feel them on me, and it makes me feel a bit self-conscious. She pauses the show on the tablet, and I squirm in my spot for a minute, trying to get comfortable.

"I don't know. I thought I heard Trey last night down by the lake..." I cut myself off before I go further, but Mom feels the missing words. "And?" she asks.

"And...I heard his screams." Urgency fills me as everything that happened last night hits me in full force. "Mom, I felt his pain. Only for a few moments, but I felt it like it was happening to me. Someone was hurting him."

Mom's eyes are wide. I can tell she is alarmed by what I am saying. However, her shock turns to sadness before she tells me, "This has happened before. When you and Greer were little and she would get hurt, sometimes you would come up to me and complain of the same thing hurting. Honestly, back then, I figured it was either sympathy pains or that you wanted the attention, too. I never really knew which."

I open my mouth to protest, but she holds up her hand to stop me. "Now, I'm not saying I don't believe that you felt what you say you did last night, and it is possible that your abilities may be making you feel the residual effect of someone in severe pain if you're focused enough on them, but from someone not close by? We don't even know where Treyton is. It is likely your worry over him being in pain could have played tricks on your mind. It was also snowing, and extreme temperatures can cause people to hallucinate. Maynard was probably messing around with his ability last night." Maynard, a ten-year-old in the community, recently came into his Water Elemental ability, which allows him to control clouds. Rain and snow clouds mostly.

"It wasn't that cold, Mom."

"Cold enough to make you sick," she points out. She takes a deep breath and then says, "Talli, I know you've been worried about him. We all have. But it's been two months. I think you should be focusing on that slipping English grade and spending time with friends. Enjoy your senior year, because I can only hold the elders off for so long before they start using you girls for missions, especially now that Treyton is gone. It's coming, Talliana, and I want you to enjoy as much of your youth for as long as possible."

"But I'm just a Healer. I'm not a fighter. I'm supposed to run from danger, not be going on missions," I argue.

"My sweet girl, I wish it were that simple. Our numbers are depleting, our people are weakening, and we can't defend ourselves like we used to. If we don't find an edge to end this war soon, everyone will be fighting for survival alone."

"What do you mean?"

Mom exhales a long breath and explains, "There have been discussions about dismantling the communities and integrating ourselves fully with the outside world."

I reel back at that, even though the line of thinking makes sense. The communities make us a target, being all in one place. Easy to find. But if we were to spread out, we would have to hide who we are daily, have no safe place to be ourselves, and constantly look over our shoulders for danger. We would be on our own.

"Do we have a timeline?" I ask.

"They are saying five years right now, but anything could change that at any time."

The hairs on my arms rise, and goosebumps spread over my body.

Mom continues, "I'm not telling you this to scare you. I just want you to understand what's going on and be prepared. Okay?"

"I know."

Mom kisses me on the head, and with a, "get some rest," she grabs the empty tray of food and leaves me alone in my room.

CHAPTER 13

GREER STROLLS INTO THE bedroom and drops a notebook on the bed beside me. I decided not to move from my bed all day, and I almost devoured an entire book from my "to-be-read" shelf. I needed a distraction to keep my mind off it all. Losing myself in a world where Brethren and house fires don't exist was perfect. I put my bookmark in and close it, setting it on my side table. Greer pulls off her hoodie and plops herself down on her bed.

"Notes?" I ask, referring to the notebook next to me. I don't bother opening it or touching it.

"Yeah. You didn't miss much. There's a test in Psychology next Tuesday and a paper coming up in English next Friday."

"Thanks, Greer."

"Don't mention it." She picks her head up and studies me. "Mental health day?" I told Greer to head to school without me this morning and that I would catch up. Then later, I texted her and told her I would be home so she wouldn't worry.

"Something like that. I need to talk to you, though," I tell her, trying not to sound as solemn as I feel.

She turns onto her side and props her head up with her fist, indicating I have her full attention. I tell her all of it. What I experienced last night and what Mom said to me today. By the time I'm done, she is cross-legged at the end of her bed with a crease between her brows.

"Do you think that lizard could be your bonded?" she asks.

"No, it didn't talk to me. If it was shopping around for someone to bond with, it clearly didn't find me up to its scaly standards." Bonded creatures always talk to their selected bonded human in their mind when they choose to bond with them. Any creature capable of bonding can understand what humans are saying around them, so the fact that it understood me is not abnormal.

"Yeah, you're probably right. About what you felt, though, our history books tell us that there were Healers that had water abilities. They were very rare, and we haven't seen any in a couple of centuries. But maybe that magical connection is rooted in your blood, and the lake enhanced your ability like, tenfold. Also, since you and Trey have a deep connection, you could sense his pain even though you weren't touching him and far away. How far, who knows, but arguably I doubt he could be that far," she suggests.

My cheeks heat a little at the word "deep." When Order members have sex with one another, it forms a connection to that person, like a heightened awareness. Continual sex makes the connection even stronger. If the relationship ends or someone dies, then it does eventually fade, but it's painful. It's like the connection puts you on a level deeper than love. Because of this, having sex before marriage in the community is not a "don't do it" rule, but it is frowned upon to try to save immature teenagers some unnecessary pain. Intimate relationships between our people and humans, though, don't form any connection. That makes it much more appealing to some and unappealing to others.

"We umm...We haven't, though. Not yet," I admit quietly.

"Oh." Greer swallows. "Sorry, I just assumed...I guess I can't be peeved anymore that you didn't tell me."

I laugh. Of course, she would be upset that I didn't tell her. I would be upset if she didn't tell me if the roles were reversed. "Nope, guess you can't be."

We both laugh.

"I guess that means my theory is no good," she says with a defeated tone.

"Maybe Mom is right, and I was hallucinating. It seems like the more logical explanation."

"No, I don't buy it. Come get me next time it happens, and we'll figure it out together."

I nod, but I hope with every cell in my body that it won't happen again. I move on to the last subject. "What do you think about what Mom said? About everything."

Greer sighs. "I wish I was surprised."

"What do you mean?"

"They keep us updated in our Strategist class. Current mission successes and failures, attacks on the communities, any intel gained, etc. I don't agree with the idea completely, but it makes sense as a worst-case scenario plan," she explains.

"Why don't they share that kind of information with all of us? Shouldn't we all know what's going on?" I ask incredulously.

"They should, I agree. But I think they don't share with everyone to avoid panic. We are losing, Talli," she admits grimly.

"I gathered as much."

We fall silent for a while, thinking about what could be in our future. It doesn't look bright, that is for sure. I don't know what happened to me last night or what any of it could mean. Trey could be in danger, or he could be perfectly safe somewhere, living a new life. Either way, I need to focus on being better, stronger, and smarter so that if I see him again one day, I'll be better prepared to survive what's coming. Survive so that I can have a future with him, as much of one as possible, anyway.

"Want to go train with me?" I ask suddenly.

Greer whips her head to me. "Really? *You* want to train?"

"I know I'll never be great at fighting, but I want to be better," I say resolutely.

She smiles at me, a full grin, and says, "Greer's school of 'How to Be a Badass' is not going to be easy to graduate from."

"Do you have a school for 'How to Not Be Killed Within a Minute' instead? That would be a little more achievable."

"Nope! Don't worry, though, I'll enroll you in the beginner class first." She jumps to her feet and grabs her matching black training outfit.

"What's in the beginner class?" I call after her as she reaches the bathroom to change.

"Strength training. We need to put some muscle on those bones." She answers through the door.

"I have muscles," I argue defensively. We already do strength training with Mr. Simon, so I'm not weak. I have to be able to help carry injured people as needed, as all Healers do, which requires strength.

"Not enough," Greer replies simply. She walks out of the bathroom and I trade places with her, getting dressed in my own training outfit.

I braid my hair to lay over my shoulder, adding an aqua blue hair tie to match my blue outfit.

We walk outside and I reach for Mom's car keys in my pocket.

"Nope. We are jogging to the community building," Greer informs me with a grin.

I roll my eyes and put the keys back into the small pocket of my thin jacket. I already regret this.

Okay, now I *really* regret it. Greer and I sluggishly amble back to the house after two hours of torture. Me because everything hurts, and she because she doesn't want to leave me alone in case I collapse on the way home. Our training gym was a bit more crowded than usual, but I'm used to sharing it with a few people. It wasn't our night to train, but the Earth Elementals were happy to share since we took up little space.

"Hey!" Ash calls out, waving from his seat on the porch steps as we walk by his house. He tucks the book he is reading into his backpack next to him and sets it aside.

Greer pivots and heads toward Ash, practically bouncing down the sidewalk in her not-so-obvious way. She has a reputation as the cool, moody one to uphold, of course. I groan and slowly make my way over there.

Ash eyes me wearily and asks, "What happened to you, Talli?"

I drop, taking a seat next to him on the step, and lean into him, resting my head on his shoulder. He laughs and puts his arm around me, Greer on his other side, leaning her back against the handrail a step below us.

"I need to lose a few pounds for prom," I answer, huffing from being out of breath.

That makes him laugh harder, his body jiggling my sore muscles. I groan. He looks at Greer. "I suppose you're responsible?" His tone is full of playful accusation.

"I did what she asked." Greer shrugs.

Ash looks down at me. I can tell by his movements alone since my eyes are closed. He says softly, "Talli, you know you are perfect the way you are, right?"

"Yeah, yeah. But there is nothing wrong with wanting to shed a couple of pounds." I brush off his remark, as sweet as it is.

"Isn't it a bit early to be worrying about that anyway? We aren't even halfway through the school year yet," Ash points out. I hate how smart he is sometimes.

"You can never start too early," I reply as I grow more uncomfortable with all this lying to him. I try to avoid it as much as possible, but it's become second nature at this point. Straightening myself, I stand up, groaning the entire time.

"I stink and need to jump in the shower. See you later, Ash?" I ask, slowly walking down the two stairs, wincing at each step.

Ash nods, and Greer says, "I'll catch up with you later, Talli. I'm going to hang back for a bit if that's okay?" She looks to Ash. He smiles at her in a clear "yes," and I walk the rest of the way home alone. So much for her saying she was going to make sure I didn't die on the way home.

I scoff at the air and wonder how much more of Greer's training I can take. The first few days are always the worst, I remind myself. I have to be strong. I have to do this. My back straightens with the return of my determination. For Trey.

All members of the Order are masters of emotion, not slaves of it. We cannot allow emotions to cloud our judgment or guide our actions. In doing so, we lose ourselves to our abilities. We will be unable to control ourselves and will become no better than those whom we have sworn to fight against—worse even.

- The Laws of Magic

CHAPTER 14

November

"Sarah, order the deep-blue tablecloths, not the navy, please. Oh, and I'll grab the colored paper this weekend so we can start making the sea life that will be hanging from the ceiling," I say to the small girl beside me and then to the room of classmates.

"Noted," Sarah responds as she writes the information in her notebook.

"Anything else we need to discuss?" I ask the room.

I get a resounding, "nope," and then say, "Alright, thanks, everyone. Let's make this the best prom ever."

The five other people in the room all shuffle to pick up their stuff, and with a few goodbyes, I'm by myself organizing the last of the plans we have finished making for prom. I'm the head of the Prom Planning Committee this year, and despite everything going on, this is the one thing I have looked forward to every week.

Each year, our school picks a different nature-inspired theme, such as Enchanted Rainforest, Strolling through the Sahara, A Long Walk on the Beach, and last year's, Snow-Capped Mountains. This year's theme, though, I am personally very pleased with: Under the Moonlit Ocean.

Along with the obvious—covering everything in deep-blue shades—we are mainly focusing on bioluminescent creatures. There will be a giant light-up octopus and brightly colored fish hanging from the ceiling, as well as neon accents to make it fun and unique. I'm so excited to see how it will all come together on prom night, even if I won't have a date. Well, am unlikely to have a date.

I haven't given up on Trey, but my hope is slowly fading. I went to Dad with what happened by the lake, as well, and got a similar response to the one I got from Mom. He did promise to look into the possible new ability of feeling people's pain from far away, but he didn't sound hopeful that he would find anything. I didn't feel hopeful that he would, either. He didn't mention anything about the search for Trey being called off; he only said he would take everything into consideration with Trey's disappearance. I didn't mention what Mr. Simon told me, either.

A knock sounds on the open door, and I turn my head to see Greer and Ash standing in the doorway.

"Ready for our mall trip?" Ash asks.

"Yep! So ready!" I reply as I stuff the rest of the scattered plan into my purple backpack. I zip it up and follow them out the door to Mom's car. Greer decides she will drive today, and Ash hops into the backseat while I get into the front seat.

We don't have a mall or stores—aside from the grocery store—directly in our community, so we have to drive to the next town over to get any shopping done. It's not a far drive, but forty-five minutes one way isn't close either.

It's the middle of November and Thanksgiving is just around the corner, so we are going to get a little Christmas shopping started. I love going shopping, especially when it's for buying presents, and even more so when I have a list ready.

"I'm going to beat Talli this year in giving the best gifts for Christmas," Ash claims from the back. His tone sounds overly confident, and it makes me laugh.

Greer laughs, too, and comments, "Impossible. No one out-gifts Talli."

"You both know that is not the point of gift-giving, right?" I scold, but I can't contain the smile on my face. The trick to giving the best gifts is being observant. I pay close attention to the things that my friends and family use often and determine what they might need or want based on that. It's not that complicated.

"You just say that because you're so good at it," Ash retorts.

"I always love your gifts, Ash, so you're good at it, too," I reason.

"That's because he asks Mom for help with ours," Greer comments.

I turn around in my seat. "Wait. Really?" He looks guilty as charged. "Well, I'm disappointed in you, then." I huff and turn back around in my seat.

"You both are so hard to shop for!" he complains. "But I'm going to do it on my own this year, and I know the perfect thing for both of you."

"Alright. If you say so," I tease.

We keep the conversation light and teasing as we make the drive to the mall. Once we arrive, we stick together through the department stores looking for parent gifts, then we grab some Chinese food at the food court, and finally, we scatter in different directions to shop for each other's gifts. Of course, not all of our gifts can be bought today. The modern-day mall doesn't have a lot anymore, but it's a great place to get ideas, and what it doesn't have can be bought online. Granted, we try to avoid online orders if they can be helped. But when it can't be, all mail and packages are dropped off at our front gate to be delivered by Ms. Molly.

I'm by myself at a jewelry store, looking at lockets for Greer. She has one good picture of her with her parents when she was a baby, and I have been saving up all my chore money to get her one so I can put a miniature version of that picture inside. That way, she can always have them with her.

I decide on a simple white gold one that has a smooth oval shape and minimal embellishment to it. Simple and perfect for Greer's taste. I pay and place the jewelry box carefully into my purse to hide from Greer. I turn to leave and bump right into something.

No, someone.

I back up quickly, sputtering out an apology, and I look up to find captivating hazel eyes, a warm smile, and a head full of pale blonde hair.

"No, it's not your fault. I was standing too close," the man says in response to my hastily blurted apology. He has to only be a couple of years older than me, likely twenty, but his presence is...I'm not sure. Like he could command any room and brighten any dark corner with that smile. It puts me on edge, despite how alluring it is.

"I was waiting in line to ask for help on a purchase, but maybe you could help?" he asks, his tone hopeful.

"I don't work here," I reply.

"I know. But I saw you make a purchase, and I'm looking for a gift for my girlfriend. I'm bad at this kind of stuff." His smile turns sheepish. He continues, "Your style looks similar to hers, so maybe you can help me decide on something if you have the time. I promise not to hold you up for long."

I tune into him and sense his embarrassment and hope, then tune back out. He seems harmless. I return his smile and ask, "What's the gift for?"

His eyes brighten, causing the green in them to stand out more. "Our anniversary, we're celebrating a year next week."

My heart warms for him. "Congratulations. What kind of jewelry are you looking for?"

"A necklace."

I move over to the necklace section of the glass counters, then ask, "What kind of girl is she?"

"What do you mean?"

"Does she like hearts, flowers, sparkly things...Maybe she's a birthstone type of girl?"

He considers for a moment, then answers, "I don't know. What do you like?"

I laugh at his obliviousness. This girl must be with him for his looks rather than his observation skills. I look over all the necklaces and spot an open heart made up of a bunch of tiny hearts attached to make the larger heart shape. Each tiny heart has an equally tiny diamond in it, and it is beautiful how it glitters under the lights. Just the right amount of sparkle without being over the top. I point to it and suggest, "I think few girls would hate that one."

He leans in closer to me to study it, the cuff of his brown leather jacket brushing up against my arm. His smile is wide. "It's perfect," he breathes.

Jealousy grabs ahold of me, its claws sharp and capable of tearing me to shreds in one swipe. I swallow and begin backing up as I say, "Looks like my job is done. Good luck."

His head lifts, and his eyes meet mine. Everything blurs around us, and I feel as though time has stopped—my breathing has stopped.

"Thank you for your help. I would have been lost without you." His voice reaches me, and things start to move again, my lungs burning with the need to breathe. Opening my mouth, I quickly force air back into my body. She is a lucky girl, this man's girlfriend. Despite my judgment of him being oblivious, he seems invested in the relationship. He isn't going anywhere. Not like...

Nodding, I leave the store quickly. I feel ill. I find Greer and Ash waiting for me at our designated spot.

"Everything alright?" Greer asks, looking me over carefully, then checking our surroundings.

"Yes, sorry I'm late. Got caught up with something. Let's go home," I answer quickly, suddenly anxious to leave.

Back in the car, Ash must be picking up on my thoughts because he says suddenly, "I don't think he's coming home for Thanksgiving."

I force my pulse to ease and reply calmly, "I don't think so either. I'm sure he'll make Christmas a priority, though," I lie. He won't be here for Christmas, either. I didn't even bother getting him a gift.

"Yeah, I hope so. I just..." Ash starts, but his word cut off as Greer swerves the car to the left. I throw my arm up to shield my face as—

CRASH.

Shattered glass is in my lap, in my hair, and all over my arm. Oh god. My broken arm. The pain of it flares to life as my shock wears off a bit. A truck crashed right into the passenger side of the car, crunching my door in, and my outstretched arm took the brunt of the force.

My ulna, one of the bones in my right forearm, is cracked in half. I bite my lip to suppress the scream I want to let loose. Tears pour down my face as I taste blood in my mouth, likely from where I'm destroying my lip.

Breathe. In through my nose, out through my mouth. Again. Again. I look over at Greer, and I realize she has been talking to me. Without asking her to repeat herself, I say, "My arm is broken. You and Ash okay?"

Thankfully, Ash is sitting behind Greer, so opening up my senses, I touch Greer's arm and then Ash's leg and can tell neither of them are hurt aside from a bit of whiplash and a few cuts from the shattered glass.

"Yes, we're okay," Greer replies quickly. She then exits the car where a middle-aged woman is waiting outside the door, phone to her ear. Likely a good Samaritan, stopping to check on us.

I look out of the shattered window to my right and see that the truck is now gone.

"That asshole is running!" Ash yells, enraged from the back seat. A little calmer, he adds, "Good thing I got his license plate number."

"Great thinking," I reply. I try to move my arm a little and cringe at the pain that shoots through it.

Greer pops her head in the car as Ash gets out. She asks, "Do you think you can crawl out? There is no way your door is opening."

"If I could just...get...to my purse...I have a...vial in there." I struggle to try to reach for it where it rests on the floor without moving my arm too much.

Greer checks to make sure Ash is out of earshot, then says, "You can't. You told Ash it was broken and I can already hear the ambulance siren. If you take an elixir this second, it would still be in the healing process when they check you out."

Fuck. The semi-foreign swear word bounces around in my head and I wish I could scream it at the top of my lungs, but instead, I bite my tongue and try to control myself. Greer's right. There would be no explaining to the EMTs or to Ash why my bone was fusing itself back together on its own. I throw my head back against the headrest and groan. I guess I'll have to heal the human way for now.

"I'm just going to sit here and wait for the nice people to get me out, then. I really don't want to move if I have the choice," I finally answer impassively. I gently wipe my face with my good arm and rid myself of the tears. I'm still in a lot of pain, but I'm done crying over it.

Greer nods and pulls her head back out of the car to deal with the jittery witnesses of the accident and now the police officer who's walking up.

I close my eyes and continue to breathe. In...and out. In...and out.

"Miss?" I open my eyes again and see a man in his thirties in an EMT uniform outside the broken window. When he sees me acknowledge him, he says, "Your sister told me your arm is broken. We are going to get you out of here and to the hospital as fast as we can, okay?"

I nod stiffly and reply, "Okay."

The man puts on heavy-duty gloves, tells me to brace myself to prevent further injury, and grabs onto the door, giving it a vigorous pull. To my surprise, it does budge a little. He calls out for someone to come help him and they manage to pull the door open without any metal jaws for assistance. The man extends his hand out to my uninjured one and helps me exit the car. I ignore the crunching noise coming from under my feet and follow him to the ambulance.

I'm quickly greeted with an option for pain relief which I gladly take, and then after a couple of minutes, Ash is hovering over me. "I'm going to go to the hospital with you. Greer is going to stay with the car and the police until your mom and dad get here."

I simply nod at him, feeling a little lightheaded and weird from whatever they gave me, but I don't really feel my arm as much anymore.

The ride to the local hospital is quick, and I am grateful for Ash being there to help with paperwork since I'm right-handed.

An X-ray, an MRI, and a cast later, Mom and Dad show up with Greer. I have no idea how late it is, but I'm exhausted by the time I'm released from the hospital and we all head home.

Once we walk through the door of the house, Mom sits me down on the couch. I want to go to bed and my eyelids are incredibly heavy. Mom is gone for about thirty seconds before she reappears with a bone repair elixir.

"Mom, what about Ash? I can't not have a broken arm tomorrow," I argue, even though I very badly want the elixir.

"You can leave the cast on for a couple of days to let it completely heal, then we'll make you a removable cast you can take on and off for show until we can say you're better," she explains.

I don't argue further. I take the vial from her and swallow the contents without complaint.

"Can I go to bed now?"

"Yes, please do," she agrees and helps me to my room so I can get out of these clothes and into bed. The hospital made sure I got cleaned up from the accident and removed all the pieces of glass from me. One of the kind nurses also brushed out my hair with water to ensure it was all gone.

I sink into my mattress, and Greer gets out of her bed to help me pull the covers up.

"Thank you," I tell her.

"I'm sorry," she softly replies.

"It's not your fault."

"It is. I foresaw that something bad was going to happen today, but it didn't feel too bad, so I didn't worry about it and I should have."

"Greer, it isn't too bad. Mom fixed me up, and I'll just have to pretend for a bit with the cast. It's not a big deal."

Her silence tells me she thinks it is and will likely continue to think it is despite what I say. I try again, "Please don't put this burden on yourself. It was a freak accident. It happens all the time to normal humans. That other driver was distracted or something, and *they* are to blame."

She's still silent, and I turn on my lamp to see that her face is wet. Getting out of bed, I go to her. Suddenly, I realize why she is so upset. It hits me head-on. I internally wince at the poor choice of words in my inner dialogue. We got in a car accident today. Her parents died in a car accident. I want to hit myself for not thinking about it sooner. Instead, I wrap my one good arm around her, my casted arm awkwardly trapped between us, and hug her tight.

I let her cry until my shoulder doesn't feel like any more tears are falling on it, and then I say soothingly, "We are all alive. We are all okay."

She nods her head against my shoulder and I pull away, getting a good look at her. Greer doesn't cry very often. The only times I have seen her cry are when she thinks of her parents or when Ash got hurt and lost his memory.

Greer reaches for a tissue on her nightstand and blows her nose. "I'll be okay. I think we both just need some sleep. Here, I'll help you get into bed again."

She follows me to my bed and tucks me in once more. I grab her hand before she can walk away, though, and squeeze it. "I love you, sister."

"I love you too, sister." She gets back into her bed, and we go to sleep.

CHAPTER 15

December

GREER AND I WALK into the training gym bundled in heavy coats. It's been a cold winter so far, and we are only a couple of weeks away from Christmas. One more week and I can ditch the fake cast completely, thank god. I'm seriously tired of slipping it on and off during the day and struggling to write at school, but I'm choosing to focus on being grateful I have a healed arm instead.

I drop my bag on a bench and unzip my coat. Thankfully, there is no reason to have a cast on at training.

"Zip it back up, Talli," Dad calls out. I whip my head around to see Dad also in a heavy coat with something long wrapped in a blanket under his arm. "You and I are going on a field trip today to the great outdoors."

I turn to Greer, who shrugs and finishes pulling off her coat and warm boots. "What about Greer?" I ask.

"Greer is going to continue with training like normal."

"Where are we going?" I walk toward him, coat zipped back up and bag in hand.

"Can't a dad want to spend time with his daughter?" Dad replies, forcing an innocent tone.

"Well yeah, I suppose."

"Good. Because you and I are going to start spending more time together." His smile sends a mixture of nerves and suspicion rolling through me. Nonetheless, I follow him through the back doors of the community building and outside up a long rocky path. The sun is on the verge of setting, and the lanterns marking the path start winking on as we get close to them.

"There is nothing to be suspicious of, Talli," Dad reassures.

Dad walks to a table that is made from trees that were cut down from this very clearing. The legs are stumps left in the ground, and the top is made of long trees split down the middle, then carved and sanded to create a smooth, flat surface.

Dad places his bundle on the table and begins unwrapping it, saying, "Talli, I know your mother and I have always told you to run if you're ever faced with danger, but things are changing in this war." He clears his throat as he opens a leather case and pulls out a long bow and quiver full of arrows. The bow looks as if it was crafted from midnight-blue stone with carved light-blue swirls and lines that lead to sharp points at each end of the bow. Although, despite its somewhat medieval appearance, I'm sure it's made from metal. The quiver matches it beautifully with the same midnight-blue colored leather and light-blue design and stitching.

Dad continues, "Pretty soon, we are all going to have to fight. I'd be doing you a disservice by not trying to teach you how to wield anything you can."

I swallow hard and ask the obvious, "So you're going to teach me how to shoot a bow?"

"If my memory serves me, you're not a bad shot with a gun. Maybe a bow would be a good fit."

He's right. I have always had good aim with a gun, and I enjoy the rare shooting practice when we have it. But even though we have guns, and that's a lot of what the Brethren use themselves, we don't use them much because of one key flaw: they are loud. We are a hidden world because we stay quiet and don't bring attention to ourselves by constantly shooting people. That's an easy way to bring the government to our doorstep. So, we use quiet weapons like bows, swords, and knives. Sure, silencers exist for guns, but we can't outfit thousands of people with them, especially when they only muffle the noise a little bit. That would also likely bring the government to our doorstep. Hence the medieval weaponry.

Dad extends the bow to me and I take it, surprised by how light it is—definitely a light metal of some kind.

"I had it made for you, so I hope you like it."

"I do. It's beautiful. Thank you, Dad," I reply as I look it over. I run my finger down each carved line, feeling how smooth and cool it is to the touch.

"My favorite weapon has always been a bow, and I'm disappointed in myself for not having you try one sooner. I just thought..." He clears his throat, and I look over at him, asking him with my eyes to finish.

"I thought this war was going to reach an end before you got to an age where you could fight in it." His voice breaks at the end, but he quickly recovers. "Hope, Talliana. Sometimes, hope means you don't prepare for the worst-case scenario, and that is dangerous. That is what has gotten the Order to this point of irrelevance and near extinction. Hope is not serving our people anymore, and it's time to change tactics."

This is the exact opposite of everything Dad always preaches to the people of the community. He is the first one to advocate for hope, especially in times of crisis, but I guess his real feelings are quite the contrary. It must be difficult to be a leader, always having to stay calm and positive for your people, when in reality you feel just as scared and defeated as everyone else. A shiver runs down my back, and all I can do is nod as I grip the bow tightly. I can sit and overthink his words later. It's time to listen and absorb.

"Now. I will take you here twice a week during your training session, every Monday and Thursday night," he explains.

"For how long?"

"Until you're a pro like me." His smile reemerges warm and bright, like we weren't just talking about our near extinction a breath ago.

I return his smile and say, "So we'll be here for a while."

"We'll be here for as long as we need to be here. We won't worry about putting a timeline on anything yet. For today, we are only going over the basics."

The basics, as it turns out, were more complicated than I had hoped. Now that it's time for me to practice with the bow, our time is about up. Dad mostly prattled on about technique mixed with stories from when he first learned how to shoot a bow in the Florida community where he grew up.

"Alright, hand here. Put your other one here. Back straight. A little closer to your body. Okay. Now release," he instructs.

I adjust as he says and let go. The arrow flies through the air much faster than I expect and hits the target two rings away from the bullseye.

"Amazing!" Dad cheers. I smile widely at him. It feels so satisfying to be good at something. It's not right on the mark, but I'm thrilled I hit the target at all.

Dad gets me another arrow. I line myself up and let it fly. The second ring again, but on the left side of the target this time instead of the right.

"Good. Good!" Dad praises. "One more, and we will call it a night."

I release the third arrow and it hits a little closer, on the line of the first and second ring. I lower the bow and hop on my toes in excitement.

"I'm actually good at something! Thank you, Daddy!" I set the bow down and wrap my arms around his neck giving him a tight hug. He hugs me back affectionately, and I suddenly feel like a small girl again in my dad's arms. I let go and smile at him. His face is surprisingly serious, though. I lift an eyebrow in question.

"Talli, honey, you know you're great at a lot of things. Just because you're not a natural fighter doesn't mean you are any less valuable or skilled." His tone is soft, and he tries to catch my eyes.

My gaze shifts to the ground, though, embarrassed. "I...It's not like I don't think I'm good at anything. I just don't want to be totally useless if something happens or a liability in a fight. I want to contribute more, other than healing," I explain.

His body tenses, but only for a moment before he shakes it off. "I understand that. Just know that no matter what, you are not useless to me or your mother, okay? We are so proud of you."

I nod and try not to cry. It's something I already knew in my heart, but hearing him say it out loud makes me feel emotional, and I believe it is having the same effect on him if his demeanor is any indication.

We pack up my bow and quiver of arrows into the leather case and start walking back toward the community building to grab Greer.

"Greer has been updating me on your training progress. I think that's great. Do you want me to ask Simon to add you to hand-to-hand training more?" Dad asks.

I think about it for a moment. Greer has started to do some hand-to-hand with me instead of all strength-training, and I'm exceptionally terrible at it, as I already knew. But I need as much practice as I can get. It's great knowing that using a bow is now an option for me, and one I'm good at, no less. But I might not always be able to stay far away from everyone. I make up my mind.

"Yes. I think you should," I answer.

"Okay, consider it done," Dad replies.

We grab Greer from the training room and head home. She eyes me and the new leather case I am carrying. After a few moments, Dad announces, "We have a new archer in the family."

Greer's eyes brighten and then meet mine. "Really?"

"Really." I smile.

"That's so great, Talli!" Greer exclaims and pulls me into a side hug. I'm not used to so much attention and praise, but it's nice coming from my family. I'm doing something right. Even though the future looks gloomy, I finally feel like I might make a small difference in it.

Bonded creatures, big and small, are sacred to our cause. The bond aids us in focusing our abilities or adding to them. In exchange, we share our life force with them, so they are our partners and guide through life. The bonded choose their Hawk, and they mustn't be refused. A Hawk is not offered a bond more than once if they survive refusing the first one.

- Bonded Creatures: Ceremony & Guide to the Bond

CHAPTER 16

"HE'S GOING TO OPEN the envelope first." The voice came from behind me. I was startled and spun around to see Trey smiling past me to where Ash was assessing presents in front of him as if something would jump out at him if he touched the wrong one first.

"Yes, because it's the least threatening, and he hates it when everyone watches him," I replied coolly, even though my heart rate kicked up a few notches. I knew my mental shield was in place, but I checked it again to be sure.

Trey looked at me, brows raised, then smiled as he looked back at Ash, who went right for the envelope. I suspect that we both took note of Greer sitting on one of the dining room chairs next to where Ash was, counting his every breath as he opened his birthday gifts—a practice not unusual for her when he isn't looking.

Trey finally said, "It's funny how he likes the least threatening route in just about everything except for his love life."

I choked on the sip of lemonade I just took. Everyone in the house stopped and looked at me. Now I knew why Ash was so uncomfortable under this kind of scrutiny. I waved a hand and said a bit hoarsely to everyone, "I'm fine."

As I finished clearing my throat, Trey's amusement was palpable. I completely agreed with his assessment but did not expect that comment to be said aloud. Without a doubt, Greer was the most threatening presence in any room.

Being known as the opinionated and outspoken elder daughter in this community, I decided to speak my mind like always, despite how nervous I felt. "If Ash likes the scary, broody girls, what's your type?" I kept my face neutral and forward, not looking at him. Play it cool. I had to play it cool.

I could hear the smirk in his voice when he said, "I like a sense of humor and a gentle touch. Someone I can take care of and will care for me by patching me up when I get hurt." My lips twitched up in the corner, and he paused for a moment before adding, "Oh, and red hair. It's kind of my weakness."

That caught my attention, and I couldn't help but look at him. How he looked at me with those dark-brown eyes made me feel seen. Unfamiliar butterflies were making a mess of my stomach.

Was this happening right now? Could Trey and I be something? I thought back to what had always stopped me from considering him.

Mei-Lien. They both are Intelligence Officers, and they always seemed close.

I didn't hide the jealousy from my tone when I commented, "That sounds nothing like Mei-Lien."

His face twisted into a confused look. "I'm not her type, and clearly she isn't mine based on the description I just gave you."

"How could anyone not see you as their type?" The question slipped out before I could think better of it.

I was on the verge of backpedaling when he retorted, "Well, you just answered my question."

"What question?"

"What your type is."

"Just because I made that comment doesn't mean you're *my* type." Not true, that definitely meant that.

"Okay then, what's your type?" His challenge left me feeling out of sorts and unsure how to proceed.

"Well..."

"Talli, I'm opening your present," Ash called out to me, interrupting at the perfect moment. I gave Trey a shrug and walked over to Ash to watch him open the new backpack I had gotten him. Something he needed, considering his other one was fraying at every corner.

In a blink, I'm on the front porch of Trey and Ash's house, on my way home after the party. "Running out on me before you can answer my question?" I heard Trey's light tone and saw him on the other side of the porch, sitting in one of the brightly colored Adirondack chairs that litter their porch.

I startled but did my best not to let it show. "Maybe some other time. I have someplace I need to be." I had absolutely no place to be, but I didn't care to embarrass myself any further in such a short period of time.

Before I could flee too far, he got out of his chair and asked, "How's tomorrow at noon? I'll pick you up and we'll have lunch at Sally's."

"Like a date?" My mouth opens once again before my brain has time to stop it.

"Yes. I hate that it took me so long, but I see you, Talli. I see you now." His lack of hesitation made my face turn pink. I could feel the heat radiating off it.

"Okay, see you then," I forced myself to say and walked away.

My eyes fly open, and I'm not surprised to find the darkness of my room. Another memory. This keeps happening. I either see him in my dreams or that fire and black lake. Compared to the latter, I much prefer the former. The dreams of him are both wonderful and heartbreaking all at the same time.

This memory, in particular, was the first time Trey expressed real interest in me. We had grown up together, of course, but it was a couple of weeks before this that he had come to the house looking for Mom to heal a wrist injury he had from a mission. She was out and I was there, so I healed him. I can still feel the way his eyes watched me while I worked my magic on his injury.

Trey was someone I had always taken note of, but all the girls were after him, so I chose not to be. It was as if it took me healing him for him to see me as the capable woman I am, not just the girl who's best friends with his adopted brother. However, once he did notice me, I realized that my feelings for him had already been a bit more than simply "taking note of."

I close my eyes again and concentrate on Trey. I've been hurting from all these dreams and memories of him, but these last couple? They are a comfort now. So, I will myself back into the memory, following it until I fall back asleep.

"I can't believe he's not coming home for Christmas," Ash complains at the lunch table. Winter break starts tomorrow. He continues in a grumble, "First Thanksgiving, now Christmas? It's clear Trey has left us for a new life. He's just too much of a coward to tell us he's not coming back."

"Hey. That's not fair, Ash. You know that's not who Trey is. There is just a lot going on for him," I snap at him, but it even sounds hollow to my own ears. I don't know what to believe at this point. I know he's still alive, but where he is? I don't know.

"Have you even talked to him lately? Or has he shut you out too? He obviously didn't care enough to come check on you when you broke your arm. You deserve better, Talli. So much better." I feel as if he has slapped me in the face.

"Ash, this is hard for her, too," Greer interjects, trying to de-escalate the situation.

Ash continues glaring at me. I don't have to tune into him to know he means well, but his anger is getting the best of him, and he's directing it at me because he can't direct it at Trey. Well, my anger is getting the best of me, too. Everything I want to say is right on the tip of my tongue.

Greer shoots me a warning look.

I stand up from the bench and zip up my lunchbox with so much fury that the zipper pull snaps off. I grab the whole thing from the bottom instead and stomp off. We can't keep doing this anymore. We can't keep lying to Ash. It's time this whole thing comes crashing down and he learns the truth.

Bailing on the last two classes I still have left for the day, I find myself face-to-face with Dad's office door. I have no idea if he's in a meeting or if he's free, but anger has now turned into desperation as I knock.

Dad opens the door a moment later and gives me a confused look. "Talli, what happened? Why aren't you at school?"

I look inside the office. Mr. Waterstone and Chief Lu are seated at his conference table. I guess I will have an audience for this impromptu plea for the truth.

I hesitate for a moment but straighten my spine and look back at Dad. "Nothing happened. I...I need to talk to you—all of you preferably. It's about Ash."

Dad opens the door, letting me in, and gestures toward an open seat at the table, which I take. Suddenly, I'm embarrassed, barging over here in the middle of the school day with no plan whatsoever. Greer would have berated me for being reckless, though I know she would back me up in what I'm about to say.

"We need to tell Ash the truth," I announce to the room.

"Talli..." Dad starts, but Mr. Waterstone cuts him off, "Let's hear what she has to say, Aaron."

Dad nods, and I swallow before continuing. "He's angry. Completely losing his cool, not understanding why Trey left and won't come home. I'm sure you see the texts he sends to him. He knows something isn't right. I think he even knows we are hiding something from him. I tuned into him shortly after Trey left, and it seemed quite clear that he was suspicious. We need to tell him the truth about everything. He has a right to know at this point."

Mr. Waterstone nods. Evidently, he has seen the change in Ash, too, so this does not come as a surprise. He says, "This is hard for everyone. I don't blame him for being angry. We are all angry."

"But we know the truth, he doesn't. He thinks his brother just left him and..." I start.

"He did just leave him. He left all of us. In consideration, he has the kinder version of the truth," Mr. Waterstone claims.

"With all due respect, I disagree, sir. Why can't we finally tell him? He's known once before, and it's honestly a miracle he hasn't figured it out on his own by now," I argue.

"He has figured it out. Three times to be precise," Chief Lu says out of nowhere. I snap my head to her, not sure I heard her right. I look to Dad, who seems exasperated as he runs his hand down his face, and then to Mr. Waterstone, who seems exhausted. Bone-deep exhaustion, like the weight of everything is getting hard to bear.

"I don't understand."

"Kasumi, is this really the time?" Dad asks.

"Yes. You need to stop sheltering them," she replies, then turns back to me. "Talliana, it's time you understand what it means to make hard decisions for the betterment of the community." I don't like what she's implying, but I focus on her next words carefully. "Due to a slip-up, or Asher simply piecing things together, he has figured out the people here are different three times now. Each time, once we realized he was figuring it out, we had Mei-Lien hide the memory from his mind."

Mei-Lien's compulsion can't wholly wipe anything away within someone's mind, but she can tell someone to forget the memories, which is essentially hiding them in a dark corner. Still there but un-available.

So many emotions war inside of me. I don't understand. What is the point of it all? I decide to ask what I need to know. "Why?"

Mr. Waterstone is the one to answer. "Asher lost his parents in a tragedy, one that could be considered our people's fault."

"We didn't set their house on fire," I argue.

"No, but their house was set on fire because they lived here, and they chose to help our people when they didn't have to. In anger, he could place that blame on us. Even though our intentions were good, trying to give him a normal life after all that happened, it would be easy to choose to mistrust us now because we didn't tell him the truth then. This is how Brethren are created. We could push him to become the exact thing that took his parents away from him."

"Asher isn't like them. He is kind and tolerant and reasonable."

"You came in here and said yourself that he is angry—losing his cool, even. That is why we must be cautious," Chief Lu explains.

I hate this. I hate this so much. Part of me wants to see their point, but the other part of me physically recoils at the idea.

Dad chimes in at last. "Talli, no one wants to see Ash endure the pain and suffering from a world he isn't from. That's not fair to him when this was not his choice. He should have a normal human life. That's his right."

"It's his right to choose," I retort under my breath. When all I'm given in reply is glares, I ask, "What's the plan, then? School is almost over. Are we just going to shove him past the community gates once he graduates?"

"Watch the tone," Dad warns sharply.

I take a deep breath, in and out, to get ahold of my emotions.

"I apologize to you all," I say sincerely. "I'm just...He's my best friend." The fire and purpose I had when I walked in here are gone now. Smothered with a bucket of water.

"We know, Talliana. He is so lucky to have you and Greer in his life. I promise he won't be dumped on the side of the road or abandoned once he graduates. We will encourage him to go to college and start a real life for himself. Angeline and I will still be his adopted parents and take care of him as best we can." What he doesn't say, I see in his eyes: *since we failed Trey.*

I only have enough energy left to nod and offer my brief apology for barging into their meeting. Then I make my way home feeling defeated and embarrassed.

CHAPTER 17

"ANOTHER RAILROAD! I CONTROL them all now," Ash brags.

"Doesn't matter. I have both of the dark blues, and the reds, and the yellows," I list out and grin at him.

"Yeah, but you don't have any money," he argues.

"Oh, you mean like all of this?" Greer asks, fanning herself with her large stack of Monopoly money.

"You can't win with money alone. You must have property for people to land on so you can get more money," Ash explains as if she doesn't know.

"Why bother when I can sit back with my stack and watch you two battle it out? You'll bankrupt each other, and I'll win in the end."

"You try that strategy every time we play this game, and you've yet to win with it," I point out.

"Just because I haven't yet, doesn't mean I won't someday."

Ash and I both shake our heads at her and her logic. Greer might be the Strategist in real life, but she sucks at board games. All except one.

"Can someone just win already so we can play Risk?" she whines. Right on queue. She obliterates us at that game every single time without fail, so of course, it's the only game she enjoys playing.

We continue playing the game, enjoying this tradition of ours. Every Christmas Eve, we make homemade pizza for dinner and sit around playing games all night. It's honestly my favorite part of Christmas, this time with my friends. Ash and I apologized to one another that same evening after our argument last week. Since then, we have decidedly avoided the topic of Trey altogether.

Ash lands on my most expensive property for the third time in a row, and it's enough for him to go bankrupt. I jump from my seat. "Yes!" I shout in victory.

Ash drops his head to the table, making a loud thump. I laugh, and he lifts his head to say, "Good game, Talli. Now it's time for Greer to beat me next."

"Hey, you beat us at dominoes earlier. Maybe we will all get a win tonight," I offer, looking on the bright side.

Greer gives me a look of surprise. I just offered a bright side. I don't think I have done that since Trey left, even though the bright side was practically my personality before he left.

Neither Ash nor I have been ourselves. We both feel Trey's loss deeply, and I think this is the closest we have allowed ourselves to feel normal since he left. Maybe we are finally turning a corner now that the topic is no longer driving a wedge in our friendship. We are learning to live our lives without him, despite how it makes my heart hurt.

"Merry Christmas, beautiful," Trey whispers into my hair.

I turn around to face him and realize something isn't right. "Trey, what happened to you?" I ask, panic leaking into my tone.

His face appears ashen, his normal golden-brown color looks gray. I look him over. He is thin and his muscle tone is no longer easily seen like it always was before. His hair is long, the frizzy black curls turning downward on his head, trying to reach for his ears. Then there are his eyes. They are hollow and tired, with visible purple shadows underneath them.

"I'm okay, Talli." He is trying to comfort me, but even his voice sounds wrong. It's gravelly and devoid of all its strength.

I place my hands on either side of his face, pulling him close. "You're not okay. Is this somehow real?" The thought now out of my mouth, I realize it could be possible.

He could be dream-walking right now. As far as he told me, though, he has to be in the same room as the person whose mind he is entering for his ability to work. A check and balance from nature on his ability to ensure he can't easily misuse it. Everyone has some kind of limitation. But what if...

"Trey, are you dream-walking?" I know it's foolish, but I can't help the hope that grips my heart at the idea.

This shouldn't be possible, but his appearance now is one I have never seen before. All the other dreams I have had have been of how he looked in those memories. This isn't a memory. He has never said those words to me before.

Trey shifts his gaze down, hurt twisting his face. But I watch as it shifts to a neutral expression, then a reassuring smile. "No, of course not. I'm just a dream your mind created. Come, let's sit down."

No, I don't believe it for a minute. I open my senses and try to feel his pain. I've never tried to use my ability in a dream before, but I must try. Actually...I don't remember ever being this conscious in my dreams before.

Another realization dawns on me. I've been this aware and in control in a dream only once before, when Trey dream-walked into my mind after I asked him to one night. Curiosity had gotten the better of me, and I wanted to know what it felt like. It felt like this.

I refocus on my senses, and sure enough, I can't keep track of the amount of bruises littering his body. A broken finger, a swollen left knee, and a gash on his right arm.

I grab ahold of his shirt and yank it off over his head, despite his protest of, "What are you doing? Talli, stop!" Panic thickens his tone, and I feel my own dread shifting inside me as I search for proof of my suspicion.

Finally wrangling his shirt free, I gasp at the sight of him. Then, a sob tumbles from me. I cry as I look at every bruise, the red angry-looking slice in his bicep, and at the ribs that are so visible, I could count every single one without trouble. I fall to my knees in front of him, hand pressed to my mouth to try to control the horrible noises coming from me. I faintly realize we are under our willow tree at the lake. That realization does something to me—my blood thrums through my veins and my vision blurs. I am so angry.

He drops in front of me and pulls me to his chest. "I'm so sorry, Talli. I shouldn't have come. I shouldn't have done this to you. I thought I was strong enough to change my appearance. I didn't mean..."

I cut him off and pull away from him to ask, "They have you, don't they?"

He gulps, his hesitation clear as day, and it's all I need. "Trey, do you know where you are? We will get you out of there. I will come to rescue you." Urgency causes adrenaline to match the wild current of anger inside of me.

Panic, horror, anger, and urgency. They all threaten to swallow me whole.

His eyes flash with fear as he grabs my upper arms and pleads, "No. Stay far away from this. These people are monsters, and they will kill you. Enjoy your life there for as long as you can, Talli, then run."

"What? What do you mean by 'run'?"

"I mean, graduate and pack a bag. Go to your Uncle Cyrus. He will help you hide," he tells me frantically.

"Trey, I can't run. I would never. I'm needed here!"

"Do it for me, Talli. Do it in my memory. I love you."

What?! His *memory*?

Before my eyes, Trey's body starts to fade.

"Trey! No, please don't leave! No! No! Please!" I wail.

He's gone. He's gone. Shock has become a familiar friend to me as of late, but the chill of it still makes my fingers feel numb.

I clench my fists and as I do, I jolt awake. I jump out of bed without hesitation and run for the door. I'm outside, running, stumbling over fallen tree branches. It's raining outside. Not a gentle rain, but a downpour of freezing water.

I slip on the slick mud under my feet and fall hard on my back. All the air leaves my body, and I lie frozen and gasping for a moment. Hands slide under my armpits, and they haul me up to my feet. I turn and see Greer's raven-black hair plastered to her face and pajamas soaked through. She's speaking to me, but I don't know what she is saying. I turn back to my goal and start running again to the lake, where I just was with Trey in my mind.

Reaching the lake, I look around for something. Anything.

"Trey!" I scream into the dark, placing all my anger behind my voice. I do it again. And again. And again.

"Talli! Talk to me!" Greer hollers over the sound of the storm.

I turn to face her and shout loudly, "He came to me. He dream-walked, and he is hurt. They have him. He told me to leave the Order and hide. He told me to do it in his memory! I have to find him."

A loud hoot rings through my ears, and I spin around to locate the familiar sound. Theora flies over my head and lands under our tree, seeking cover from the rain. I scramble in her direction and drop before her.

"Theora, is he here? Where is he?" I ask, frantic.

The barn owl closes her round black eyes and lowers her head.

"I know he's still alive! He isn't gone! He can't be!"

She lets out a loud screech in answer and drops her head again.

"Talli. Talli. Talli!" Greer is pulling me away from Trey's bonded creature, trying to jar me back to life. "Talli, listen to me. Please, let's go inside and talk this out."

I'm exhausted. My body is bone-deep exhausted, but my brain is running at a million miles a minute. Fighting, searching, doing anything to explain how it's not true. Trey can't be dead.

Greer's grip tightens on my arms, preparing for a fight, I realize. I don't give her one, though. All I do is nod and let her guide me back home. All my emotions still feel like a raging storm inside me, but I push them down. I need to clear my mind. Come up with a plan.

This can't be happening.

CHAPTER 18

January

THE LAST TWO WEEKS have been hell. Absolute fucking hell.

After Theora came to me, she went to Mrs. Yvette, the one person in our community who can talk to any bonded creature. She, unfortunately, is the one who always receives news of a community member's death when they aren't at home. The surviving bonded creatures go right to her to share the news.

This time was no different.

When Greer and I returned to the house that night, Mom and Dad were up after hearing us run out the door. I, still in my shocked state, explained everything that had happened. Mom gave me a sleeping elixir after Greer and I got warmed up and dry. Then, I woke to the official news that Trey was dead. Theora confirmed that he was captured by the Brethren and held as a prisoner until they killed him.

I didn't believe it and still don't believe it to be true. My intuition is telling me he is alive. I have researched and called Dream-walkers from other communities and have done everything possible to try to reach him. There is just no way to do it. Only he can reach out to me and not the other way around.

Dad asked me to share what happened and my conversation with Trey with Mr. and Mrs. Waterstone, as well as Chief Lu and Mei-Lien, along with her two older siblings who were visiting from other communities for the holiday.

On Christmas Day.

Of all the days, that was how our Christmas went. Ash was told he died in Virginia where he believed he was attending college. The lie they spun was that he died of a heart condition no one knew he had. A horrible but completely human cause of death that had nothing to do with the Brethren. I don't even remember which one they said because I was so infuriated. Greer left a hand-shaped bruise on my forearm when the elders informed us of that decision.

I don't blame her. Her squeezing grasp was the only thing reminding me to keep my emotions in check. I wanted to scream and rage at the continued lies. When do they end? When do we stop keeping him in the dark? The Great Hawk gave us our abilities to weed out the deceivers and liars, not become them.

Even though we were on school break, a rumor started to spread that I was lying about seeing Trey before he died. Apparently, it was all so I could get attention because how could that be possible anyway?

Greer and I haven't been able to confirm it, but we know Mei-Lien is the one who started it, even though she knows the whole truth of the situation. She will do anything to throw salt in my wounds and discredit me to everyone at school. Her mistake is thinking I care about what anyone at school thinks of me. Or what anyone in this community thinks of me, when it comes down to it.

A week after we got the news about Trey, a funeral was held. A tombstone was placed in his memory with no casket. No body, no need for a casket. His isn't the first tombstone in our cemetery without a body buried underneath it, and it won't be the last. Many of our dead only have ashes left, which we gather if we can and place in a small hole by the gravestone.

Something. It is something. But for Trey? There is nothing.

From the rumor, or because of the simple fact that no one knows how to act around us, Ash and I have been given a wide berth at school. Greer, too, since she is usually with at least one of us. It makes it harder, being treated differently. It's a constant reminder that something has happened, and there is no way to pretend everything is normal.

I don't blame them, though. Finding out that someone they know, someone they walked the school halls with, was taken and held prisoner without anyone realizing it. That kind of thing puts everyone in a gloomy mood and desiring to avoid that truth as much as possible. I suspect that Ash and I carry that truth on our faces.

A knock comes at our bedroom door and Greer goes to answer it from where she was at her desk. Ash walks in, face red and wet. I get to my feet and go to him, wrapping my arms around his neck. I tune into him and know he isn't physically hurt, but mentally, he is brokenhearted. First his parents were taken from him and now his adopted brother.

We hold each other for a moment, and then I step back, allowing Greer to take over. She pulls him in and leads him to rest on the floor with her. He rests his head on her shoulder and cries into her hair. I have seen Ash shed a tear here and there since news of Trey reached him, but I'm starting to think this is the first time he has allowed grief to consume him.

I sit at the edge of my bed, allowing him to receive every bit of comfort from Greer he needs. When he finally pulls back and collects himself, he confesses, "He died thinking I hated him."

I don't need to think before I reply, "That's not true."

"It is true. The last text I sent him when I found out he wasn't going to make it home for Christmas was horrible. So much so that he didn't even reply to it."

"Maybe he never got it," Greer reasons, still sitting next to him on the floor, only now she is turned so that she is facing the both of us.

"I don't see why he wouldn't have. He has gotten all my others."

"Did he reply to all your others?" I ask.

Ash wipes his nose with a tissue Greer hands him and answers, "Yeah, he always replies."

"Then it's possible he never got that one if he didn't reply. Either way, he loves you, Ash. He knows that if you said anything horrible to him, it would be out of anger and not real hate," I reason.

"Loved. He loved me. I do know that, but did he know that I loved him?" Ash clarifies, responding to the perceived mistake in my wording. It wasn't a mistake, but he doesn't need to know that, at least not right now. Not when he won't understand.

Greer steps in and answers, "He knew you loved him too. You two did stuff together and were friends, not just brothers."

Ash nods. "I am just worried...I'm not good at expressing how I feel when I care about someone. What if I wasn't obvious enough?"

There is absolutely nothing funny about this situation or conversation, but Ash is one of the most transparent people I know. If he had made that statement any other day, I would have laughed. Instead, I say, "You may not be the best at saying the words, but it's obvious through your actions how much you care. So give yourself a little more credit."

"It is?" he asks. He turns to Greer, and I pretend not to notice that he is looking for something in her eyes. She looks away, and his face falls. I could strangle her right this second.

I stand up, walk over to Ash, and hold out my hand. He takes it and uses it to pull himself up off the floor. "It is," I answer him.

He hugs me again and says into my hair, "Thank you, Talli. I couldn't have asked for a better friend."

He pulls away, and I meet his eyes. "We will get through this together."

He gives me a weak smile and, heading toward the door, says, "I should get back home and try to rest."

"Goodnight," Greer and I say in unison.

Once the door clicks shut and I can hear that he has also walked out the front door, I turn on Greer as she rises from the floor. "You are an idiot."

"What did you just say?" she asks with surprise in her tone.

"He was looking for *you*. He was trying to see if you knew he cared for you, and you rejected him," I accuse.

"That is ridiculous. That is not what happened," she protests.

"Then what happened?"

"He...I...Ugg. I can't do this with you right now. I need some air." She heads toward the door.

"Do you love him?" I challenge.

She stops and quietly answers, "More than I should."

"Then why? Why waste all this precious time you could have with him?"

She turns to me, her eyes shifting into daggers. "He would never know who I truly am. And if he did eventually learn the truth, I would only be putting him in danger. Ash is the one person who can get on a lifeboat and get away safe from this sinking ship that is our lives. If we get to graduation and he leaves for college, he is safe. If I act on these feelings, then I am damning him to the same fate we have. Do you want that for him?"

I shake my head no. Tears threatening to fall again as the truth of her words sink in.

"Then stop making this harder for me. It's the least you could do."

She's almost out the door when I ask, "Why didn't you tell me this? How you felt?"

"You wouldn't have understood before." She leaves the room.

I wouldn't have understood before. Before I lost someone I loved, someone I was close to and cared for so much. Regardless of if Trey is dead or not, I have lost him. I have spent more time mourning his absence now than I did in a relationship with him.

How foolish does that sound? I don't regret the time I had with him, and I will always cherish my memories with him, even if they are now all laced with pain. But if someone had told me before we got in a relationship that I would lose him like this? Or told me I could have saved him if I simply didn't date him? Would I sacrifice all those memories I didn't realize I would have so he would be safe?

My head is spinning, and my heart feels like it's breaking all over again.

For Greer.

For Ash.

For Trey, wherever he is, dead or alive.

For my people.

For myself.

Our abilities are powerful. The magic within us can build just as well as it can destroy. The Great Hawk foresaw this capability and placed limits on our magic. This wisdom ensures that no individual Hawk can stand against many Hawks and be evenly matched.

- The Great Hawk & Our Call to Order

CHAPTER 19

February

IT'S LATE FEBRUARY NOW, and my eighteenth birthday has come and gone with no fuss, per my request. Mom argued it was a big birthday for me and that we should celebrate, but I didn't feel up to it. We still had a delicious dinner at home with a small cake. Just Mom, Dad, Greer, Ash, and myself. Everyone got me small gifts, which I appreciated, and I did my best to accept them graciously, but I'm sure they all could see my heart was not in it this year.

Greer and I are in the middle of training. We are sparring with Mr. Simon when Dad walks into the training gym.

"Sorry to interrupt training, but girls, I have your first mission." We all stop to look at him. Not just Greer, but a mission for both of us.

My jaw drops, and I look to Greer, who seems equally shocked. We hustle over and stand at attention in front of him. It feels unnatural, the military stance, but Mr. Simon has been teaching it to us for when this day came. I guess it's here.

Dad gives us a small smile. He isn't a rigid man who enforces military attention, but when an elder has a mission, we are taught to respond like soldiers in a war. Because, well, we are at war, and it's a matter that should be taken extremely seriously. It could be life or death.

"We need to discuss this in my office." He turns on his heels and leads us to his office on the other side of the community building. The training gym is located at the basement level next to a small area for holding cells which are rarely ever used, whereas his office is on the third floor with a very nice view of the forest and distant mountains behind our community.

Once we reach his office, we stand at attention in front of his desk while he plops unceremoniously into his overstuffed chair. Melisandre is curled up on a giant white bed beside Dad's desk, paws elegantly crossed under her head. At a glance, she seems to be catnapping, utterly undisturbed by any of us, but her rounded ears are perked up instead of relaxed. Dad's bonded panther is always listening. In contrast, Chief Lu's bonded pit viper, Midori, is always watching. Then there is Lemon, Mr. Waterstone's golden retriever. I guess she is always there for cuddles. I always prefer her presence of the three, and her soft blonde head would be calming to pet right about now.

Bonded creatures, as a general rule, are not to be petted by others unless permission has been given. Seth and Lemon are the only two that I can comfortably reach my hand out and pet because of the consent they gave me prior. Melisandre is a special case since she is Dad's bonded. As in, she had to deal with me as a toddler pulling on her ears and trying to climb on her back. But, as soon as I was old enough, it became clear that she did not want to be touched and I've never crossed that boundary. Mostly because I like my arm staying intact.

Dad waves a hand at us, "Girls, sit please. What I have to tell you isn't going to be easy, but I need you to let me speak my piece, and then you can ask questions." We both nod, but our joint tension is palpable in the room. Oh god, what is he going to tell us?

"I'm just going to rip off the Band-Aid. We believe Ash's parents are alive."

Greer, who never reacts without thinking, bolts upright from her chair and says, "What?!" way too loudly. Dad gives her a look, and she sits back down, face still contorted in shock. I am so distracted by her reaction that I forget to have one of my own.

Dad continues, "When their house burned down, we did not find any human remains in the fire. We suspected then that the Brethren had kidnapped them and staged it to make it look like they died to cover it up." He pauses to let everything sink in for us. When we both seem like we are with him and ready for the rest, he continues, "We have been looking for them ever since, and we believe that we have finally found them."

Dad turns his monitor screen around so we can see it. There are surveillance pictures of what looks to be an abandoned prison that's four stories high and made of cinderblock. "We believe they are being held prisoner here. We need you two to infiltrate the prison, confirm that they are there, pass a message to them, and get out. I cannot stress this enough: *this is not a rescue mission.* Just confirm they are there and give them the message." He gives us a hard look, and we both nod.

Dad then gives us all the details of when we leave, flights, and who we are to meet when we get there. When he finishes, he asks, "Okay, any questions, concerns, or grievances?" He looks right toward Greer, knowing it will come from her first.

"Why weren't we told that you thought they were still alive? Why let Ash think they are dead?" Greer's tone is dangerously close to anger.

"We didn't know for sure what happened, and adding the new worry of kidnapping to your kids' plates did not seem like the best idea at the time."

"Because that is so much worse than dying," Greer snorts with her arms crossed over her chest.

After so many months of her comforting me, it's finally my turn to try to do the same for her. I place a hand on Greer's crossed arm, and she releases them with reluctance. I don't think she actually is that angry with anyone, but she is overprotective of Ash, and it's all hitting a bit too close to home for her because of the loss of her own parents. We do know that her parents are gone, though; their actual bodies were recovered, cremated, and placed in our cemetery.

"It very well can be, Greer. Being tortured for information can have you wishing for death," Dad scolds. Greer looks away, crossing her arms once again. She knows he is right.

Torture. The word hits me like a physical blow, and my ears start to ring. What happened to me a few months ago when I thought I felt Trey's pain, heard his voice. It was likely real, and he was being tortured. I saw it with my own eyes when he walked in my dreams almost two months ago. All those bruises...My fists clench.

Dad looks at me sharply. Greer asks, pulling his attention back to her, "Why us? Why doesn't the Colorado community take care of this mission?" The prison is in Colorado, so it would make the most sense for them to take this one, being a mission community themselves.

"When they lived in our community, we kept their identity safe, so no one outside our community knows them. We could get the local community pictures, of course, but we don't know if they will trust the message coming from people they don't know. They have every reason to be suspicious of anyone offering them hope of escape, so if it comes from you two, we can trust they will do what is asked. It also helps you both are small compared to the others here who are mission-ready."

"What is the message?"

"You will receive it when you get there. It's essentially an escape plan. We need them to play a part to give us the opening to grab them," Dad explains.

Makes sense.

I look over at Greer to make sure there is nothing else she wants to say or ask. She shakes her head, and I look back at Dad. The ringing in my ears is finally clearing up.

"Do we think Trey could have been there?" I ask. *Be there now* is what I actually mean, but I am trying to choose my words carefully.

Dad audibly lets out a noise that's either exhaustion or frustration. He rubs his face with his hands, then looks at me. "We don't know. If he dream-walked before he died, then it's likely he was held somewhere close. Intelligence is still working hard to identify all the Brethren bases and determine if prisoners could be held at any of the local ones." Two months later. Guess there is no rush when he is already dead as far as they are concerned.

"Do you think it might be beneficial to have a look around at that prison while we are there? Just in case..." I start.

"Talli, this better not be about Trey still being alive," Dad warns.

"I just can't shake this feeling..."

"I thought we were past this," Dad groans. "I know losing someone important to you is hard, and it's hard to believe they are gone, but, honey, you need to come to terms with it. Trey was one of our finest, and I would have loved to call him a son one day, but he didn't make it. End of discussion." I have heard Dad be blunt and harsh to other people on rare occasions before, but having it turned on me makes me want to crawl into a hole. I fight the urge to flee and instead hold my ground. I am a grown-ass woman now, and I will not back down.

"It's not just me not letting go. I know it inside of me! He lied for some reason!" I stand and brace my hands on the desk in front of me, the urgency to get him to understand driving my actions.

His expression goes quickly from exhausted to stern. "Talliana, don't even think about looking for him while you are there. Do not risk the mission and your own life, as well as Greer's life, on this notion with no real evidence to back it up."

"But, Dad!"

"No! Greer, you're the lead on this. Promise me that you will not let her run around looking for Trey. You go in, find the Hansens, give them the message, and get out. Not up for discussion."

"Yes, sir." Even though she is angry, Greer is the ever-good soldier who agrees with the order.

"Now, both of you go home and pack. Simon will take you to the airport in two hours."

Greer and I shuffle out. She shuts his door behind us and we drive home in silence. Once we are in our room, I whirl on her, but she cuts me off before I even have a chance to start. "No, don't ask. I agree with him."

I inhale a deep breath, ready to argue, but she cuts me off again, "I am lead on this mission, and I say it's too risky." Her tone is hard, but she softens it when she sees my face on the verge of tears. "Talli, I do believe you and agree that the timing of his death in relation to you begging him to share where he was is too coincidental. We will keep our eyes out for him while we are looking for Ash's parents, but we cannot stray from our mission to do so. Deal?"

I search her eyes for a minute and know she is genuine. I sit at the end of my bed and let my shoulders fall before I whisper, "I miss him so much. He is out there somewhere, and if what I saw and felt both nights at the lake is real...they are torturing him."

"We will find him one day, Talli. I will search with you for as long as it takes, but we have to be smart. We can't find him if we are locked up ourselves or dead."

"I know. Thank you, Greer."

Her smile is warm and reassuring. "Get over here and get yourself packed. If I am forced to pack for you, I will pack every thong and tight sock you own, so you will be forced to only think about how uncomfortable you are the entire time." There is the cruel Greer I know.

I laugh. I do not doubt that she would do just that, so I get up to pack without any more arguments.

CHAPTER 20

"THERE WILL BE GUARDS stationed here and here," Jarod, one of the members of the Colorado community, says, pointing at the large screen in front of us.

Jarod is a tall, bald man with a warm-sepia skin tone and dark eyes hidden behind his thin-rimmed glasses. If Dad hadn't already told us that he was an Intelligence Officer, I would have guessed it on sight by the way he dresses in a casual suit. Intelligence usually tend to have a flare to their wardrobe.

To any human passing him by on the street, it would be a safe assumption that he is a very successful business professional. Although, knowing better, I can see he is a person who isn't quite built for fighting, but he's seen enough of it to wear permanent creases of concern on his face despite only being in his thirties.

The first thing he did when we arrived was offer his condolences for Trey. He understood that we were close, and he knew him as well, having had the opportunity to work with him a few times on missions. All I could do was nod and swallow my wish to ask him his thoughts on how Trey died.

We are looking at a map of the prison where they believe the Hansens are being held. Since arriving yesterday evening, we have had information drilled into our heads, then drilled in again, and again. This is the fourth time we are reviewing where the guards will be stationed and I am on the verge of slamming my head down on the table we are sitting at, whereas Greer is intensely concentrating and soaking in every word. This is why she is the Strategist, and I'm the Healer. I am confident, though, that I have memorized all the information, and where I may falter, I know Greer will not.

Dad said Greer was the lead on this, and it's our first real mission, so I know she is taking this extremely seriously. Aside from the whole we-could-be-killed-if-we-are-caught thing, a successful mission for a Strategist means a good resume for better missions in the future. Not that I think Greer would ever struggle with getting whatever mission she wanted, but she is always determined to be the best.

I have no intention of messing up this mission for her, either. But I can't let go of this feeling that we need to search for signs of Trey. I asked Jarod if there were signs of other prisoners, and to my dismay, he said no. It seems the prison is used more as a headquarters than anything else, for command and temporary housing for members of the Brethren.

The Brethren don't keep prisoners—they kill us and burn our bodies without hesitation. End of story. Or so we have always been taught. However, evidence keeps suggesting that there is more to the story. I don't want to believe the elders are keeping a vast amount of secrets, but I've uncovered a few big ones in the last few months. I won't say it out loud, but my faith and trust is starting to waiver. If

Greer's is too, she hasn't voiced it, but I believe I see it there, a hint of doubt behind her eyes.

"Do either of you have any last questions?" Jarod asks.

I let out a sigh of relief that we are finally done. Greer and I both shake our heads.

"Good. I want you two to meet your backup team."

We follow him out of the dining/briefing room and toward the backyard of the safe house we are staying at. It's a good-sized house right in the middle of a busy human housing community. Jarod explained to us when we arrived that having a safe house positioned like this makes it very easy to blend in and hide from the Brethren. A newer concept that he created himself, and it has proven to be effective because it's the last place the Brethren expect us to be. I can't help but think back on what Mom told me, that we might have to dismantle the communities one day. It seemed like a terrible idea at the time, but maybe it isn't so terrible after all.

Once outside, we are met with three new faces.

Zephyr, an Air Elemental who is built like an ox with a face just as pleasant looking as one. His chestnut hair looks unnaturally greasy in the sunlight, and his protruding eyebrows and jaw give him a very distinguishable face. His bonded pigeon, perched on his shoulder only makes him look bigger.

In contrast, Javier has a small frame with a plain face, his skin is medium brown and he has black hair. He recently transferred from the Texas community to Colorado because he has a compulsion ability like Mei-Lien. I have an idea that many communities tried fighting for him, but I'm not surprised Colorado won, given that they are a mission-oriented community like Massachusetts. He does not have a bonded animal, or not one that I can see, anyway.

Lastly, there's Frankie. She's sleekly dressed with cropped light-blonde hair and steel-blue eyes, and, to my bubbly delight, resting in her palm is a little hedgehog. Her finger idly strokes its belly while it is on its back. One of the cutest bonded creatures I have seen in a long time. She is also an Air Elemental, but she proudly explains that her ability allows her to move very fast. Greer is particularly interested in how she uses that to her advantage in a fight.

With the introductions now concluded, Jarod explains that they will be on standby in a separate van to get us out if something happens on the mission. Greer explained to me earlier that if we get caught, the Brethren will likely see us as such a small threat that they will want to question us first to discover our purpose. That will give the backup team enough time to get us out before we get *too* hurt. So even though this mission is dangerous, it's clear that Dad is only willing to risk our lives so far.

Greer and I are dismissed to our shared room to get some rest before the mission since we will be going in at two in the morning. The sun is starting to set now, and even though I know I should be tired, I am jittery with nerves.

I take a long shower for the third time today, the water being the only thing that helps my nerves. When I get back to the room, Greer is calm as can be, sketching on the pad she brought.

"How are you so calm?" I ask.

She glances up at me and points out, "You must be extremely nervous if you think I am calm. You know better than that."

I do know better than that. Greer has a way of portraying the picture of serenity when she is at the peak of anxiety. Granted, she always looks calm compared to me, whether she is stressed or at ease. Only Mom and I can genuinely tell the difference between her moods when her mental shield is up or without trying to tune into her when it is down.

I finally voice the question I wanted to ask Dad after receiving the mission from him, but withheld, fearing he might send Greer without me. "If we are successful and they end up getting Ash's parents out, do you think they will finally tell him the truth about everything?"

Greer shrugs, which I immediately spot as a defense mechanism, and goes back to her sketchbook saying, "It will likely be up to his parents, but it would be hard to explain their absence otherwise."

"We should tell him." Greer's eyes meet mine again, and I continue, "We will give them a chance to make the right choice, but if they don't, we will do it. We will have to explain to him that he can't tell anyone he knows to avoid his memory getting adjusted again, but we are his best friends, and he has the right to know the truth behind everything."

Greer's eyes light with a fire that I love to see in her, and she smiles as she agrees, "Okay, let's do it. After we are sure they won't tell him."

I am relieved that she agrees with me. I wasn't so sure if she would after the way our last conversation about Ash went.

I smile back at her and walk over to her bed to see what she is sketching. It's a staircase. Like one you might see in a medieval castle leading down to a dungeon. It spirals around a stone wall and looks ominous.

"Do you think we will find them at the bottom of a staircase like that?" I ask.

"No, all the images and layouts we have seen of the prison have nothing like this."

"Your imagination running away with you, then?"

"I'm sure of it," she replies, and puts her pencil down.

Before climbing into bed, we both take some time to ensure everything is ready. I take a moment to look over my first set of fighting leathers that I have laid out. It felt so weird to wear them when I tried them on this morning. Custom-made yesterday to fit me like a thick second skin, they are black and cover me from the top of my neck to the bottom of my ankles. I never noticed how severe my curves were until I wore them. I've also dropped weight and gained muscle over the last few months of training with Greer. This morning was the first time I really stopped and looked at myself.

So different. I am so different now than who I was half a year ago. It feels like an eternity has passed, but it's only been six short months.

I check the inconspicuous pocket on my left arm and ensure all three of my standard-issue elixirs are full and secure. Again. Three thin cylinder glass vials containing three different healing elixirs: freeze it, blood replenish, and tissue restitch. Only enough for one dose each. I argued with Jarod earlier on the merits of having extra on me, but I was assured there was no need for it. Still, my Healer instincts tell me that more is always necessary.

I rezip the pocket and look at the pants where I have four knives tucked into their built-in sheaths at my thighs. Two knives on each side. To the right of the ensemble is my bow and quiver of arrows. I run a finger down the familiar cool feel of the metal. A weapon I have come to love over the last three months. It's not the smallest thing to carry, but it's the one weapon I can use confidently, and I know it won't fail me.

I finish my inventory check as Greer finishes hers. Taking one final breath, we each climb into our own beds, and then I proceed to stare at the dark ceiling for the next few hours.

CHAPTER 21

"HIT YOUR PANIC BUTTONS the instant you think you have been caught," Jarod tells us a final time, helping us wrap the constricting bracelets around our wrists. There is a hidden button on the side of the flat black band that will signal back to where Jarod will be in the van. The backup team is in another van behind ours, prepared to run in and save us if needed. I pray to the Great Hawk that they won't be.

They have spent months trying to tap into the prison's surveillance cameras in preparation for this mission so that Jarod can erase the footage, open doors, and help quell any alarms we may trigger as we move through the prison.

We check ourselves one more time, place our communication devices in our ears, and exit the van. Jarod gives us a quick, "good luck," and we start our small trek through the trees to get to our first obstacle—the huge electric fence.

Greer pulls out a small round silver disc from a pocket located between the knives on her thigh and her knee. We stay back a yard and a half from the fence as she throws the disc at it. The fence makes a zapping sound when it impacts, and then the sound quickly fades. I find a small stick and mimic Greer's movement by throwing it at the fence, but nothing happens. Perfect. The disc was made courtesy of the Hansens a couple of years before they were taken to disable the electricity in a small section of the fence. That way, we can cut through it with the industrial wire cutters Jarod's team left hidden next to a tree close by.

Carefully, we cut through the fence, making a small square for us to crawl through. Greer goes first, then my bow and quiver of arrows, then I squeeze through. If I had worn normal clothing, the wire would have sliced through the cotton with ease, but the leather keeps me protected.

Crouching, we creep to the back door of the prison. It looks like we are walking through what used to be an exercise area when this was a state prison. We reach the door and as soon as Greer touches the handle, we hear it unlock. It's comforting, the evidence right away that Jarod is keeping such a close watch on us.

Greer slowly eases the door open and we hear, "Be ready to sprint in five...four...three...two...now." Greer pulls open the door and we run down the long hallway, ducking into an empty storage room to our left. Hiding in the shadows, we see two men walk past the door. We count to fifteen and hear, "Clear." After easing out of the little room, we run to the next door. As we put ourselves flush with the wall behind it, the door opens, just barely brushing up against us, and a man walks down the hall with his back toward us. Greer grabs the door before it locks, and we slide into the next room.

There is a large glass window to the right that we have to get past. That is the security room. We drop to our knees and crawl against the two feet of wall space below the window. Before we can reach the end, the door on the right wall directly in front of us opens, and we freeze. A man walks out backward, saying to the room, "I'll have her begging for me within the hour. Mark my words, boys." We hold our breath, and he spins around to walk away, luckily keeping his back to us the entire time.

Once he is out the door we used to come in, we move even quicker to the door straight ahead to the next hallway. Jarod unlocks the door for us and we are through it in a flash.

Next, we locate the staircase that will lead us up to the fourth floor, where the cells are. Finding it easily, we climb and climb and climb. I'm out of breath by the time we reach the floor we need. Thankfully, it's a moment before Jarod says, "Clear. You should have five minutes to locate them and give them the message."

We start our search, running down different hallways and looking through every small square of bars on each metal door. After what has to be the thirtieth cell, we finally find them.

Mr. and Mrs. Hansen's cell is decently accommodating with a full-size bed, two desks and chairs, a bookshelf full of books, lamps, lots of notebooks, and a jar full of pens. It appears that being residents for almost four years gives them some kind of rights. Mr. Hansen is in bed fast asleep, his dirty-blond hair obscuring half of his face, but luckily, Mrs. Hansen is sitting at a desk reading.

Her light blue eyes, almost twins to Ash's, lift to see us, and she freezes in shock. Greer tries waving her over to the cell door, but instead, she runs to her husband and shakes him awake. He stirs, and with his wife's wordless insistence, he looks and sees us standing there.

He scrambles out of bed and runs over to us. "Greer? Talliana? Oh my god, girls. I am so happy and terrified to see you both."

Greer quickly relays the plan to get them out, while I shift from checking the time on my watch to looking around, trying not to think about who else could be here. My heart aches, and my pulse races with the need to find him, but I do my best to push it all down.

Greer jars me back to life after two minutes have passed by whispering, "Time to go." One minute to spare to get off of this level.

We slip back down the way we came and down the stairs to the main level. We are almost back to where we have to crawl past the office window when I see a shimmery blue out of the corner of my eye. I turn and see a lizard.

No wait. *The lizard.*

The one that I saw the night at the lake. It's looking at me, and it keeps moving its head back and forth like it wants me to follow it. I grab Greer's arm to bring her to a halt. When her eyes meet mine, I point at the little creature.

She gives me a "so what" look, and I silently indicate to her that we have to follow it. Greer makes it very clear with her expression that we are not following the lizard. I hesitate when the lizard darts down a hallway to the right of us, and with one last look from Greer that tells me she is about to strangle me, I run after it.

I have probably lost my mind, but this lizard wants me to follow it, so there has to be a reason. I have to trust my intuition. Let's just hope I don't get us both killed for it. Or grounded.

Jarod is in my ear asking us what we are doing and to turn around, but we can't talk back to him to explain, so he is going to have to just go along with us for the ride. I pull my communication device out of my ear so I can focus better. I know Greer will keep hers in.

I walk carefully with Greer right on my heels, making sure to check every door we walk by, peeking around hallways before we pass them, and, of course, watching the lizard to make sure we stay close to it. It leads us down a narrow winding staircase, one that was not on any of the maps we looked at of this place but is exactly like the one Greer drew last night. Coincidence? I think not.

Greer and I make quick work of the stairs while the lizard, too small to hop down the stairs quickly, deftly crawls on the wall next to the staircase. Once we reach the bottom, the lizard transitions to scurrying along the floor again, leading us past more cells until it stops in front of one. My heart nearly beats out of my chest as I slow down my pace and approach the cell. Peering in the open room with wall-to-ceiling bars, I can't believe my eyes. This wonderful, amazing, perfect little lizard led me right to him.

To Trey.

He is curled up in a ball in the corner of his cell, shivering from the cold, trying to sleep it seems. Greer stops next to me, eyes wide and mouth open. I have no idea who or what might be down here, so I don't dare speak aloud. Instead, I take down my mental shield, causing all the carefully laid bricks to come crashing down and letting all the confusion and anger and sadness I've felt over the past six months come flooding forward. If my emotions are intense enough, he doesn't have to tune into me to feel them. Greer cringes beside me, so I know she at least feels them.

Trey jerks out of his position and immediately locks eyes with me. Fear and panic pour off of him when he runs over to me and cups my face through the bars.

"Talli? Oh no, no, no. What in the hell are you doing here?" he whispers. He appears okay for the most part, better than how he was when I saw him in my dream two months ago. There are no visible signs of serious injury, and I can't sense any either; that's good.

Joy surges through my veins like an adrenaline rush. We found him. He is alive.

I was right this entire time. There's no time for a happy dance, though.

"Rescuing you."

I look over at Greer, who is already trying to assess the lock on the door. Her head is shaking. It's not something we can try to pick. Damn it. I need a plan. I need a plan *now*.

"You need to get out of here. Leave me and go." Trey's fear triples, and I can feel it in his grip on my face. I pull his hand away and look him in the eyes. "Where is the key? Tell me, or so help me, I will bring the whole place down looking for one.

"Please, Talli." His plea makes me flinch, but I cannot back down.

"I will not leave without you."

Trey knows that there is no convincing me otherwise. The longer he keeps trying, the higher the chance we get caught. He nods his head toward a door almost directly across from his cell. "That door should be unlocked. Inside is a man. He will have a key. He keeps it on a small red carabiner clipped on his side."

I nod once, and I am at the door before Greer can protest. I open the door an inch and look inside to make sure all the lights are off, and no one appears to be awake. When all is quiet, I ease the door farther open and tuck myself inside without a sound. My eyes only needing a second to adjust to the darkness, I quickly search the desk, walls, and drawers, all while keeping an eye on the man asleep in the bed in the small room adjoining this one. The key is not here. Maybe he sleeps with it on him?

I creep into the other room where the man sleeps on a small cot, and luckily, I see a glint of silver coming from the crack in the bedside table drawer. I grab ahold of the handle and start pulling the drawer open when a loud creak comes from the drawer.

I still, waiting to see if the man moves. When he doesn't, I grab the key and begin to flee out of the room. In my rush, I hit a stool with my foot and flinch knowing that definitely woke him up.

"Who's there?" he asks gruffly as he gets himself to his feet.

I think about running for a minute, but he could sound an alarm. I curse myself for leaving my bow on the floor by Trey's cell. I reach for my dagger strapped to my thigh instead and throw it. Even in his haze of sleep, he darts to the side and misses getting hit. He runs straight into me and uses his force to put me on my back.

The man is on me, trying to grab hold of my arms, but I grab my second dagger right as he grabs my neck. I struggle to draw air into my lungs.

He is choking me. I can't breathe.

I stab him in the side, and he flinches, but his grip starts to tighten. I pull the dagger out, and desperation grips me as I plunge the dagger into his chest. He lets go, falling backward with a thud, and I am instantly trying to gulp in air. I push his weight slightly off me and slide out the rest of the way.

Before I can completely get away from him, I can sense that he's still breathing. The knife just missed his heart. My vision darkens at the corners and without thought, I grab the knife and plunge it back in his chest, hitting the mark this time.

I hear a gasp, then turn to see Greer, staring at me. My vision clears and I scramble to my feet, looking at where the man lies.

Dead. I...I killed him. Why did I kill him?

Greer rushes over to me, grabs the key from my shaking hand, and runs back out. Taking a deep breath, I grab the knife from his chest. Nausea sweeps over me at the sickening sound it makes, but I push it down and run after Greer.

I can think about it later, once we are all out and safely away from here. As soon as I walk out of the room, Trey is running for me, arms encircling me, and I allow myself the moment of relief feeling his arms around me again brings me.

"We have to go now. Jarod does not have eyes on us." Greer's voice is frantic, and she doesn't wait to see if we're following before she runs up the stairs, taking them two at a time. Trey and I hustle behind her, following her lead and finding our way back to where I spotted the lizard. Wherever that little creature went, I hope to see it again so I can give it a proper thanks.

After Greer's quick but thorough assessment that none of the guards have changed positions, we get on our hands and knees and follow her, crawling past the office window. We hop to our feet as soon as we pass, slowly going out the door, and race down the next hallway until we are out the back door and running for the fence. We don't stop until we are back at the van parked about a mile away from the prison.

Jarod opens the door and goes rigid at the sight of Trey. "Treyton? What in god's name...You should be...Nope. Explain later. Get in the van." We don't hesitate and jump in. The door isn't even fully shut when the van speeds away into the night.

IT IS STRICTLY FORBIDDEN FOR A MEMBER OF THE ORDER TO SHARE THEIR TRUE SELF OR DETAILS OF OUR CALLING WITH A HUMAN. OUR SECRECY IS PARAMOUNT BECAUSE HUMANS DESTROY WHAT THEY DO NOT UNDERSTAND. THIS DECISION IS FOR OUR ENSURED SAFETY.

- COMMUNITY LAWS & GUIDELINES

CHAPTER 22

IT IS AN HOUR's drive back to the safe house, and I have positioned myself opposite Trey on purpose with my knees up, pressed to my chest, and my arms holding them close. I'm relieved Trey is alive, and we are all safe, but I'm furious. He forced Theora to lie and make everyone believe he was dead. He tried to convince *me* he was dead. That will not go unpunished.

Our only interaction since climbing into the van was me giving him an elixir to help heal any minor soreness he was feeling, as well as help with his malnourishment. He took it without question. Greer gave me a look, clearly communicating that I should take something, too, but I couldn't. Not yet. I have to see the evidence of what happened to me. Maybe seeing what that man did to me and what he was trying to do will make me feel better somehow. Like what I did to him was justified. Can an unnecessary, violent act be justified though?

Jarod keeps trying to ask questions, but it is clear Trey is not feeling chatty about it, so he eventually relents. Now, halfway through the drive, Jarod pulls out his phone and calls Dad. I listen while he explains how he sent in two of us and now he has three of us. It doesn't take long before Jarod hands the phone to me.

"Now, before you yell, we are all okay, and it will be morning before they likely discover we were there."

Silence for three heartbeats, "Talliana, this is the most reckless, disobedient thing you have ever done in your life," another prolonged silence. "But I am sorry. You were right. You trusted your gut, and it paid off." Now it's my turn to be quiet.

"Really? You're not mad?"

"I am furious. You better enjoy every second you get with Trey now because once you get home, you'll be lucky if you ever see daylight again." It's an idle threat, but I still can't stop myself from meeting Trey's gaze for the first time since getting in the van.

When I don't respond, I hear a sigh through the phone and then, "Get some rest. We will go through a detailed report when you get home. I will call Orsen and Angeline and let them know their son is alive and coming home because neither of my daughters can follow orders. Make sure your sister knows she is in trouble too."

"Yes, sir. Love you, Daddy."

"Love you too." The call ends, and I hand it back to Jarod.

"Is he pissed?" Greer asks without looking at me. Her head is leaned back against the back door of the van, eyes closed.

"Yep."

"Awesome." Her sarcasm would almost be funny if I weren't so tired and angry.

It's another twenty minutes before we get to the safe house. As soon as we park, I'm running into the house, heading straight for the bathroom. I need out of this van, I need out of these blood-coated clothes, I need space to deal with my emotions. I am on the verge of bursting at the seams with everything I'm feeling right now.

I hear Trey trying to keep up with me as I run through the house. I go right to the bathroom, but before I can shut the door, Trey catches it with his hand and pushes his way in. He closes it behind him and turns back to look at me. This is the first time we have been under any kind of real light, and the expression on his face tells me I must look pretty bad. I avoid the urge to turn toward the mirror.

Not yet.

"Why?" is all I ask.

"I didn't want you looking for me. Though, I should have known better because you did anyway." I don't miss the frustration in his tone.

"Don't you dare start accusing me of things!" I shout at him. Taking a deep breath to calm myself, I then ask, "Did you know they had Ash's parents there? Alive and well?"

"I found out a month in. I can promise you they are not well, though."

"I'm sorry, you're right. I'm sure they're not." I pause momentarily, thinking over my words, then explain, "We were there on a mission to get a message to them. Apparently, our parents have known they were alive. They are working on getting them out."

His eyes widen. "I hope rescuing me did not jeopardize that plan."

My heart sinks. I didn't consider that. I only saw my own need to get Trey out of there. *Sorry, Ash,* I say in my head. "We'll figure it out if it did. With how thorough Jarod is, I suspect he is already on top of it."

He nods and doesn't say anything further. Trey has never been a big talker, but now is not the time to be quiet. Not when I literally just killed someone to get him out.

I killed him...I had to. He would have stopped us otherwise. Even if he didn't, he saw me. That could have put me in further danger.

"I never believed you were dead, even as I attended your funeral. My intuition wouldn't let me, not for a minute. But you know what sucks? Your parents and Ash believed it, and I couldn't tell them that I thought you were lying because I couldn't bring myself to put them through that. So I pretended to mourn with them. I pretended not to know anything more than they did. Seriously, I have no idea how they will explain this to Ash. The story they decided to spin was that you left to go to college in Virginia, and you died because of some freak heart condition no one knew you had. Serves them right, though, for continually choosing to lie to him."

Trey rubs his face with his hands. He's tired. In the light, I can fully take in his appearance. I have never seen his hair this long. As far as I know, he has never let it get this long before. He inherited his mom's thick black hair, and he told me once that if it got too long, it would have to be considered an Afro. He was right. What has always been a well-trimmed curly poof on top of his head with shaved sides is now full of long curls that jut out in every direction and just about cover his ears. I examine his eyes, which look like they are sunken in a bit more, and his jaw is hidden behind a thick layer of scruff. He has been a prisoner for six months. *Six months.* The least I can do is let him rest before I rip into him for doing what he did.

Finally, he says, "I'm sorry, Talli. All I have ever wanted is for you to be safe and not to have to make the hard choices like the rest of us."

I swallow hard and it sends a dull ache through my throat, a re-minder of the hard choice I made tonight. "I'm angry. Very angry with you. But now is not the time. I can yell at you when we get home."

On that note, I reluctantly turn toward the mirror over the sink, and it only takes a blink before tears well up and start to fall.

Even though it's dry at this point, the faint shine of the man's blood is still visible on my face, my leathers, and in my hair. I unzip my top and drop it to the floor, leaving me in my sports bra while I scrutinize my neck. It's covered in purple and green bruises and slightly swollen. Seeing it doesn't make me feel better about what I did like I had hoped it would. I am still horrified about what came over me.

Through my tears, I turn on the shower and start trying to remove the rest of my clothes. I feel like I'm suffocating.

Wordlessly, Trey moves from his frozen position at the door and helps me peel my clothes off. I don't think about the fact that he has never seen me completely naked before. It doesn't matter. Nothing matters right now aside from getting clean.

In the shower, I let the hot water wash over me, trying to absorb as much warmth and reassurance as I possibly can from it before the images flash back through my head. He was choking me; he would have killed me without a second thought; he would have stopped us from leaving; he likely participated in Trey's torture. Those are all facts, and I don't deny them. But he was human. He had a life, maybe a spouse and kids. I could have taken someone's loved one away from them and they will never get him back.

Our training with Mr. Simon focuses on self-defense which can and often does lead to the death of your adversary, so it's not like the possibility of killing someone never crossed my mind. But I am a Healer, not a fighter. I didn't think I would need to, at least not so soon. I can still feel his body pressing me down against the hard floor while I struggle. *But I got away from him without killing him*, I reason to myself. It wasn't life or death. Not really.

The image of Mei-Lien underneath me, the urge to squeeze over-whelming me, the desire to make her pay all comes back, too. I'm no better than them.

My slow-falling tears turn into body-racking sobs.

Trey is safe. Trey is here. Trey is with me. I repeat it like a mantra to keep myself from drowning in my guilt and fear. I grab the soap I brought with me and start scrubbing every inch of my body in an attempt to get the feel of that man off me—the feel of Mei-Lien's pulse under my thumb.

When it doesn't work, I give up and pull back the curtain, finding Trey sitting on the floor. He is quietly crying. I'm not sure what the exact reason is for his tears. He has so many reasons to cry, just like I do. Grabbing a towel, I wrap it around myself and then crouch in front of him. He carefully runs his hand down the side of my neck. It hurts, and I'm ready for it to go away. I close my eyes at his touch and let my forehead rest against his.

"Your turn to shower. I'm sure you want one," I say gently.

We both get to our feet, and I turn away while he undresses and gets in. Realizing we don't have clean clothes, I ensure my towel is in place and go to the door to get some. I'm surprised when waiting on the floor outside there are two piles, one for me and one for Trey. Mine has an elixir resting on top. Greer. I need to remember to thank her for literally everything at the first opportunity.

I take the elixir without question and watch the coloring around my neck fade in the mirror before getting dressed. When I hear the water turn off, I hand Trey a towel and indicate where his borrowed clothes are toward the sink. I turn to the door and let him get dressed.

His hands touch my upper arms, and he turns me around to face him. I let myself fall into his arms and take his warmth in.

"I missed you," I whisper to him.

He squeezes me tighter for a moment, then pulls away enough to see me. He takes in my now normal neck and asks, "I know we said we would talk later, but you are okay?" He sees right through me. That hasn't changed.

"I'm working on it. You?" I try to keep my voice steady, but the resolve I just worked so hard to build starts to crumble already.

"I'm working on it." One side of his mouth quirks up at his copied reply. The softness in his eyes fades quickly as he becomes visibly uncomfortable.

"I. Uh. I did want to know..." He swallows hard. "It's been six months. Has there..."

Knowing where he is going with this, I cut him off before he can say it. "No. Not even a thought of anyone else."

He releases a deep exhale and eliminates the small distance between us again. His lips crash against mine, sweeping me into a kiss so urgent and so desperate, it takes me a moment to comprehend what is happening. Trey has only ever kissed me like this once before. The night before he left. He likely knew in that moment what was going to happen, but he pretended otherwise. I use my anger at him to fuel the intensity of my movements. Trey takes it in stride, kissing me through all the anger, pain, and relief that's starting to flood in.

After a few moments, he pulls away, grabs our dirty laundry with one hand, and takes mine with the other. "Stay with me tonight in my room? I don't want you out of my sight right now."

"Good. I don't want you out of arm's reach. Ever." That is probably a dramatic statement to make, but he smiles in response and leans over to kiss me again, just a quick, soft one this time.

I follow him to the laundry room to drop off our clothes and then we head back to the room he is staying in. It's right across from where Greer and I are staying. Unlike our room, though, this one has a queen bed instead of two twins.

We crawl into bed and I can barely adjust my pillow before he pulls me back against him, cuddling me close. I don't protest, but settle in as the little spoon and close my eyes. I take three deep breaths in and carefully blow them each out before I let exhaustion pull me under.

CHAPTER 23

THE NEXT DAY ON our long flight home, Trey, Greer, and I devised a plan. Ash needs the truth, regardless of the consequences. Trey coming home changes everything. What everyone else thinks is best be damned.

Greer texted him and told him to meet the two of us at the lake after dinner. She instructed him not to believe anything he was told and not to let anyone touch him in the meantime. Honestly, we have no idea how the Waterstones will try to explain Trey to him or explain his parents, for that matter.

It's already dark outside when Mr. Simon picks us up at the airport. When we get home, Trey heads over to see his parents while Greer and I make a beeline for the lake.

Ash is sitting on the bank by the lake, reading a book with a book-light attached so he can see. He stands up, hearing us approach, and quickly stashes his book into his backpack. "What's going on?"

"Did anyone say anything to you about Trey today?" I ask.

"No. Why? Dad said they wanted to talk to me after dinner, but I managed to convince them that I needed to bring something by your house first, and then I would be right back. They're probably worried by now."

We anticipated this. If they bring it up, Trey will tell them that Ash is with us.

"Sit, Ash. We have a lot to tell you," I begin.

To my surprise, he doesn't sit. Instead, his sea-glass blue eyes bounce between Greer and me, seeming to hesitate about something.

"Ash, what is it?" Greer asks, her tone low.

"I know," he answers quietly.

"You know what?" I ask.

"If you are about to tell me who or what you two are, I already know."

"You already know?!" Greer's surprise and annoyance explode out of her.

"Ash, tell us what you know," I prompt, trying my hand at being the calm one for once.

"Sit, please."

Greer and I do as he says. Oh, how the tables have turned. Ash starts pacing and tells us everything.

He does, in fact, know exactly what we are and what the community is. He explains to us how, when he started becoming suspicious, he had written down every weird thing he had witnessed in a "research journal." After he had his memory tampered with the first time, it took him a while, but he eventually found the journal he had hidden and resumed his "study" of us. After the third memory tamper, he realized he had to hide his suspicions better and become the clueless human we all thought he was.

179

"It is. Let's call it a night here, though, and talk again more when you are ready," I suggest.

"We still have the dilemma of what to do. We want to leave that up to you, Ash. Do you want to continue to pretend like you don't know, or do you want everyone to know that you know?" Greer asks.

Ash seems to be at war with the decision but finally answers, "I'm tired of the secrets, and I trust you both to keep telling me if they erase my memory again."

"Alright. I guess it's time to walk you home and face the music. Greer and I are already grounded, I'm sure. We might as well add to the sentence. You ready?" I ask Ash.

He nods. "I want to go hug my brother and go to bed."

Greer and I walk with Ash back to his house. It's a long walk full of awkward silence that I didn't think was possible between the three of us. But I understand why it's there, and I have no doubt that it will go away over time.

When we walk into his house, all the downstairs lights are still on, and I hear quiet voices coming from the dining room. They cease abruptly, and Mrs. Waterstone comes around the corner.

"Asher, we have been so worried about you. We were told you were with the girls, but you shouldn't run off like that," Mrs. Waterstone lightly scolds.

"I'm sorry." Ash looks around. "Where's Trey?"

Mrs. Waterstone freezes, then pins me with a look. Trey rounds the same corner she just came from, still in the borrowed clothes he had on when we parted a couple of hours ago.

"Hey, brother." Trey gives him a broad smile, and Ash walks down the hall to meet him. He wraps his arms around Trey and holds on for dear life. Everyone stays in silence for a moment, waiting for Ash.

He pulls away and examines Trey. "Is it all true?"

Trey meets my eyes, and I nod.

"Yes. I am so sorry for what you've been through," Trey says gently.

"I should be saying that to you," Ash replies.

Trey's jaw clenches, but he nods. Ash hugs him again, and Mr. Waterstone enters the hallway. Trey and Ash move over toward Greer and me so that the four of us are facing the parents on the other side of the hallway.

"I think he knows, Orsen." Mrs. Waterstone tells her husband. If I am not mistaken, her posture suggests relief.

Mr. Waterstone looks to her, then to us in surprise. "Asher, what do you know?"

Almost imperceptibly, Greer steps in front of Ash and answers, "He knows everything, and it's going to stay that way."

Hell yeah!

"I agree with them. We all decided this together on the trip home," Trey adds, looping his arm around my waist.

"I didn't realize you three were the new elders in this community." Mr. Waterstone says tersely.

Mrs. Waterstone grabs her husband's arm and says to all of us, "I think we all need some sleep. We can discuss this in the morning with Aaron and Kasumi present."

Mr. Waterstone places his hand over his wife's and smiles at her. "I think that is best. It's been a long night."

Greer doesn't budge from her spot, and I can see from my position behind her that her spine is straight and her stance is wide. "I want to be assured that Ash will not be touched and he can rest peacefully tonight without fear that you will try to tamper with his memories the minute he closes his eyes."

Mr. Waterstone narrows his eyes on Greer but places a hand over his heart and says, "You have my word. He is safe in this house like he has always been."

Greer relaxes and then opens the front door, promptly walking out of it. Ash goes right up the stairs to his room, and Mr. and Mrs. Waterstone go back in the direction they came, leaving Trey and I standing alone in the hallway.

"Is it silly that I don't want to leave you?" I ask, looking up into his dark eyes.

"Not one bit. I feel the same way, but I think I need to be here for Ash tonight. I'll see you tomorrow the first chance I get," Trey reassures me.

"Okay."

He pulls me close and kisses me. Soft and slow, sending warmth flooding through my entire body.

He pulls away after a moment and walks me out the door to where Greer is waiting for me at the bottom of the porch steps.

"Goodnight, you two."

"Goodnight," Greer and I say in unison.

CHAPTER 24

THE NEXT MORNING, I wake up to Greer dressed and pulling on her sneakers. I check the time on my phone: eight o'clock. It's not that early, but I'm still exhausted since we didn't get to bed last night until two a.m. My brain is still foggy with sleep.

"Why are you up so early?"

"I have something I need to take care of," Greer answers.

Sitting up in bed, I rub my eyes and ask, "What?"

"Go back to sleep, Talli. I promise to tell you later."

Usually, I would argue, but I really want to go back to sleep. So, I lie back down and close my eyes.

The next thing I know, I am being woken up by a kiss on my cheek. My eyes flutter open to find Trey standing over me, so close...

I smile at him. "I guess you found a chance pretty early, huh?"

He laughs softly. "I have never known you to consider noon as early."

Noon? I want to care. There is definitely a version of myself inside that cares that I slept in that late, but I'm choosing not to listen to her right now. Instead, I laugh and cover my face with my comforter. The bed shifts and dips. Trey pulls back the blankets and slides underneath them to lay beside me. A twin-size mattress is not enough space for two people, which means it is perfect.

Rolling to my other side so that I am facing him, I wrap my arms around his neck and kiss him deeply. Butterflies flutter in my stomach as he puts his arm around my waist and pulls me as close as possible. He devours my mouth as I open it for him. He tastes like coffee and smells like vanilla.

I run my hand through his tight curls and down his smooth jaw. He shaved. I didn't even notice when I saw him. That is where the vanilla smell is coming from, his aftershave.

His lips move faster, and the grip of his hand on my waist tightens. He nudges me so that I am on my back, and he follows me, shifting his weight so that he is only halfway on top of me. His hand moves up and down my side, and my pulse quickens. I want so badly for him to touch me. *Really* touch me. But he always stops short. I groan in frustration. He pulls his lips away, breathless, and rests his forehead against mine.

"I came up here to get you, but you have seduced me into your bed instead. Now you have less time to get ready."

"I did no such thing!" I protest, indignation rising.

Trey laughs, and my heart smiles from the sound. It's so beautiful.

"Really, though. We have to be on our way to your dad's office in..." he looks at the watch on his wrist, "ten minutes."

"For what?"

"My mom said it was about Ash, but I think we will end up in there for a few hours talking about everything that's happened in the last two days."

"Right. I guess there is a lot to debrief them on." When Greer and I walked into the house last night, we got quick hugs from Mom and Dad and were then sent promptly to bed since it was so late.

Trey climbs out of bed, and I do the same. He doesn't move or stop watching me as I collect some clothes and then stride into the bathroom to get dressed.

When I come out, he is standing by my desk, looking at a picture I have pinned to the wall above it. It's one Mom took of Greer, Ash, and me on Christmas Eve. We have flour on our clothes and faces from making pizza. Ash is trying to spin out the dough on his finger while Greer and I laugh at him. That was the night I had felt my lightest since Trey left, just for everything to come crashing down on me a few hours later.

I move to his side and say with a light tone, "You are under every obligation to help me fill up this wall with pictures of you and me or the four of us."

The corner of his lip lifts. "I have every intention of doing so."

On the way out, I grab a granola bar, and we race over to Dad's office at the community building in Mom's car.

When we enter his office, everyone is already seated around his conference table waiting for us, bonded creatures included.

"Sorry, everyone. I guess I slept in," I apologize, and we take the last two remaining seats. Dad sits at the head of the table with Mr. Waterstone at the other end. Mrs. Waterstone, Chief Lu, and Mr. Simon sit to his right on the far side of the table, across from Ash, Greer, and now me and Trey. The formality of it all is very intimidating. The bonded creatures are scattered around the room in various spots. Melisandre,

Lemon, and Seth are sitting on the floor next to their people, Midori is coiled up over Chief Lu's shoulder, and Pebble is resting on Mrs. Waterstones head, nestled between her braids.

Ash is across from Chief Lu and Midori, and it seems he is trying to push himself as far back into his chair as possible. I don't blame him. The viper is pretty terrifying to look at.

"Alright, everyone is here. I don't want to take up too much of everyone's Saturday, but we have much to discuss today. Let's get started," Dad says to the room.

We discuss Ash first, and the elders allow him to plead his case. I remain quiet while he speaks, and Greer and Trey do the most to back him up. It becomes evident that the three of them made a plan this morning while I was sleeping. As much as I would have liked to have been part of that conversation, I am okay with letting them handle it. I will have plenty to answer for today.

The elders decide to let Ash keep his memories for two reasons: his parents are about to be rescued, and he has a knack for figuring every-thing out anyway. We didn't voice the fact that, if they had decided unfavorably, Greer and I would have told him the minute we were away from everybody.

Next on the agenda was the mission. This is the uncomfortable part for me. Greer, as lead, outlines how everything went and what happened, avoiding any serious details surrounding what happened to me. *What I did.* When she finishes, all eyes turn to me.

Fuck.

Trey gives my hand a squeeze, and I rise from my seat to explain my side of it.

Dad looks thoughtful when I mention the lizard since he knows I have seen it before. Everyone else seems baffled by it. The whole room goes quiet when I detail what happened with the guard I killed. My slightly altered version of it. The version missing the part where he wasn't dead after I stabbed his chest the first time.

"I just..." My voice cracks. "I didn't think past my desperation to breathe. I stabbed him in the chest to get away. Then I grabbed my dagger and we all left like Greer said."

Mr. Simon looks at me closely. I didn't lie, so he shouldn't have picked up on anything. I just skipped over some details. Greer also looks at me. She is the only one that knows exactly what happened and I hope to keep it that way. I know the moment we are alone, she will want to discuss it with me, and I won't be able to avoid it.

My skin feels feverish, and my stomach is begging to throw up that granola bar.

Trey grabs my hand and gently pulls me back into my seat.

Chief Lu argues for some consequence for disobeying orders—for me, not Greer. I don't disagree with her point that Greer only disobeyed to keep her partner, me, safe. Dad sides with her. To my surprise, the Waterstones both defend me. They claim that good Hawks follow their intuition and listen when nature calls them to do something, and I apparently did both. If I had to guess, those words sound more like Mrs. rather than Mr. Waterstone.

Mr. Simon chimes in for the first time and defends my actions as well. Ultimately, I get off with only a verbal lashing and warning to never disobey orders again.

"Alright, Talli, Greer, and Ash. You three are free to leave," Dad tells us.

I look to Trey, realizing his trial is next. "Can I stay?"

"No," Dad answers. I want to protest, but I am already treading on thin ice at the moment.

"I'll meet you once I am done," Trey tells me, meeting my eyes. He doesn't want me here either. I hesitate, but leave with Ash and Greer.

Once outside, Greer tells Ash, "I want to show you something."

We both follow her to the library, and I know exactly what she is up to once we walk through the doors.

She leads us through all the rows in the history section, then stops in front of the blank wall. Greer kicks the baseboard in at a particular spot, releasing a latch that allows her to push the door open. Through the door is a room with a floor-to-ceiling bookshelf on one wall, which houses books about the Order.

Ash's eyes light up at the sight, and he smiles widely. For him, this must be a close comparison to heaven.

"I can read all of these?"

"Yes, you can check them out like any normal library book," Greer answers.

Ash slowly walks from one side of the wall to the other, not touching any of the books but skimming over their titles. I suspect to determine which ones he wants first.

Greer and I lean up against the wall casually, enjoying the sight of Ash's absolute happiness. We know that soon, he'll have a lot more questions, and we'll answer any of them that we can. But giving him access to this will aid in his obsessive need to collect information.

"Where did you go this morning?" I ask Greer, keeping my voice low.

She sighs. "I was putting a contingency in place in case things didn't go our way today with Ash."

My eyebrows lift in question, and she explains, "I made sure Mei-Lien wasn't going to mess with his memories again."

I stand from my casual position. "How did you manage that?"

"I owe her a favor now that she can call in whenever she wants."

"You think that was a good idea?"

She shrugs, standing up as well. "It doesn't matter if it was or not. It's done."

"What if things didn't go our way? Was she going to just pretend to mess with his memory?"

"That was pretty much the plan."

I let out a low whistle. Mei-Lien is clever. She will not call in this favor for something small. She will hold onto it until the absolute worst time, then call it in.

"He is lucky to have you at his back. *I'm* lucky to have you at my back." I turn to her. "You have done a lot for me, Greer. Most of all, you believed me when even I questioned if I was crazy. I haven't said it enough lately, but thank you. I couldn't have asked for a better sister."

She nods, then says, "You know we'll have to talk later, right? I'm not going to just cover for you like that and let you off the hook."

"I know."

She puts a hand on my shoulder and smiles. Then, without saying anything, she strides off to help Ash carry his armful of books.

"Talli, tell me what really happened. No bullshit."

I let myself fall onto my bed. I've been dreading this conversation all afternoon. How do I explain something that I don't even understand myself?

I scrub my face with my hands trying to will thoughts into existence. Exasperated, I explain, "I don't know what happened, Greer. One minute I was trying to get out from under him, the next I was looking at his dead body."

"You blacked out?" Greer asks incredulously. She is both right and wrong. My vision darkened at the corners, but I was fully conscious.

Her arms are crossed, and she is hovering over me from where I am sprawled on my bed.

"Will you please sit? You are making me uncomfortable."

She slowly backs up until she is sitting on the edge of her bed, arms still crossed and eyes still narrowed. Well, that's slightly better.

"I didn't black out, not really. I felt my body make the movement to kill him, but I acted without thought. It wasn't until you walked in and looked at me that I realized what I did."

Greer seems to think that over a moment. Then reasons, "Okay, it is like your survival instincts kicked in."

Maybe? It is sound logic, but it doesn't quite feel right. I know there is more to it than that. Does Greer really need to know that right now, though? Why should we both worry about something that is likely nothing? Probably just adrenaline or hormones. My body has felt strange lately, and my mood has been...different.

Finally, I reply, "I think you're right, Greer."

She scrutinizes me a moment longer and then relaxes. "Why lie to the elders then?"

"I didn't lie. I just didn't provide all the details." Her eyes narrow again, so I add, "I didn't know what it was at first. I was scared of how the whole thing would be perceived."

"Fair enough. I just thought I saw..." she trails off.

"What?"

"I thought I saw black swirling in your eyes."

An icy chill shoots down my spine, and my hands start to shake.

"I wasn't that close to you, though, and it was dark. It must have been the lighting."

My eyes really did darken. Not adrenaline or hormones, then. Something else. I feel all the blood in my face drain and Greer is suddenly in front of me, hand on my shoulder. "Talli? Are you okay?"

I blink a few times and look up into her eyes, her pewter-gray irises clear. I jolt out of my spiral and reply, "Yeah. I just...Talking about killing someone and what I did...I don't feel well."

She nods in understanding and gives me space to escape to the bathroom where I continue my spiral.

MAGIC IS NOT INFINITE IN ANY ONE INDIVIDUAL OR CREATURE. IT IS MEANT TO BE NURTURED AND USED IN MODERATION. IT REQUIRES REST, MUCH LIKE OUR PHYSICAL BODIES. DRAINING IT TOO QUICKLY CAN HAVE LASTING EFFECTS. DRAINING IT COMPLETELY CAN COST A PRICE THE HAWK IS NOT PREPARED TO PAY.

- THE LAWS OF MAGIC

CHAPTER 25

March

"A WEEK IS ENOUGH time, right?"

Greer gives me a look from her corner of the room. "I think a week is generous, all things considered."

Trey has been home a week, and I still haven't asked him for any answers. Not about why he left us those notes when he left, what happened while he was gone, or his conversation with the elders after they told me to leave.

I have dropped subtle hints each day when I see him, but he has pretended not to notice. I know he does, though. I'm just so scared to push him to talk about things he isn't comfortable talking about yet, but there are some things I need to know. My hope that he would offer up the information without me having to ask has disappeared entirely.

I'm also at a disadvantage because, as it turns out and if my lack of sleep is any indication, I am the type of person who doesn't easily let things go. I thought I would sleep better once Trey was back, but honestly, aside from that first night home, I still have been sleeping as fitfully as before. It's as if an internal battle is going on inside of me.

One that I think I am losing.

"You're right. I'm going over there this minute, and I'm going to demand some answers." I stand up, confidently at first, but then wonder, what if he is busy or in the middle of something? "First, I will text him and make sure he is free."

I sit back down and grab my phone to do exactly that. Greer chuckles softly and returns to her sketch pad resting on her bent legs.

Me: *Hey, are you free? I want to see you.*

Trey: *I'm free. Want to come here or meet by the tree?*

I am not sure how this conversation is going to go. Even though I think as much privacy as possible would be best, I am afraid to tarnish our spot if this doesn't go well.

Me: *I'll come over. Be there in 10.*

I put on my shoes and head to the door, my back straight with renewed determination.

"Good luck," Greer calls to me.

"Thanks. I think I might need it."

The walk to Trey's house is too short. Not nearly enough time for me to organize my thoughts. Instead, I focus on the setting sun before me.

Looking toward his house, I smile, realizing Trey is sitting on his front porch, watching out for me as I approach. When I reach the top steps, he pulls me to him in an embrace and kisses me gently before leading me inside and up to his room. I've been in Trey's room plenty of times, but this is the first time since he got back.

He has clean white walls dotted with framed pictures and not much else. Soft gray carpet covers the floors, and simple dark wood furniture fills the space. His desk is on the far wall underneath the window, his queen-size bed to the right of me, a side table beside it, and a dresser across from it.

As I cross the room and climb onto his bed, I notice collapsed boxes in the corner. "What's with the boxes?" I ask.

"Mom had started to box up my things before I came back, but luckily she only made it through a small amount." He gives a slight shrug and closes the door behind him. He climbs onto the bed as well, but to my relief, he keeps a small distance between us.

"What's on your mind, Talli?"

I sigh in frustration. "Am I still that easy to sense? I'm using the brick method now, and I've really been trying hard to keep them sturdy."

"I'm sorry, but I didn't even have to try. You wear everything on your face."

Note to self: work even harder on shields and do it in front of a mirror.

Seeing my dismay, Trey adds, "It's one of my favorite things about you. I always know what you're feeling, so it's easier to know how to make you happy."

My gut twists. If he knows how to make me happy so easily, why isn't he doing those things? Like offering me up some truth.

"Trey..." I start but stop to rethink my words. "Trey," I start again. "I have been trying to give you time, but I have questions. I don't expect you to tell me everything right now. But there are some things I need to know."

He slowly nods, and I plunge forward.

"Did you leave of your own accord?"

He swallows and folds his legs in front of him, getting comfortable. "On the last mission I went on, I was captured. I was told to go home for a night and then leave, making it appear like I left for my own reasons. Then, I was to turn myself over to them. Otherwise, they promised to burn the entire community to the ground."

My heartbeat kicks up at his explanation of what happened. It doesn't make sense.

"Why did you go along with it? You had to have known they could have been lying to you."

"That was a risk I was willing to take in case they were telling the truth."

"Did you not think the community could handle it? Why didn't you tell someone?"

"Next question."

"Trey."

"Talli, next question." His tone suggests there is no room for argument.

I grumble but move on, putting those unanswered questions aside for later.

"Why did they want you?"

"Next question."

I throw up my hands in frustration and climb out of his bed. My body needs to move. I start pacing, trying to think of one he might answer. When it comes to me, I ask, "How did you dream-walk from so far away?"

He closes his eyes, looking tired, but answers me. "Theora. I sent her to check on things while I was...away. To make sure the Brethren were being honest and everyone was safe. When she was checking on you, I felt something—a faint connection. Normally, when I walk into someone's dreams, there's a door I have to open to enter. But that night, when I felt that connection, I found a long, dark tunnel. I followed it, and when I reached the end, I could slip into your dreams. She and I believe that since her bond acts as an amplifier for my ability, it may also be used to reach people who are far away from me but close to her, almost like a satellite."

"That sounds like an extreme amount of energy use," I comment, brows furrowing. How did he survive that much power? Something like that shouldn't be possible.

"It was," he agrees grimly. "It knocked me out for two days. That's how I found out the Hansens were still alive. They were the ones to help me wake back up."

That makes sense. It was lucky that the Brethren decided to consult them for help before just killing Trey for no longer being of use. Whatever that use was.

A realization takes hold in my brain. He told me before that he found out about the Hansens about a month in, meaning he started dream-walking in September. Not just the one time in December when I realized it.

Anger, red and hot, starts to sizzle inside of me.

My words quickly shift to a demanding tone instead of a questioning one. "How many times? How many times did you walk in my dreams?"

Trey grimaces. "I lost count."

My mouth falls open.

He lost count.

He fucking lost count.

All of those memories of us that I was forced to relive in my dreams each night. I thought I was losing my mind.

Were they all really me? Was it my subconscious choosing it, or was he plucking them out of my head and forcing them to play?

"The only time I manipulated your dreams was on Christmas Day. Every other dream I walked in, I was merely a fly on the wall. I promise," he explains, clearly reading my face.

"How do you know that my brain didn't recognize you in it and thus forced me to relive those memories because of it?"

"Because that is not how it works."

"Are you sure?" I question, accusation sharpening my tone.

"Yes."

I force myself to relax. My anger feels like it's about to take over right now, but I can't let it. I need to remain calm. After taking three deep breaths, I ask, "How long were you out after Christmas?"

"A week."

My heart sinks. Hawks are not meant to drain ourselves so entirely that we get knocked out for even a minute. Our ability has limits for a reason. Limits we shouldn't pass because there are consequences when we do. The Great Hawk put them in place to maintain balance and ensure no single person can have too much power. Push too far, and it could kill you.

It hits me then what he did and why.

"You didn't expect to survive it, did you?"

He shakes his head, confirming my suspicions. I swallow down the pain in my chest. That's why he was basically saying goodbye. He thought it would kill him.

I can't fall apart. Not yet. I need to know a little more.

"Did you ever try to reach anyone else in the community?" I ask.

"I did, but I couldn't reach anyone else except Ash. One stroll in his dreams, though, and I never went back." His nose scrunches.

"You have to tell me." Curiosity flairs to life in my chest, temporarily replacing my anger. It's incredibly nosey to ask, but Ash is my best friend. I can't help it.

"I'll just say what he dreams about doing with a certain someone is disturbing. That image will be forever burned into my mind." He rubs his eyes with the palms of his hands like he is trying to wipe the image away.

I don't miss the fact that he tells me that story to lighten my darkening mood, but I allow myself a small laugh anyway and say, "Hard to look at Greer now, huh?"

"It's fine most of the time, but sometimes it will randomly appear in my mind like a bee that won't leave me alone."

I wish I could say I pity him, but I don't, even if the situation is funny. Pity is the last thing I feel for him right now. He had a way of communicating with me and telling me what happened, but he didn't use it. And the one time he actually risked his life to talk to me, he wasted it.

"I want to make sure that I am clear and understand. You knew for about five months that you could talk to me and tell me what happened, but it came with the risk of draining your ability to a fatal level. Finally, you decide to do it just so that you can wish me a Merry Christmas and tell me to run away before hoping you would die from it. Instead of doing the sensible thing and trying to quickly tell me what was going on so that I could rescue you."

His dark eyes look pained. "I didn't want you to be reckless and get yourself killed!" His breathing is rapid. "I know you. You wouldn't have let me stay in that cell one extra minute. If they had gotten their hands on you, they would have used you, hurt you in front of me to get me to tell them everything."

"You really think I would have run right in without a plan? I would have gone to the elders, and we would have found a way to get you out. I wouldn't have done that on my own."

"You think they would have believed you?"

I wince. I don't know if they would have or not. Everything that has happened to me in the last few months has not been entirely believable. But then I remember.

"Yes! You could have quickly explained to me that Theora was amplifying your power. But no. You would rather die by your own hand or stay in that cell and let god only knows what happen to you to keep me from being reckless?" I stop pacing in front of him and look at him directly before adding, "Hate to break it to you, but it's my recklessness that saved you! With no help from you. If you had given me the chance to convince them that you were in danger, then maybe I..." I break off, trying not to choke on the words.

"Maybe what, Talli?" he challenges.

"Maybe I wouldn't have had to kill someone!" I scream at him.

He drops his head, and I turn my back on him, my tears starting to fall. I can't stand to argue with him; it feels wrong, but I have no other choice. I can't ignore the past if I expect to have a future with him.

I know the man at my back is Trey, but the old Trey would have never challenged me before like that, he would have never made me feel small.

And I do right now. I feel so small.

I walk toward the door, making my way to leave, when his hand grips my arm, holding me back.

"Talli." Trey's voice is broken as he explains, "I only have ever cared about protecting you. I have done everything to protect you. I'm sorry if I was selfish and wanted to see you that night, but I needed to feel you. Touch you. Even if it was the last thing I did."

"You promised." I turn my face back to him, bearing my tears to him and continue, "you promised that you would always do everything you could to get back to me. You broke that promise."

"If there had been a way to without endangering your life, I would have."

I want to believe him. I want to fall into his arms and let him, with a few comforting words, take all the pain away.

"I love you," he whispers.

Those words are like a sledgehammer to my defenses, and I give in. I believe him. I fall into his arms and let him take all the pain away with comforting words.

CHAPTER 26

April

"AH, TREY. NICE TO have you back at training with the rest of us," Mr. Simon says.

I turn and see Trey in his regular exercise ensemble—black basketball shorts and a black athletic tank top—walking through the door.

"Good to be back. You'll have to go easy on me for the first couple of sessions, though. It's been a while," Trey replies.

"Don't worry. I'll make sure you get plenty of warm-up time before we get back to our usual pace."

Seven months of inactivity has quite an effect on a body that is used to at least three workouts a week. He will indeed have some work to do to get his body ready again.

Trey nods his thanks and catches my eye. I give him a small smile, and he heads my way. He looks fully back to normal now, like the old Trey. His skin is back to its usual golden-brown color, his face is full again, but in his eyes...something is different.

It's like the light that was there has been snuffed out, and now all that consumes him is fear. I attempt to tune into him but feel nothing. Using my inner eye as Ms. Horn has taught me, I look and find an ironclad mental shield. Again. I have been trying to catch him with his shield down for a month now, but it never slips or comes down.

He's still Trey, without a doubt, but there is an aggressive anxiety inside of him now that I can't figure out how to deal with. I hoped peeking at his emotions would give me a clue, but I can't seem to manage it.

Since our last conversation, Trey has been excessively paranoid. He's wanted me to be close to him every chance possible. I hardly leave his sight aside from school. I suspect keeping me close is the only way he feels like I'm safe.

Evidently not realizing what I just attempted, he reaches me and pulls me into a hug, then kisses me deeply. I get completely swept up in it, and everything in my mind and around us fades away. There is only us. Nothing else matters.

A throat clears. Trey pulls away unhurriedly, but gets the point Greer is trying to make. Before, my face would have reddened, but now? I don't care. I simply do not care anymore. He is here. He is mine again. I saved him, and I deserve this even if I got him back a bit broken.

Trey walks over to the treadmill and starts at a slow pace. He gestures toward the other treadmill beside him, expecting me to join him. He doesn't know I rarely run anymore. I train to fight now. I hesitate. Maybe I should do some running today; it wouldn't hurt. I start to walk toward Trey.

"Talli, I want to work on your offense today. On the mat, please. Grab your bow and arrow from the chair," Mr. Simon calls out.

I give Trey an apologetic look, and he gives me a confused one in return. I turn on my heel and do as I am told.

Going to the benches, I find Ash sitting on one of them with a book in his lap reading. I catch the title: *"Ability Registry: 1750-1800".*

Since Greer showed Ash the secret door in the library that hides all our people's books, he always has one in his hand—from the boring to the extremely boring ones. He has also started hanging out at our evening training sessions, watching Greer...I mean *us*, train.

It's been nice having him around and wholly a part of our lives again—no more secrets.

"Doing some light reading before your entertainment starts?" I ask Ash, my tone teasing.

"Watching you get your butt handed to you is not much entertainment. I've seen it too many times," Ash answers playfully.

I swat at the air, pretending to hit him, then move to my bow.

As I pick it up and the arrow next to it, I notice some kind of clay on each end of my bow and covering the head of the arrow. I touch it, and to my surprise, it's hard, like a tennis ball.

"It will keep you from accidentally stabbing anyone. Don't worry, it comes off. You need to learn how to use your bow or an arrow in close combat situations," Mr. Simon explains.

I stop examining it and walk to the mat. Mei-Lien meets me there with a wooden sword.

"Just defense and no powers, Mei-Lien," Mr. Simon barks at her.

She nods, but her smile tells me she has no intention of listening to that order—just like I have no intention of holding back.

From the edge of the mat, Greer calls out, "Start!"

I immediately go for it, using my bow first. I raise it above my head, swing it down like a baseball bat, and collide with the wooden sword.

"Good, Talli, but that move took too long. It was too easy to see and defend. Try less dramatic movements."

We restart on Mr. Simon's direction, and I run, pointing the clay end right at Mei-Lien's chest, trying for a stab. She blocks with her sword again, but the bow slides along the wood toward her face, and I jab her in the jaw.

"Shit! That hurt!" she yells and rubs her jaw.

I beam at the blow I was able to make. Greer gives me a thumbs-up. Then I look over to Trey, but he isn't on the treadmill anymore. Instead, he is standing on the other side of the mat. I didn't notice him move. His arms are crossed, his stance wide, and concern is etched into the lines on his face.

Mr. Simon's voice brings me back to the mat. "Well, don't let her hit you."

We start again.

Again.

And again.

Fourteen starts and seven bruises marring Mei-Lien's body later, she is seeing red. She has tried a few times to get her own hits in, but Mr. Simon has yelled at her the minute she made the move to do so.

We line up for our next start, and Mr. Simon says, "Alright, girls. No more offense or defense. But still no powers, just clean fighting."

Trey protests, "I have to disagree, Simon. They don't have clear minds..."

"There are no clear minds on the battlefield. You know that, Trey."

"Talli won't see battle."

"You've been gone for a while. Things have changed. Now start!"

I startle back into focus and see Mei-Lien charging me, wooden sword primed to strike. I raise my bow and meet it straight on. She bares down on it, trying to out-strength me. I hold firm. She lifts her sword back and goes under my arms, getting me in the ribs. I stumble back and get my bow in striking position once I regain my steps. I run toward her, meeting her in the middle, and manage to land a blow on her shoulder. She grabs ahold of my bow with her other hand and pulls it out of my grasp, tossing it across the room. I quickly move away from her and grab the arrow that's strapped to my back, holding it like a knife.

Her jaw clenches, and she races toward me again. I spin at the last minute, pushing her to the side. I get a grip on her from behind, arm around her shoulders, and arrow pointed at her neck, the clay ball on the end digging in.

I win? I win! I finally beat her!

I wait for her to yield, but my arm holding the arrow moves on its own, and I hit myself in the head with it, causing the clay to shatter and my body to tumble to the ground.

"Talli!" Trey is at my side, though I can't see him. My head is spinning, but I don't think I'm that hurt. He pulls me onto his lap, and I feel him brushing my hair away on the injured side of my head.

"The arrow cut her. Greer, go get her something for this," Trey orders. I also faintly hear Mr. Simon lecturing Mei-Lien.

"Everyone quit. I'm fine," I say, trying to sit up.

"You're not fine," Trey insists, keeping me down.

"She's not made of porcelain, Trey," Greer chides. She crouches next to me and places an elixir in my hand. The world spins, but I carefully take the elixir and swallow its contents. I stay in my place on Trey's lap while the magic works.

"She's a Healer. She should not be fighting and taking blows like this."

"She asked to learn. It was her choice to make," Greer says.

"Was it really a choice? Or does she feel that unsafe here that she thinks she has to learn?"

"If she ever felt unsafe, it was because you left."

"I left to protect her!"

I crack my eyes open to try to put a stop to all this arguing, but before I can, Mr. Simon walks up. He puts a hand on Trey's shoulder and says, "She's alright, Trey. Need I remind you, you've taken much worse hits on this mat."

"But that's not her role. She should only be learning how to run away from danger, not confront it head-on. Those men will kill her without even working up a sweat. Her powers can't protect her or aid her. She is powerless against them."

Each word slices through me—a blow worse than the one I took to the head. "I'm not powerless, or weak, or fragile. It's not an ideal situation, but I can do this. I can fight," I try to reason with him.

"You can't, and you won't."

"That's not your decision to make!" I pull myself out of his lap and work to stand on my feet with only a slight wobble to my movements. I sway to the left but find a soft, furry body there keeping me up. Seth. I give him an ear scratch before turning toward Trey. He follows suit, getting up, and I give him a piercing stare, matching his frustration.

"I rescued you in that cell. I killed that man and saved your life! Not the other way around. You can't come back after being gone for so long and think you can make all the decisions for me like you know best."

Before he can argue further, I walk away, snatching my stuff off the bench as I walk out the door.

"Let me at least walk you home," he calls out behind me.

"They aren't going to snatch me in the middle of the day," I snap at him without stopping my stride, then add, "If they do, then maybe I'll see why you liked that cell so much." It was a stupid comment, but one that felt appropriate, seeing as how he was determined not to leave it.

It takes effort not to run, but I hold myself steady as I walk out the door and toward home. Greer is behind me, silently following, but I don't say a thing as I take the storm raging inside down the street. I can feel Theora trailing me at a distance, watching me for Trey, but I don't turn around to confirm.

We get to our room, and Greer shuts the door. I throw myself onto my bed like a dramatic and hopeless princess, decidedly done with the day.

"You did amazing. I'm proud of you," Greer commends.

"Which part? The fighting or the yelling?" I ask.

"Both."

"He has no right to treat me that way."

"No, he doesn't."

"He doesn't own me. I own myself."

"Yes, you do."

"But am I being too overconfident? I still have nightmares from killing that man. Maybe I don't have the stomach for it. Maybe he has a point. Maybe..."

"Talli, stop. You're letting him get into your head. If you didn't feel something after killing that guard, I would be really worried about you. Remember, fighting isn't about killing. It's about trying to protect yourself and others. You only kill when you have no other choice. Trey...What Trey is going through is something that neither of us can understand, but that does not excuse his actions today."

She's right. Trey is scared, that is why he follows me around and can't seem to get rid of that look in his eyes. How does someone feel safe after being locked up for six months?

I was so harsh on him. My response was ugly, just like his was.

"I should apologize. He was worried about me, and I blew up on him," I say, getting back to my feet.

"Give him space. Taking some time to think will do him good, and then you two can make up tomorrow."

I nod and plop back down on my bed.

Space.

I have given him so much space since he got home. Aside from that one day a week after he got home, a month ago now, I have not pressed him for explanations. I have not pestered him with all the questions that have been swarming my brain and I have allowed him to tell me only what he decides, which has been not much at all.

Small bits and pieces.

Scraps to keep me happy.

I'm over it.

CHAPTER 27

My phone buzzes later that evening, and I peek at the screen to see a new message from Trey.

Trey: *Meet me at our spot. I want to talk about earlier.*

I put my phone back on my desk where I am working on homework and close my eyes. I guess this means he doesn't need any more space.

Is he going to apologize, though? Or is he going to just press the issue further?

I thought I knew Trey so well before he disappeared that I would have known exactly what he would say or do. But now, he is different. He is no longer the soft-spoken man with the primary goal of making me smile. His new goal seems to be to protect me at all costs, and that...That makes him unpredictable in my eyes.

Though, I'm not the same cheery girl he left behind either. Perhaps we need time to reacquaint ourselves with one another instead of trying to force ourselves back into our old relationship. I grab my phone again and reply.

Me: Okay.

Ten minutes later, I'm walking down the familiar path I know so well. I stretch my hand out to the tree branches, feeling the sticky maple leaves as I pass. With the arrival of spring, prime syrup season is almost over, but the oak and hickory trees are showing the promise of new leaves and new life here in the forest.

Through the dense branches, I can make out a bit of the sky, which is painted pink and purple. The sun is setting on another day and the air is chilly but not unmanageable with my thick sweatshirt and jeans.

Sometimes, I wish this path to the lake was longer. I want to stay in this cocoon of trees and keep the world small for a bit more time. Small and peacefully quiet. But of course, the path ends where it always does, and I'm greeted by the sight of Trey staring out at the lake.

I take up a place standing beside him and say, feeling suddenly very calm, "I never told you, but when you were gone, I woke up one night in a panic and ran here. When I got here, I heard you." He turns to me, but I don't move my gaze away from the line of trees on the other side of the lake.

I continue, "You were screaming in pain, and every time...Every time they hurt you, I felt it. I felt the pain slice through me for a brief moment before it faded away. I don't know how I heard or felt you, but I did. It was one of the worst moments of my life."

He steps in front of me, capturing my attention, and says, "I'm so sorry, Talli. I don't know how it could have happened, either. Maybe it was our connection to one another, the one that allowed me to walk in your dreams. Maybe it was the magic in this place making you strong somehow. Maybe it was something else. Regardless, you never should have had to go through that."

He grabs my face between his hands and adds, "I know you probably think I am crazy, but being at the end of their knife for so long, I can't bear the idea of you experiencing the pain they can inflict that I felt firsthand. They got to me, which means they can get to you. They can get to anyone here if they want to. We have underestimated them for so long, but they are much smarter and more organized than we could have ever imagined."

I pull my face out of his grasp and take a step back. I need space to breathe.

"What are you not telling me, Trey?" I ask carefully.

"I can't tell you. I want to tell you everything, but I can't. At least not while the Brethren are still a serious threat. Everything that I know is in the hands of the elders, and that has to be enough for now."

I can sense his quickened pulse. I don't resist the temptation to check his shield, but yet again, I am faced with it. However, looking closely...The iron covering his bricks is gone, and fear is seeping out between their seams. I will get to the bottom of this—maybe not today, but one day.

"If you can't trust me with the truth, then how can I trust you with my heart?"

His jaw clenches, and I continue, "I am no longer the naïve little Healer girl who is blissfully in the dark about everything happening around her. And you are no longer that guy who can make everything negative disappear simply because he wishes it to. We have both changed from what has happened, and there is no going back to who we were. So how do we move forward as who we are now when we don't know each other anymore?"

My question hangs in the air like lead while I await his response. Two heartbeats. Five heartbeats. Twenty heartbeats.

Finally, he answers, "We move forward by compromising."

My jaw nearly falls open. Compromising? That's his solution to all of this? I have to at least hear him out.

"What do you suggest?"

"I will be okay with you continuing to train for battle if you allow me to watch over you. Just for my peace of mind."

I take a moment to consider, but he quickly adds, "I don't want to start over, though. I don't want a clean slate with you. I want what we have already built, even if it's messy right now."

My chest warms. I don't want to start over, either.

"Alright. I agree to your terms."

Trey smiles and pulls me to him. I nuzzle my face into his chest, using his warmth as reassurance.

"Let's sit for a while. I'd like to hear more about what happened while I was gone."

I swallow. I'm not sure I want to dredge up all those bad memories. However, I can't expect him to open up to me if I don't open up to him. So, I follow him to the blankets laid out underneath our tree and tell him everything.

"I have been doing a lot of reading," Ash announces before we start our planned movie for the night, a week after Trey and I met at the lake. Trey, Greer, and I are already on the couch with snacks and blankets, ready to hit play. We watch him as he stands in front of the TV and wrings his hands together nervously.

"We have noticed," I say in reply.

Ash gives me an unimpressed look and pushes forward, "It was bothering me how both Trey's and Talli's power seemed to surpass extraordinary limits, basically out of nowhere with no explanation as to why. So, I decided to do some research."

"And?" Greer prompts.

"And I found an interesting rule you all seem to have about controlling your own emotions. The Order has a lot of rules, but this one appears to repeat itself constantly in everything I have read."

"What do you think it means, Ash?" Trey asks.

"I think emotions are the key to unlocking power. I'm talking about a lot of power. It basically says it in one text, how dangerous emotions lead to darkness getting inside of you and taking over. You both were at an emotional high when you experienced your power boost. It's like emotions are what fuel you."

A hundred dots in my mind start to connect. He is right. Every weird thing that has happened to me has been when I felt out of control. But I have told both Mom and Dad about these instances. Well, some of them. Do they not know about this rule? Dad, at least, has to know of it. Right?

"Our parents know about what happened. Why wouldn't they have come to the same conclusion and told us so?" I ask the room.

Trey and Greer subtly look at each other, sharing something between them.

Trey answers, "It is possible that they did come to that conclusion but decided not to say anything."

"It wouldn't be the first time they have withheld the truth in the name of protecting us," Greer adds.

"How would that protect us? It could be more harmful for us not to know that we need to control our emotions better," I argue.

"Because, in the hands of the power-hungry, that's an easy way to achieve what they want," Greer answers.

"Then why make that information so accessible?" Ash asks.

"I doubt they are hiding the truth, but they aren't advertising it either," Trey answers.

I repeat Ash's words in my head, and I get caught on one word in particular, "darkness."

"Ash, what exactly does it say about darkness?" I ask.

He reaches into his backpack and pulls out a book called, *The Great Hawk & Our Call to Order*. Multiple colored tabs litter the top and sides of the book. He flips through it, and then quotes, "Anger, hate, lust, greed, fear, sorrow, and grief are all catalysts for darkness. We must not fall prey to those dangerous emotions. Darkness is always lying in wait for us to allow it in, and even if only a sliver of it is permitted, it will take over and consume until all of the light within us is gone. No one has ever come back from this." He closes the book, putting it back into his backpack. "That is one quote out of many. It is the most direct one that I have seen so far, though."

I let the words sink in.

Anger. Hate. Fear. Grief.

I felt anger when I was fighting Mei-Lien on the mat that day after Trey left. Then fear and grief when I felt Trey's pain at the lake. Hate and fear when I killed that man. I've also felt those four emotions in many moments in between. Greer has said before that she saw me go a little dark, but I didn't think she meant *actually* dark.

What if she was right, though? And all along, I have been losing myself to the darkness inside me. I have been letting it in and fueling its power over me. Is there any way to reverse it? Will it eventually take over?

Trey lightly grabs my face, pulling me out of my spiral. "Talli, when these books were written, the dramatics were normal. Nothing is going to happen to me or you. If this were the case, thousands of our people would have fallen prey to the darkness, and we would be much more aware of it."

"I've felt those emotions several times, though. What if something got in?" I ask carefully.

"Those emotions are a part of being human. We all feel them at times, but that doesn't mean we are dark. It is saying that if you let those things *consume* you and drive your actions, then you are welcoming the darkness. So, you have nothing to worry about. You are the light of this place. You embody truth and justice, and you always do what's right. Don't doubt yourself. We don't."

I meet his gaze and then look at Greer and Ash. All their eyes convey the same thing. Trust. They agree with him, meaning they all have faith that I do not have darkness inside me. My chest warms, but I can't help but notice the small part of me that feels cold inside. I swallow hard, pushing it all down. "Let's watch the movie."

Hawks are meant to be mated for life. Once together, a connection between the two is formed. With time, mental shields no longer matter, and an acute awareness of the other is built. Only separation and time can weaken the connection. However, it is not yet known if the connection can ever entirely be severed, even after death.

- Community Laws & Guidelines

Chapter 28

"I HAVE TO ADMIT, you are a natural at archery."

I turn to Trey, where he is leaning up against the table at the Range, his arms crossed over his chest. His t-shirts fit him snuggly again. They no longer drape over him, and I can see the hard lines of his pectorals and biceps. Especially now with his arms the way they are. I bite my lip, ignoring the desire to drop my bow and trace my fingers along those lines. I smile at him instead. "Told you."

He hands me another arrow and I get back into position, lining up my next shot. I pull the arrow back and then let it fly. It lodges itself into the bullseye of the target—the sixth in a row.

Trey crosses the distance to me and wraps his arms around me from behind. I lower the bow to my side and close my eyes, taking in his warmth. The gentle ring of Trey's phone interrupts, and he pulls away to answer it. After a moment of listening to the person on the other side, he looks at me with a wide grin.

"Yes, sir. We will be right there," he says to the phone, then stuffs it back into his pocket.

"What is it?" I ask, already putting my bow away into its case.

"They got them—the Hansens. They are arriving in thirty minutes," Trey tells me. My eyes brighten with excitement. Ash's parents are coming home.

Ash has done his best to hide it, but he has been anxious since we told him they were alive. Over the years, Greer and I have told Ash about his parents, but he's been asking us questions about them more than ever. Now that he knows the whole story, it is clear that he is proud of their bravery and sacrifice for a people that aren't their own. Though, I suspect his research-driven mind has been running in overdrive between his parents and the knowledge about the Order being opened up to him.

Trey and I clean up and race down the path to the community building where Greer and Ash are already waiting in front. Ash is nervous, as evidenced by his constant fiddling with his jacket zipper. I march right up to him and pull him into a hug. "It'll be okay," I say, trying to soothe him.

"I don't remember them. What if they are upset with me?" He pulls away enough to meet my eyes.

"I'm sure they have been briefed on what happened to you. They won't expect anything more than what you are comfortable with, I have no doubt," I reassure him.

Trey puts his hand on Ash's shoulder and says, "They have been a bit battered by what they have been through, but they stayed strong, hoping they would see you again one day. I'm sure that is all they care about."

Ash nods.

All four of us wait for a few minutes, and then Dad and Chief Lu arrive to join our welcome party. Mom and Mrs. Waterstone are the next to arrive, happily chatting about plants and elixirs with Lemon and Seth on their heels. Ten minutes later, Mr. Waterstone's SUV pulls up. He and Mr. Simon exit the front seats, and then the back doors open to reveal Killian and Stella Hansen.

Ash goes still at the sight of them. Mrs. Hansen does as well, taking in her son, whom she hasn't seen in four years—four critical years. He was a boy when she left, but now he has matured into a man. Slowly, she walks up to him, her husband at her side. I can see tears streaking down her cheeks as she reaches out and embraces Ash.

He looks uncomfortable at first, but after a moment, he wraps his arms around her. Mrs. Hansen is a small, petite woman, so Ash appears taller than normal in her arms. She pulls away, and Mr. Hansen takes a turn hugging his son. Their heights and builds are about equal now, after so many years apart.

Mrs. Hansen wipes away her curly dark-brown hair from where it sticks to her face. Joy and relief roll off her in waves as she watches her son. Ash pulls away from his dad, and I can see tears clouding his eyes from behind his glasses.

So many people I know, myself included, have features that favor one parent over the other. But not Ash. He is a perfect combination of his parents, with his mom's hair and eyes, but his dad's olive-colored skin and narrow features.

Tears well up in my own eyes as I bear witness to this beautiful moment.

The Hansens work their way around the group, giving hugs and smiles to their old friends. When it is Greer's and my turn, Mr. Hansen grabs one of each of our hands and says, "Thank you, girls. You both have done an unimaginable amount for Asher—much more than any parent could have asked of you two. Thank you for finding us and helping us back to our son. Stella and I will always be in your debt."

"It wasn't duty or favor that dictated what we have done for Ash or what we will continue to do for him. He is our best friend, and we will always be there for him," Greer answers.

Mrs. Hansen pushes her husband out of the way and hugs us tight, offering no words herself, but her warm embrace conveys everything she could have said. Mr. Hansen is next to hug us, Greer and I squished together into his long arms.

Noticing Greer scrub at her face when they walk away, I grab her hand and give it a comforting squeeze. She returns it with a gentle smile. Ash appears next to us, and Greer grabs his hand. I also loop Trey into our line when he comes over to us. The four of us stand together, hand in hand, and it feels as though we can take on the world.

Mr. and Mrs. Hansen take up a center spot, with their loved ones surrounding them in a crescent. I notice Mrs. Hansen look at her husband and give him a nod. He wraps an arm around her and starts to speak. "The last four and a half years have been extremely difficult. Stella and I have been through things that we will never recover from. We do not wish to share all the horrors with you. We want to move forward with renewed passion for our work and only focus on a better future. However, with that being said, there is one horror that we feel is necessary to share, as it is a reality we must live with every day." Mr. Hansen looks to his wife again and gives her a gentle kiss on her forehead. He continues, "My brave wife, in an attempt to free other prisoners, lost her tongue as a result. She screamed about a fire to distract the guards while they attempted to make an escape. The plan proved unsuccessful, though, and those souls are no longer with us." He swallows hard and finishes, "It will be an adjustment because she can only speak to us in American Sign Language now. Thankfully, we both already happened to know the language. However, we do not expect everyone to learn, so she will always have a pen and paper on her to aid in communication difficulties. Thank you all."

Shock hits me with such force that I almost double over. Our magic can mend a severed tongue if we get to it before it heals itself, but it sounds like this is an old wound. There is nothing we can do to heal it or ease the trauma from that day.

Barbarians. They are violent, wretched men. They did this to humans, the people they claim to protect from us.

A heavy silence falls upon our small group, standing in front of the community building. Mrs. Hansen is staring right at Ash, trying to gauge his reaction. His face is filled with horror. It seems no one is sure what to do or say.

Dad steps out from his place. "I am so sorry for everything you've had to endure. Rest assured, we will be the ones to bring down the Brethren. We will wipe them out of existence so that they become a long-forgotten nightmare for future generations. I speak for all the elders of the Massachusetts community when I say we will never let harm befall either of you again. We failed you once, and that is one time too many. We have a home awaiting you, and you will have our strongest guards on watch to protect you at all times. Sleep, my friends. Rest and recover. When you are ready, resume your work, and together, we will bring peace to our people."

Trey lets go of my hand and wraps his arm around my waist. He pulls me close like he is trying to protect me now from whatever path my father intends for us to achieve that peace. I'd be lying if I said that I wasn't afraid. I am. I have seen Dad give plenty of passion-fueled speeches, but this one feels different. There is a gleam in his eye that promises violence. I obviously want peace and a bright future; everyone does, but at what cost? What price will our people have to pay?

Goosebumps cover me from head to toe as the wind kicks up around us. It's as if nature itself is responding to Dad's words—in support or defiance, it's impossible to know.

Everyone in our group seem to have similar thoughts, and we all break apart, dispersing down different paths. Trey and I lead with Greer and Ash on our heels. Mrs. Waterstone approaches our group, stops us, and pulls Ash aside. Her hushed tone indicates she means for her words to be private, but the wind carries them to me. "You will continue to stay with us for now. Your parents need some time to reacclimate to the world, and Orsen is going to ensure they get some counseling to help them recover. But nothing has to change unless you want it to. You are my son, too, despite the wedge that has been between us lately."

Ash gives her a weary smile and nods. She embraces him and then walks away, meeting back up with Mom.

We continue our walk back to my house, quiet except for the wind whistling around us.

CHAPTER 29

I WIPE MY SWEATY palms on my jeans for the dozenth time as I pack my toothbrush into my small bag. That is the last item I need, but I run through my mental checklist again before zipping my bag closed.

Trey's parents are out of town this weekend for an Order-related trip and he asked me to stay with him tonight at his house. Immediately after asking, he made it clear that he didn't have any dishonorable intentions—I internally rolled my eyes at that—and he just wanted me close.

He has kept his word, though, and has backed off when it comes to my training. There are no more meltdowns when I get hurt, and he's even thrown in a useful tip here and there. If his being so close all the time is the tradeoff for peace while I'm training, then I'll take it.

Unlike Trey, I do have dishonorable intentions for us tonight. My cheeks heat at the thought of what I have planned. Greer will have Ash away from the house for the night, apparently with the intent of keeping him up too late with movies and having him accidentally fall asleep on the couch in the living room. So Trey and I will be completely alone. Like *alone*, alone.

The butterflies in my stomach flutter around, and when I am sure they won't make me sick from all the commotion, I do one last check in the mirror and head to Trey's house with my bag slung over my shoulder. Those stupid butterflies flapping harder with each step I take.

What if he says no? What if he isn't ready? Does the guy normally ask, or is that just what happens in the movies?

I wipe my hands again as nerves and, if I am being honest with myself, fear try to sink their teeth into me. I force myself to slow down my breathing, which is bordering on labored at this point, and I keep myself moving, focusing on my steps and pushing everything else away.

I'm at the door, and I ring the bell. I ensure my mental shield is firmly in place, and Trey opens the door with a smile. It is soft and reassuring, and everything I need right now.

"Hello, beautiful." His voice is deeper than I remember, and he ushers me inside, closing the door behind me. Maybe it's my imagination. "I am finishing up an assignment, but come up and get comfortable."

Trey started taking online college classes a few weeks ago instead of starting on campus like he was supposed to. He was able to get into some shorter courses for the second half of the spring semester, and he jumped right on it, not wanting to waste more time.

"What class is this one for?" I ask as I follow him up the stairs to his room.

"Biology." His tone suggests he would rather be doing anything else. Apparently, this class has not been his friend.

"That bad?"

"No, not really. I shouldn't complain. It's just a lot of work since it's an accelerated course."

"I would trade you your college Biology homework for my high school English any day," I offer with a laugh.

He turns to me with a grin. "Be careful. I might take you up on that."

We walk into his room, and he drops into the chair at his desk, his computer open to what looks like a paper he's in the middle of writing. I sit at the edge of his bed and set my bag by my feet. I can smell the fabric softener, a gentle lilac scent, coming from his comforter. My cheeks go pink at the thought that he might have washed them today just for me.

"Just five more minutes, I promise," he throws over his shoulder.

Now, Talli. It's time to get ready. I grab the handles of my bag and grip them much harder than needed before asking, "I am going to use the bathroom and get in my pjs, if that's okay?"

"Of course." I can feel the intensity of his determination to finish his assignment from here.

Trey has a bathroom attached to his room in a jack and jill style, the other side of it leading to Ash's room. Walking into it, bag in tow, I get to work getting ready. Aside from getting dressed, and not in my pajamas, I did everything at home.

I pull out a silky navy-blue piece of lingerie from my bag and try not to think as I change into it. Greer and I made a quick trip out of town last week to the mall to pick this out for tonight. A trip I did not tell Trey I was going on, otherwise he wouldn't have let me go without him.

I was looking at a flowery pink one, but the saleswoman insisted that the dark blue would match my eyes and have a beautiful effect. She was right.

I take a moment to admire myself in the mirror. The silk lays delicately on my body, somewhat covering my breasts with two triangle pieces that connect in the center. A black lace band is connected to the bodice, and then the navy silk flows out at the bottom like a babydoll-style top. The whole thing comes to just above the bottom of my ass, the matching thong barely visible but giving quite the tease in the back. Or so the saleswoman said it would.

I arrange my hair to be just right, with just a few auburn waves in front of my shoulders and the rest behind. The makeup I did is more severe than I am used to, and it makes me look older. I don't want to be a girl that needs coddling tonight. I want to be a woman that needs to be touched.

I take another deep breath and level a stare at my reflection. *He loves you. You love him. This is right, and it will be great. It may hurt at first, but it will get better. Trey is your true love. You will marry him, take care of him, and have at least three of his babies.*

My smile curves up at that thought. Weirdly, that is enough to calm me. Not that I have any intentions of having those babies any time soon, but the promise of the future we will have together soothes my racing heart.

Leaving my bag and stuff in the bathroom, I open the door and step out, feeling exposed and comfortable all at once. Trey stays looking at his computer for a few heartbeats longer before he says, "Perfect timing. I'm..." He freezes as he swivels his chair around and sees me, stopping mid-statement.

"You're done?" I finish for him. I don't think he heard me, though. He is taking in every inch of me as I try to stand, not quite as still as a statue but not wanting to break the caress his eyes are giving me. I feel the heat from it, like a physical touch to my skin. After a moment, he swallows hard, his Adam's apple bobbing, and then meets my eyes.

"I'm pretty sure I said there wouldn't be any dishonorable intentions for tonight." There is humor in his tone, but his face shows no sign of it.

"I'm pretty sure *you* said you wouldn't have any dishonorable intentions, but I did not make the same promise." I grin widely at him.

Trey stands, carefully walking over to me and placing his hands on my hips. He takes me in again as he feels the fabric under his palms. Those brown eyes lock onto mine, and his face grows serious. "You want this then?"

I nod.

"I do have condoms ready in case something like this ever came up." My heart warms. He has been thinking of it, too, ready in case the moment came.

"That won't actually be necessary. Mom got me the contraceptive elixir when we started dating. I didn't start taking it until I got you back, but it is well into my system by now," I explain.

He seems equally pleased with the knowledge that I have been planning for this too. "I knew that it might be coming soon, but I didn't expect it tonight."

"Is it okay? That I did all this?" I gesture to what I am wearing and continue, "If you're not ready or want to wait, I..."

"Talli, I want this. I want you. Just promise me first that this is completely coming from you and that you didn't feel any pressure to do this from me or anyone else."

"I promise. I decided this all on my own."

His hands shift from my hips to lightly gripping my upper arms. He gives a little squeeze when he says, "I love you. Please, please tell me if you want me to stop at any point."

"I know. I love you too. And I will, I promise."

And I do. Know he loves me. I feel it deep down. I wouldn't have done all this if I didn't know for sure that he loves me and that I love him. I know he would stop if I asked, but I have no intention of wanting him to stop.

"You are so beautiful, and I am completely unworthy of you, Talliana."

"I think we are plenty worthy of one another."

He scoffs and pulls me in, looping his arms around my back. He pulls an arm away to cup my face and slowly lowers his lips to mine.

His kisses are unrushed like how they used to be. Since we rescued him from that prison cell, most of his kisses have been needy and urgent. But now? I feel like I have my old Trey back. His lips and his touch are both soft and giving.

There is nothing greedy about Trey. He always gives more than he takes, and I doubt what is about to happen between us will be any different. He has one hand curled around the back of my neck, holding my lips to his, but also kneading it, working out knots I didn't realize I had. The other hand is on my lower back, gently rubbing and warming up my skin, removing the goosebumps that formed when he walked toward me earlier.

I want so badly to give him everything tonight, all of me. Even if I don't get all of him. I know there are things he is still not telling me about from when he was imprisoned, but I don't care right now. He will tell me when he is ready. I have to believe that.

I break our kiss but don't pull away as I quietly tell him, "I'm going to take down my shields. I want you to feel and touch all of me—body and mind. I don't expect you to do the same, but I'm giving myself fully to you." At that moment, I take down my shield, letting him access all my emotions.

What I'm doing is something that is usually only done between spouses, and even then, I'm not sure many do this. It is an offer of complete intimacy. Trey will be able to read every pleasure, discomfort, and every bit of love that I feel while we share our bodies for the first time.

Trey's eyes close, almost like he is in pain. He touches his forehead to mine and says, "I want so badly to give that to you, too, but I..." He takes a deep breath, "I don't want you to feel everything that happened to me. Not yet. I need more time."

"I know. When you are ready to share your horrors, then I'm ready to help you bear the weight. But right now, try to forget about them and focus on what's right in front of you," I say softly, pulling his lips back to mine.

We stay there for a moment, holding each other and kissing until he leads me to the edge of his bed. Walking slowly, still connected to my lips.

We break apart long enough for me to climb into his bed and for him to climb in next to me. He pulls off his shirt and lies down on his side, pulling me to him and pressing his mouth against mine once again. His hand runs down my neck, arm, and then thigh. He glides it back up, slipping underneath my lingerie and scorching my skin with heat.

Touching my ass, then my hip, and finally, my breast once he works his way under the band of the garment. He cups it, kneading it under his palm and running his hand over my nipple.

Oh god. I let out a moan, and that only encourages him to do it again, playing with me all while still tasting my mouth.

I lift my leg up and place it on top of his, both pulling him closer with it and opening myself up to him. Trey takes the hint and glides his hand back down, and slides a finger along my core over my too-thin thong. I jerk at the sensation and, much to my embarrassment, almost come undone at that touch alone.

He reaches back down, moving the thong aside, and touches me down there, exploring, feeling everything, until he splits me open by sliding his finger inside of me. I arch, pressing my aching chest into his warm and solid one. The feel of his skin is so perfect against mine. I need more of it.

Trey works his finger in and out of me in a rhythm that is perfect—so, so perfect. His finger glides easier each time.

There is more pressure, and suddenly, I realize two fingers are feeling me and stretching me. I adjust and slowly start moving with his rhythm, my body feeling like it's on fire.

Slowly, he removes his fingers, and it takes me a moment to realize he stopped kissing me, too. When, I'm not sure.

He stands up and before I can ask what he is doing, he starts removing his jeans. My breath catches as I prop myself up on my elbows. His jeans come off, and then his underwear.

My throat dries as I take him in. This is happening.

"Can you scoot up on the bed and get under the covers? It's best if we can get comfortable," Trey says, standing completely at ease in his nakedness.

I do as he suggests and climb up the bed, getting under the covers. He walks around the side and gets in next to me. His body heat warms up the sheets instantly.

He doesn't lie down, though, but stays sitting up as he turns to me. He grabs the bottom of my lingerie and asks permission with his eyes, which I grant. Then, he pulls it over my head, fully exposing my upper body to him. But to my surprise, his eyes only lock onto mine and pays no heed to my bare skin. He just grabs my face again and pulls me to his lips.

As I melt into his kiss, relishing each sweep of his tongue, we lower to the bed on our sides. His hand moves from my cheek and trails down my body again until he gets to the strap of my thong. He carefully works it down until I can pull up my legs and wrestle it off, having to break free of his kiss in order to be successful.

With his hand back on my side, he asks, "Are you ready?"

"Yes," I breath.

Trey moves so that he is on top of me, holding his weight with his arms on either side of me. He bends back down and kisses me softly. He pulls his lips away, and I feel him get in position.

I count my heartbeats. One heartbeat, three heartbeats, five...He pushes slowly into me. The pressure is so overwhelming, it's almost too much.

"Breathe, Talli."

I do as he says, taking deep breaths, and everything is much easier. When I feel so full, there is a slice of pain. I hiss through my teeth, and he stills, giving me a moment.

The pain eases, and I nod. He starts moving again in the same rhythm that he used with his fingers. And, like with his fingers, he moves easier each time he goes in and out. My body slowly adjusts until just like that—like a light switch being turned on—every muscle unclenches and loosens as a wave of pleasure washes over me.

Oh god. How can something that feels so weird at first feel so natural? So perfect? Because he's perfect, and we're perfect together.

I feel the muscles on his back loosen beneath my hands as he increases his speed and groans. He also just now started enjoying it himself. I tighten my grip on him and allow myself to feel every thrust and movement of his body inside of mine. We both fall into a chorus of moans and panting as we move together. Faster. Harder. Until everything inside of me tightens and falls apart with my release. It's so overwhelming that my body starts to shake and tremble. Trey pulls himself out, and he loses himself as well. My inner thigh grows wet as he comes.

Our warm breath mixes as we breathe hard, our chests moving rapidly as we try to calm our racing hearts. He moves, toppling beside me, and I laugh. He laughs too—one of the best sounds I have ever heard.

When our laughter dies down, Trey says, "I love you." He smiles at me, and I return it.

"I love you too."

"I guess we should wash up and get new sheets."

"Yes, I guess we should."

Instead, he pulls me on top of him and places my head on his chest. I count his every heartbeat and commit the sound of it to memory. He kisses the top of my head and says gently, "I could never be happier than when I have you in my arms."

"I couldn't agree more."

Thirty minutes later, we are clean and back in his bed. While snuggled up tight in his arms, I realize something is different. Something inside of me is different. Like there is now something there that wasn't there before.

"What is it?" Trey asks, and I remember my mental shield is still down.

I sit up and study him. "Do you feel it? Like something new in your chest? It's hard to explain."

"Like a string that starts at your heart but doesn't end in your own body?" he guesses.

I search myself, "Yes, actually. Is it...?"

He nods. "It's the connection between our hearts. I feel it too." His face softens, and the expression is full of love.

We are now connected, even if it is a small connection that could easily disappear in time. The urge to want that thread to strengthen is overwhelming. I don't want it to fade or disappear. Panic rises, but before I can even vocalize my feelings, Trey sits up and says, "Nothing is going to happen to it. It will strengthen in time the more we... have sex." He smiles widely, then continues, "I promise it won't fade tonight or even next week. You need to rest your body for a bit before we do it again. Okay?"

I nod and relax back into his chest. He's right. We have plenty of time to strengthen it. I allow myself to focus back on him, his warm skin, his steady heartbeat, his arm wrapped around me. With a light heart now tethered to the man I love, I fall asleep knowing he will keep my dreams pleasant and happy tonight.

Violence is a price our people must pay to fulfill our order. Diplomacy and manipulation of the mind are not always enough. Sometimes, the only answer is the simplest answer, and a threat has to be removed permanently. This is not a choice our people revel in making because all life is created by nature, but sacrifices must be made to ensure survival.

- History of the Original 142 Bloodlines

CHAPTER 30

May

Baked Ziti night is my favorite, especially when it's me and the most important people in my life around the table.

Dad and Mom are out of town for a few nights, so Greer, Trey, Ash, and I decided to have a nice dinner together at the house. I made the food while Greer supervised, and Trey and Ash picked up dessert from Elemental Pizza.

"You won't believe how good the glowing fish look. Sarah came up with the best idea to put glow sticks inside of tissue paper and it looks amazing. They are insanely delicate and hard to hang, but I think they're going to look great," I finish telling Trey about everything we have planned for prom.

I have little doubt that he couldn't care less about prom, but he indulges me anyway, and I know it will be important for him because it's important to me.

"Speaking of prom..." Ash starts when the silence stretches for longer than a minute. "Mei-Lien asked me to go with her."

I choke on the noodle in my throat, causing me to cough and sputter until it dislodges and lands back on my plate. That crisis now averted, I catch sight of Greer seated across from me, and she is still—deadly still, like she is frozen in time.

Only Trey has the sense to respond. "What did you tell her?"

Ash looks at his plate, uncomfortable. "I told her I would think about it and let her know on Monday."

"Ash, you know you can't go with her, right?" I finally say.

"I know you both have your issues with her, but she has always been nice to me."

"She's not nice to anyone," Greer counters slowly.

"That's a bit dramatic, Greer. Maybe I just actually want to go with someone instead of third-wheeling it with these two," Ash points at Trey and me.

Fair point.

"Who says I'm not going? I could have had plans to third wheel it with you," Greer asks.

"We can't both be third wheels. It's mathematically impossible. Besides, you told me that you weren't going."

"When did I tell you that?"

"When Talli first started working out with you. Remember that day you hung back, and we talked while she limped home? You said you would never be caught dead in a fancy dress just to impress someone else."

Trey's eyes shoot to me at the word "limped," and I outwardly cringe. That's not something he needed to know.

"Ash, Mei-Lien's primary goal in life is to get at Greer and me. I know how this will sound, but she's jealous of us. Between the two of us, we always best her in one way or another. So this must be some weird game to try to take you away. Don't let her win it," I try to reason with him.

Ash's face hardens. "I know it's hard to believe, Talli. But not everything is about you and Greer. You don't have ownership over me. I am allowed to have other friends."

His words hit like a physical blow. I know his intent isn't to hurt me, he's just trying to tell me how he feels, but I hate myself for making him feel this way.

"Ash, I didn't mean it like..." I start. Greer's phone pings, alerting her to a new message. She reads the message, and her empty hand clenches into a fist before she slaps her phone down on the table a little too hard.

Greer says, tone low, "No, Talli. He's right. Let him find out for himself what it's like having other friends. Ash, if you want to take Mei-Lien, then take her. You will not find me caring one bit."

I cringe again, knowing that she does care very much. Too much.

"Why don't we all take a breath?" Trey suggests, trying to defuse the tension. He is rewarded with glares from both Greer and Ash.

"Fine. I will take her. I'll get her flowers, match her dress with my tie, and I'll enjoy every bit of the attention she gives me," Ash shoots back at Greer.

"Good," she says.

"Good," he echoes.

Greer gets up from the table and stalks out of the room. Ash watches her go, then gets up, too. He walks out the front door, practically slamming it.

Trey closes his eyes, and I comment, "They could have at least picked up their plates before leaving. Rude."

His shoulders shake from laughter. "More dessert for us," he says, then gets up to take care of their plates.

"Oh! And more room on the couch during the movie." I wiggle my eyebrows at him.

He grins at me, pulling the dessert from the refrigerator. Placing the plate full of goodness in front of me, I am forced to contemplate how many cannolis I can realistically eat without regretting it.

Two. I can eat two.

I grab one and sink my teeth into it. The shell is the right combination of crunchy and soft, and the ricotta filling in the middle is creamy and delicious. Then the mini chocolate chips on the ends have the right amount of sweetness to bring it all together.

Trey follows my lead and devours one, then two.

My mind turns over what Ash said. Does he really think we don't allow him to have other friends? We never once stopped him if he talked to other people. But we did always stay close because we had orders to ensure he didn't find out about everything. Would he have drifted away from us if we weren't under orders to stay close? Do I really make everything about Greer and myself?

Before I start running through my memory to look for answers to all those questions, Trey covers my hand with his. "He didn't mean it."

"But he made a good point."

"No, he didn't. You care about so many people. You are kind and generous to all those around you. The fact that you are so worried about his words is proof enough of that."

I sigh, letting his words comfort me. "I should go talk to Greer. Make sure she is okay."

"I think they both need some time. I think we are getting very close to the point in their story where they finally admit to one another how they feel. And I say this with love, but stay out of it. Let them figure this out on their own." Despite the "with love" and the soft smile on his face, I still scowl at him.

"So, what would you have me do?" I ask incredulously.

"I have many things in mind." His smile turns mischievous, and my heart rate kicks up in anticipation.

I smile widely back at him. "Alright, I am open to suggestions."

I place the rest of the uneaten cannoli's back into the refrigerator, and Trey and I retreat to the living room—all my worries about what transpired during dinner a distant concern now. We turn off the lights, curl up on the couch, and turn on the movie we planned to watch tonight.

Too bad we don't pay attention to any of it.

Reality did come back eventually, and Trey and I went our separate ways to at least check on our two siblings. Not to interfere, according to Trey, but just to make sure they are okay.

I knock at Greer's and my bedroom door. Receiving her okay to enter, I open the door to find her curled up in her bed, staring at the wall.

"Enjoy the movie?" she asks.

"Yes. I watched all but a minute of it."

She snorts and goes back to her staring.

I close the door and then sit at the end of my bed. "What was that text about?"

"Mei-Lien. She called in her favor."

"Wait. Already?" I hardly believe it. I thought she would drag that favor out longer than a little over two months.

"Yep," Greer answers, clearly annoyed.

"What, she wants to take Ash to prom? That's her favor?"

"Yep."

My face twists up. That's an odd favor. "What did she say exactly?"

Greer reaches across the space between our beds and hands me her phone.

Mei-Lien: *I'm calling in that favor. Lucky you, I found something I wanted quickly. Ensure Asher goes to prom with me, and we will be square. Thx.*

Wow, it's creepy how perfect her timing was on sending that text. Choosing not to think about that fact for too long, I hand Greer back her phone and say, "Oh, she definitely has an ulterior motive. She has never expressed any level of interest in Ash before."

"I'm sure she does, but I don't have a choice."

"You always have a choice," I argue.

"I gave my word, and I am not backing out of it, no matter how suspicious I am or how much I hate it." Greer lies back down, propping her feet against the wall, turned away from me.

"So, you are going to let her do this?"

"I am. I am also going to stay home and pretend that it's not happening. She is doing it to flaunt him in my face, and then she will toss him aside. If I don't give her the satisfaction of being there, she will quickly get bored and back off," she explains.

"Solid plan, but I disagree. I think she will dig in her heels until she gets the reaction she wants from you."

Greer twists her head to look at me thoughtfully. "Shit. You might be right. I hadn't considered that."

I bounce to my feet and clap my hands together. "That is why you need to show up and cause a scene."

I'm terrible at listening and currently fueled by my annoyance that I couldn't just stay on the couch with Trey all night. Good thing I didn't pinky promise him that I would stay out of it.

Her face scrunches up. "There has to be another way."

"There is no other way. Trust me." I'm buzzing with energy as I grin at her.

She groans. "Do your worst."

CHAPTER 31

"GREER, YOU LOOK AMAZING. Now get your ass down the stairs and into the car."

I look up at Greer from the bottom of the stairs as she stands at the top. After getting her ready, I've been here for fifteen minutes trying to convince her to come down. I don't think I have ever seen her so scared.

She grabs her stomach and hunches. "I don't like this feeling in my stomach. Just go without me, and I'll meet you there."

"You're being a chicken, and your body is physically rejecting it, that is what's happening," I retort.

Trey comes up from behind me, looping his arms around my waist and pulling my back to his chest. "Talliana," he whispers in my ear, "I don't think you can force her to do this. She needs to overcome her fear and get herself to prom tonight."

I huff, even though it's completely at odds with how Trey is making me feel right now. "I'm not making her do anything. She agreed to go tonight."

"I know, but she needs more time, and I need to fulfill my promise to take you before it's over," he urges gently.

"Please, Talli, I'll see you there," Greer calls from the top of the stairs.

I relent. I hate leaving her right now, but Trey has a point. This is something she needs to figure out for herself, and prom only lasts for so long. "Alright. But Greer, I better see you there. Do this for yourself. Clearly, he isn't brave enough to do this for the both of you."

She nods, and I let Trey pull me away toward his truck. Mrs. Waterstone came over and took pictures of us with Mom already, and both of our fathers are already at the school, so all that's left to do is go.

When I imagined going to prom with Trey, though, it felt like something that would be ours—our night to dance and forget about everything else. But now that it's here, I can't help but feel like tonight needs to be about Greer and Ash. They have barely spoken since the fight a week ago. Only offering each other brief acknowledges of existence, then not speaking beyond that. But my plan should fix everything. If only she can get herself there.

Trey offers me a hand, helping me climb into his truck in this dress. Before everything happened, I knew exactly what kind of dress I wanted to wear to prom. Let's just say there was a lot of tulle involved in my vision. But now? This year has changed me more than I could have ever imagined. I'm in a sleek, form-fitting, midnight-blue dress, with silver beads stitched all over to look like the stars. The way the sheer overlay moves on top of the bottom satin layer, it almost looks like the stars reflecting on the water's surface. It's perfect for tonight.

When Trey first saw me in it, I could tell his mind returned to the last time I wore this shade of blue, and my cheeks warmed at his expression.

Now, Trey looks over at me from where he is driving, "Have I told you yet how amazing you look tonight?" His eyes are dreamy as he steals a glance before focusing back on the road.

"Only about half a dozen times," I tease him. He laughs, and I realize we are already at the school, and he is parking.

I'm not the only one who looks great tonight, though. His tux is the same shade of blue as my dress, and his white shirt and silver tie are a beautiful contrast. I've never been a guy-in-a-suit type of girl, but Trey can make anything look perfect.

Once we park, he looks over at me and asks, "Ready?"

"Haven't decided yet. I really am worried about Greer and Ash."

"You know, I had a long conversation with Ash after he told us that he was taking Mei-Lien tonight instead of the obvious choice."

My eyebrows lift in surprise. "Yeah? How did that go?"

"All I can say is, tonight will end how it's meant to," he answers simply, reaching for my hand and giving it a squeeze. He knows something. This both comforts me and makes my nerves stand on end even more. I give him a small smile, though, and tell him, "I'm ready."

Before we can walk through the door to the school gym, we stand in a small line to get in where security guards are checking IDs and comparing them to a list. Security measures are always tight at the school, but I guess since it's nighttime and half of the community's kids are in one spot, the danger is a bit higher.

When we reach the guards, though, they waive me and Trey in. Mr. Harris and Mr. Hank know all of us elder's kids well, so IDs are not usually necessary for us.

"Looking good, you two. Have fun tonight," Mr. Harris says with little flames dancing around his fingertips and a grin plastered on his face. Mr. Harris and his family, who are all Fire Elementals, live in the house next to us. I offer him a smile while Trey thanks him.

When we enter the gym, I can feel Trey's surprise. I wouldn't let him meet me at school all week so that I could try to maintain the surprise, and it seems I was successful.

It looks perfect. It looked perfect yesterday, too, when we finished the decorations, but now that it is dark with all the neon lights and glow sticks illuminated, it is absolutely magical in here. The white brick walls are covered in dark-blue paper with the occasional 3-D or 2-D sea creature attached to make it look like we are in the middle of the ocean. On the ceiling is a combination of large clear spheres that look like bubbles, glowing tissue paper fish, and a giant octopus in the center. Its whole body is aglow with neon lights, and its tentacles are spread out in all directions, attaching at different points and levels to give it a natural effect.

"This looks amazing, Talli. Best prom decorations I have ever seen." He smiles at me, and I smile back, vaguely aware that someone is snapping our picture. He bends down and gives me a quick kiss. We hear hooting coming from some of the other students around us, and we laugh, pulling away. This is going to be a great night.

Swaying to a slow song, our fourth dance of the night, I eventually shift my gaze over Trey's shoulder toward the gym entrance, and I see Greer standing there. Finally, she made it, and her black dress looks devilish and perfect from here. I saw it at home, of course, but it looks so much better under the lights in the gym.

Something I picked out and forced her to try on, the bodice is made of two pieces of fabric that start a couple of inches below her breasts and flow over them, then around her shoulders to attach in the back, leaving the middle of her chest exposed. The skirt is a high-low cut with tulle edging that looks like it was razored off. It is one hundred percent Greer, while also being very outside her comfort zone, since so much of her alabaster skin is on display.

She takes a few steps in, then pauses, seemingly frozen in place. I pull away from Trey and look behind me. Ash is dancing with Mei-Lien. Her arms are wrapped around his neck like mine were a second ago with Trey.

Ash also freezes, and he locks eyes with Greer. Mei-Lien glances behind her shoulder, spotting where Ash's attention went. She turns her face back to Ash, places her hands on either side of his face, and kisses him.

What?! Oh no. That bitch!

Ash's eyes go wide as he darts them to Mei-Lien. Then, what the...? A glaze passes over his sea-glass blue eyes, just for a moment, then vanishes. I turn to Greer and see her back as she runs out the door. Ash looks wildly at Mei-Lien, then yanks himself away from her and runs after Greer.

My anger becomes a *living thing*.

No longer is it an emotion or a feeling that overwhelms me. It is tangible now. I feel it inside of me, expanding and shifting uncomfortably. It's asking for an escape. It wants to tear Mei-Lien to shreds for this.

I push away from Trey. If he protests, I'm not paying attention. I march right up to her, almost nose to nose with her, and demand, "What the hell did you do?"

Her smile is smug, almost gloating, as she replies, "Something that should have been done a long time ago."

"Explain now, or we'll see who the strongest elder's daughter really is—right here, right now." Energy buzzes in my fingertips, ready to make her pay for hurting my friends.

Her eyes narrow. "Despite what you think of me, I did that for her."

"You are a twisted..." I start, but she cuts me off. "I gave him back his memories. The ones from before the fire."

She could have slapped me in the face and I wouldn't have noticed, I am so stunned by her words. "You did what?" I take a step back, needing the space to process.

"I compelled them back to the surface of his mind where he could reach them."

"Then why didn't you just do that? Why all the theatrics?" I ask, wanting to be as incredibly angry as I was only a few moments ago, but I don't feel it anymore.

"They needed a push. If I hadn't done all this, Greer would never have stepped up to tell him how she feels, Ash would never have realized that she is exactly what he wants, and this whole agonizing show of 'will they, won't they' would never end. And I know you are as sick of watching it as I am."

That actually makes sense. Manipulative, no doubt, but it worked.

"And the kiss?"

She shrugged. "I've been touching him all night trying to coax the memories out, but they were being stubborn. The kiss got me close enough to him to bring them to the surface."

That also makes sense. Mei-Lien's power needs touch to work, and the bigger the compulsion, the more she has to be connected to the individual. Any lingering irritation fizzles out with each intake of air. But how is her magic strong enough to compel that many memories? I could see her being able to do it, minus the permanent part.

"How long does he have until he loses them again?"

"This will be permanent."

My eyes bulge. "How?"

"All I can say is I have spent an unsavory amount of time in the labs lately." Her face twists with disgust.

Oh shit. What does that mean?

Knowing I won't get any more than that on the subject, I ask, "Why do you even care?"

"Like I said, I did it for her." She turns and walks away. I don't watch her go, I just stare blankly ahead, taking everything in.

Mei-Lien has feelings for Greer.

Trey places a hand on my shoulder. I turn to him, and he says, "I told you she was misunderstood." He has said that to Greer and me a few times throughout our lives.

"You knew?" It is both a question and a confirmation.

"I had suspected." I meet his eyes now, and as I am starting to feel the comfort of his presence reach me again, I remember.

"You told me you weren't her type at Ash's birthday party last year. You meant that you weren't her type because she doesn't like men."

"Yes."

"You could have said something."

"It wasn't my truth to speak."

He has a point. God, everyone is making points and making sense tonight. It's starting to get annoying.

Oh, wait! Greer and Ash! I turn, realizing some people are staring, likely watching in anticipation of a fight that is about to break out. Ignoring them, I run off toward the door.

"Where are you going?" Trey calls out, trying to keep up behind me.

"I have been waiting for this moment for so long. I am not missing it."

I cannot miss whatever is going down with Greer and Ash. Should I give them full privacy? Yes, most definitely. Will I? Nope. I'm going to go spy on whatever is happening.

As I reach the open doors, I carefully step out, scanning for them. Mr. Harris sees me and instantly points toward a cluster of trees next to the outdoor basketball courts. I nod in appreciation and creep over to where they must be. It only takes three yards of careful steps before I hear their voices.

"I feel like an absolute idiot, being the only one here who was completely in the dark!" Ash shouts. I hide behind the side of the building and peek at my two best friends standing under the trees. It's so dark that I can barely make them out, but Greer is standing defensively with her arms crossed over her chest, and Ash is pacing with his hands clenched into fists.

"It wasn't our choice. Talli and I wanted to tell you a hundred times, but we were under orders..."

"Fuck orders, Greer! This was my life!" My jaw drops. I have never heard a swear word come out of Ash's mouth before. It sounds strange, like a small child trying it out after hearing it for the first time. Also, we did tell him the truth of everything. Why is he bringing it back up now? A renewed sense of anger that came with remembering knowing before?

"Yes! And it was my life too. And Talli's life. We were all hurt by this!" Greer shouts back at him.

"I lost so much! Other friends that I didn't even realize I had. Experiences that shaped who I am. I lost my true self. Now I have two of me inside trying to fight for custody over my thoughts and feelings. Do tell, what did you and Talli lose?!"

"You! We lost you, Ash!"

"Then you should have broken the rules earlier!"

"I didn't know you could get your memories back. I didn't know that Mei-Lien had the ability to do that."

"Despite that, you could have told me as much as you could about my past and allowed me to try to figure it out."

"I was scared! They told me you could have a chance at a normal life if your memories didn't come back. Do you know how much I would give up to have that chance? The chance my parents tried so hard to give me."

"But you took away my choice."

"Because I love you."

Her quiet admittance causes Ash to pause. He looks at her. Really looks at her.

"That night. A few weeks before the fire," he says cryptically.

Wait. What night?

I have no idea what he is talking about. Trey is pressed up behind me, and he whispers in my ear, "Talli, this is wrong."

I wave my hand in dismissal, shushing him. This is just getting good.

Ash takes careful steps toward Greer. "Why didn't you tell me at least that or try to talk to me about it after everything happened?"

Greer chokes out a laugh, "How? What would I have said? You just went through an insanely horrible thing in your life, losing your parents, your home, and your memory, all in one night."

"It's been almost five years, Greer. There has been plenty of time for you to tell me," he says calmly. It's like her telling him that she loved him immediately ironed out all his nerves and rage.

"I was hoping it would just happen again, and I wouldn't have to force feelings onto you. After two years, though, I honestly lost hope and tried to forget about it myself. I decided it was for the best."

What the hell happened? We were fourteen at the time they are referencing, so what could have happened?

"It seems you didn't forget about it." Ash tentatively puts his hands on her still-folded arms. "And you would never have been forcing feelings on me. I lost my memories, but not my feelings for you. Those have always lived in my heart."

Greer opens her mouth and then closes it. Greer speechless? Excitement rushes through me like adrenaline, and my cheeks start to ache from my smile.

"I'm sorry, though. For losing my memory, I mean. For forgetting the first kiss we shared," Ash apologizes.

That's it! They kissed! They kissed? Greer didn't tell me. Oh, hell no. She is lucky I am too happy to care right now.

Greer still doesn't say anything, but I catch the moonlight reflecting off her cheek. She's crying.

"You look beautiful tonight," Ash says, moving even closer to her and way smoother than I thought was possible from him. He leans into her and kisses her.

I quickly turn around and press my back against the wall of the building, holding my hand over my mouth in shock at what I just witnessed. Trey looks like he is trying to suppress a laugh.

I literally want to break into a happy dance right now, but instead, I let Trey grab my hand and lead me back inside.

CHAPTER 32

AFTER SOME FOOD AND three more dances, my feet ache. People are slowly starting to trickle out, and I am relieved when Trey suggests the same. The rest of our evening plans consist of returning to my house to change and heading to our tree with blankets and pillows in tow to spend the night under the stars.

We walk out of the entrance doors, me using Trey for balance while I try to take off my heels. I open my mouth to speak when a siren blares—the fire alarm.

The Brethren are here.

Mr. Harris and Mr. Hank look at each other and then at us. Trey ushers me back inside the doors with such force I end up falling backward on my ass. He runs back out, and the doors close.

NO!

I scramble to my feet just as the doors close. I throw myself at the door, and one of my teachers, Ms. Cinder, says quickly, "Talliana, they locked us in because we are safest in here right now. Those doors are not going to budge."

"But Trey! He's out there!" I cry out, panic threatening to choke me.

"Calm down. It'll be okay. You need to wait until it's safe," she instructs, gripping my shoulders.

I nod but start frantically looking around for Greer and Ash. I don't remember them coming in after their moment outside; they must still be out there, too. When other students start realizing what's happening, some look for places to hide away from the doors, some begin crying, and some are angry they can't get out either.

Think Talli. Think.

Racing to the other side of the gym, I find the doors that lead to the rest of the school. I check every door I come across, but they are all locked and guarded. Fury quickly adding to my panic, I scream in frustration. I run back toward the gym but turn right before going to the locker rooms.

Please work, I silently pray.

I go to the big metal garage-like door used for bringing over-sized equipment into the school, find the chain that manually opens it, and start to pull. Relief floods me when the door moves. I pull and pull and pull until it is open enough for me to crawl out from underneath it.

I crawl, my dress getting tangled between my knees. Frustrated, I drop to my stomach and drag myself out the rest of the way. Scrambling into a standing position again, I run, bare feet smacking the asphalt. I pass someone on my way, another guard for the school, and shout over my shoulder, "The big metal door by the gym is open and needs guarding!"

I don't look back to see if he did what I said, but I have faith that he did.

The air is smoky around me, black smoke, and I follow it. The streets are empty except for the occasional emergency officer on the lookout for Brethren. I turn the corner, the smoke getting worse as I get closer to my own house. I run harder.

Then I see it.

Trey's house is alight with raging flames. Four Water Elementals surround it, trying to put it out.

Mr. and Mrs. Waterstone are outside their home, hugging onto one another, mourning the loss. Lemon is sitting beside them with Pebble on her head. I'm so relieved to see them both okay.

I hear an angry roar, and as I turn to it, I notice Mr. Waterstone doing the same. Trey is straddling a man on the ground, one hand on the man's chest and a gun at his head. "I know they gave you a message! Tell me!" he yells.

"I think the message is obvious. We are coming for you and everyone you love," the man sneers.

BANG.

I jump from the noise. Trey slowly gets off the man, and as soon as he stands up, Theora swoops down and clings to his outstretched arm.

"Talli!" Greer yells. I turn away from Trey in time for Greer to capture me in a hug. "I thought you were in danger," she says breathlessly.

"I thought you two were in danger." I pull away and see Ash close behind Greer. We are all safe, it seems—for now, anyway.

"You should have stayed at the school, where it was safe." Trey's tone startles me, and I spin back around to him. He's right behind me, his quiet rage evident in his clipped words.

I shouldn't push him. I should tread lightly. Instead, I poke the beast. "You can't lock me up and run into danger. I will always find a way out so that I can chase after you."

His eyes flash, and he opens his mouth to say something, but gets interrupted. "Treyton, my office, please," Mr. Waterstone says sternly.

We both look at him, and I take in my surroundings again. The house fire is put out, but the home is scorched black. I doubt anything can be salvaged from it. Mom has her arms around Mrs. Waterstone, convincing her to go back to our house and let others deal with what happened. Pebble is on her shoulder now, the poor little mouse looking terrified.

There are five police officers with three men handcuffed and on their knees in front of them. Chief Lu is there, and Mr. Hansen is with her. I watch them converse for a moment, but I can't hear their words from here. Chief Lu turns from him and motions to the officers to take the men away. Weird.

Trey gives me a quick, "We will discuss this later. Go inside with your mom." His eyes shift to Greer, giving her a look that I can't decipher, and she nods in response. Mr. Waterstone, with Lemon at his side, and Trey with Theora still perched on his arm, walk away. On his way, Trey stops when he comes across an unburdened officer. "Please stand guard outside the Hoffman's home until I or Aaron Hoffman say otherwise."

The man looks confused, receiving orders from someone with absolutely no authority, so he looks to Mr. Waterstone, who says, "Do as my son requests. I promise it won't take long."

I huff. He couldn't lock me up at school, so now he will try at my own home. I want to protest, but Greer loops her arm with mine, Ash copies her movement with the other arm, and they walk with me to the house, the officer trailing us the entire way.

Once inside the house and in my room with my friends, I finally breathe. How did this night go from wonderful to awful so quickly? Trey was angry enough that he just killed that man with little hesitation. He wasn't an immediate threat. It wasn't life or death, but he killed him anyway.

Looking down at myself, I am not surprised to see my dress is completely ruined. It's filthy, torn, and most of the beads are missing from the front. My feet are even dirtier from running barefoot. I groan, realizing my shoes are probably still outside the gym's door where I dropped them in the confusion of everything. Greer and Ash seem unscathed, appearing as they did at prom last I saw them. Although, if I look closely enough, I can see Ash's lips are swollen, and Greer's cheeks are a little pink.

I realize then that the longing tension between them is gone, replaced instead with looks of desire. Ash lost his home tonight. The second time this has happened to him, but he doesn't seem to care. He just keeps looking at Greer.

"I'm going to go take a shower. I'll knock before coming out so you two can have some privacy," I announce.

Greer walks over to me before I shut the bathroom door and asks, "Are you okay? Like, really okay?"

I give her a small smile, one that I don't have to force because I am happy for them regardless of being very unhappy for me and the impending argument with Trey that's on the horizon. "Yes. I will be. I'm very happy for you two."

She smiles back and allows me to close the door. I turn on the shower, and resting my back against the empty wall, I slide to the floor. I don't have the energy to cry or even feel right now. All I've done these past few months is cry and feel. It's exhausting.

I should probably take the time to think over what happened earlier with my anger, but I must be a coward, because I am terrified to face *it*. Especially if *it* is exactly what I think it is.

I know Trey will probably come back here ready for a fight, and I fully plan to give him one, so I will save my energy for that by getting back to my feet and allowing the warm water to bring me back to life.

Now ready to leave the bathroom, I knock on the door. To my surprise, it isn't Greer or Ash who tells me to come out, it is Trey. I pause, not sure that I am ready. I found a sense of calm in the water, and now he is going to ruin it.

I reluctantly open the door and find Trey standing a couple of feet away from it, arms crossed. I notice he has changed too. Likely to get the blood off him. Trey has never told me if he has killed before, but if his lack of hesitation earlier is any indication, it appears as though he has.

We survey each other for a moment, and finally, Trey breaks the silence. "There was an active Brethren attack alert, and you deliberately escaped from a safe place to run through the community unarmed and with no one watching your back."

I cringe. Alright, I guess what I did was extremely reckless. But he did the exact same thing. He was unarmed and ran into danger, too. He shoved me inside and ran off to go play hero.

The *thing* inside of me pulses, infuriated.

"Don't be a hypocrite. You could have run inside and stayed safe, too, while the proper authorities dealt with the situation. But no, you ran out without a weapon and someone to watch your back."

"Talli, we are two very different people."

"You're not kidding," I reply, deadpan.

He glares at me and continues, "We are two different people because I have much more training than you do. I have been on twenty-three missions, and you have been on one. I have had to battle these monsters on multiple occasions. I know how to fight them with or without a weapon. You are..."

"Inferior? Incapable? Unpracticed? A liability?"

"Not ready. You are also too important for me to risk."

"Answer me this: you have been just playing along, trying to make me happy by allowing me to train, but you will never let me actually fight for our people, will you?" I already know the answer but I have to hear it from him.

He uncrosses his arms, and his jaw clenches. No, then.

"Treyton, if you want to redeem yourself with me in any capacity right now, it is time to come clean. Tell me everything. Tell me what happened at that prison. Tell me why the Brethren are clearly after you. Tell me why you killed that man in cold blood." There they all are. My demands laid out.

He stares at me in horror. No for this too, then. I ache to go to him and beg him on my knees. Because deep down I know this is an ultimatum for me, not a request. My heart cracks at the thought of walking away from him, but I cannot go any further with him if he isn't going to offer me at least the truth.

"I will consider your wish for me to stay safe and out of the fighting if you simply tell me the truth. That is all I am asking of you right now," I implore him.

He turns around and gives me his back.

"Please." My voice breaks on the word.

Without facing me again, he whispers, "I can't."

Tears roll down my cheeks. Why is this happening? Why are we here? I fought so hard to get him back, just to lose him anyway.

"I need you to leave."

He turns back to me, and seeing my tears, he starts toward me, but I take a quick step back.

"No, Trey. We can't continue with this in between us."

"Talli, this is a disagreement. We will resolve this. We will compromise." Panic leaks out from his tone, and the crack in my heart deepens.

"Compromise!? You seem to think the definition of 'compromise' is you getting your way. I have allowed you to string me along with tiny shreds of the truth. Just enough to make me think you will actually tell me everything one day. I'm an idiot for letting you manipulate me for so long. It's over."

"Don't do this."

"I already did. Please leave."

His face falls, and he walks to the door. Before he exits the room, he says, "I am only trying to keep you safe."

"You will make an excellent elder one day. Seems you already have the misconception that hiding the truth equals safety."

He winces and then leaves, shutting the door behind him.

I collapse to the floor when the string between our hearts shutters as a tiny strand snaps. I breathe through the pain until it subsides. The string is still there, just weakened. It would be too kind for it to disappear altogether. No, it will exist until it eventually fades—a constant reminder of what I've lost.

I force myself to stand when there is a knock on the door. Mom peers in before fully entering with Greer right behind her.

"Oh, honey." Her tone is full of grief for me. She wraps her arms around me from one side, and Greer follows suit on the other side.

I sniffle, trying to pull myself together. "How did you two know there was something wrong?"

"We saw Trey on the way out," Mom answers.

"We could also feel your emotions from the kitchen," Greer adds.

"Well, that makes me feel even better," I mutter sarcastically at my sister.

They slowly ease off me, and Mom ushers me to my bed. She sits next to me while Greer climbs into her own bed.

"What happened?" Mom asks.

A new ache seizes my heart at the idea of giving voice to what just happened, but I have to. First, to give myself at least one more minute, I ask, "Where is Ash?"

"Your Dad is helping him set up the guest room for the night," Mom replies.

"He didn't want to go to the new house with the Waterstones?"

"No. You can't blame him for wanting to be somewhere familiar tonight. Somewhere he feels comfortable."

Greer nods, and Mom gives her a warning look. "I also suspect he doesn't want to be far away from my other daughter. Which, might I add, there will be no funny business in my house tonight."

Greer's cheeks pinken, and timidly, she responds, "Yes, ma'am."

Seeing Greer pink and timid makes me laugh. We all laugh together because, despite my circumstances, Greer finally has to be told "no funny business," and that is music to my ears.

"Okay, enough stalling, Talliana." Mom moves her eyes to me.

I take a deep breath and explain all the recent sour spots of Trey's and my relationship—all the ones that led us to tonight and my decision.

Using our past mistakes in history as our guide, those gifted with powerful abilities of mind manipulation, such as compulsion, memory-seeing, dream-walking, and thought-reading, should not be the only ones in power. We have always led with three elders, but now we must ensure that each elder represents a different classification and is elected into their role by the people.

- Community Laws & Guidelines

CHAPTER 33

TREY HAS HARDLY LEFT me alone.

If he isn't lurking behind every corner, Theora is doing his dirty work. The worst part is he doesn't even have the decency to not be obvious about it. He is outside waiting for me every time I get out of school so he can trail me home. Then he is back outside our home an hour later, ready to walk me to the community building on our training nights. After the first few days of yelling at him to go away with no success, I started ignoring him. It's so bad that it has become a new running joke at school. Apparently, I am so weak and fragile that I need a bodyguard wherever I go. It doesn't matter how good I've gotten on the sparing mat or how well I use my bow. Mean kids are going to be mean kids.

Surprisingly, Mei-Lien has kept her mouth shut through it all, not starting or adding to the ridicule. It's almost like since the prom, something inside of her has shifted. Maybe she's afraid to give me a reason to share her secret? No, it doesn't feel like that's it. I haven't told a soul about my conversation with her, and if I had, I'm not sure if she would see it as a betrayal or a relief. Greer had insisted that she wanted to go talk to her after what she did for Ash, but I convinced her not to. I think it's best to leave the whole thing alone and simply be happy about the outcome. Perhaps Mei-Lien is done putting up the mean girl front. That must be exhausting, constantly finding opportunities to be cruel.

With distance and more time to think about it, fixing Ash's memories was probably not Mei-Lien's choice. The Hansens likely asked her if she would be willing to try with their help, or she was ordered to do it by an elder. However, how she did it *was* her choice. Even if she believes she did it that way for Greer, it was still unnecessarily cruel. Something I have no intention of forgiving.

The school bell rings overhead, marking lunchtime. I grab my notebook, stuffing it haphazardly into my backpack, and head out of the classroom with Greer on my heels.

"I'll meet you at our table," Greer says before going left down the hall instead of to the right. She's going to collect Ash from his class. If I weren't so happy for the two of them, I would roll my eyes at her endless need to be with him. Although, it wasn't that long ago that I did the same thing with Trey as soon as school let out.

I stroll down the hallway to my right, not talking or looking at anyone. Since the breakup two weeks ago, I have lost all my energy for socializing. Someone bumps into my shoulder, racing past me. Looking up, I find a girl from our year laughing at me. Fucking Ariela. She used to be one of Mei-Lien's minions.

The *thing* inside of me stirs, causing me to clench my stomach and divert to the bathroom. Finding it empty is a relief as I run to the sink and clench the base until my hands hurt.

Breathe. Breathe Talli.

My eyes move upward to the mirror, and I jump back as if burned by the sink.

My eyes. What is wrong with my eyes? I race back to the mirror and gasp when I see it's still there. Black swirling over my irises.

No. This isn't happening.

As the water runs out of the faucet, I splash my face, hoping that it will go away—that everything will go away. I slowly lift my gaze back to the mirror and nearly drop when I see my normal deep-blue eyes, clear and without any black. Not wanting to test my luck, I quickly dry my face and exit the bathroom.

The halls are empty now since everyone is at lunch. I head in that direction until a hand grabs my wrist and pushes me against the lockers lining the wall. The shock causes me to freeze as I stare into Balor's pale-green eyes. He is a Strategist and the only one in our class who gives Greer a run for her money on the mat. His tall and muscular frame makes him feel like a giant hovering over me. The smirk that graces his face is terrifying. We both know that he has me trapped, and there is little I can do against him.

"Where is your bodyguard now?" His taunting question brings back what I had just forced down a moment ago. *It* clenches onto my chest.

"Let me go." I try to force my voice into a calm tone, but it comes out strangled.

"I wonder if you scream if he would come running for you? Go on. Do it. I think screaming is all you're likely good at. Besides spreading your legs, of course."

Fury tightens its grip and I lift my knee, hitting him hard right where it counts. I bet he didn't expect me to do that. I slide out from under his looming form, trying to get down the hallway and away from him quickly, but he grabs the back of my neck and throws me toward the lockers. I slam into them face-first and fall hard on my ass.

My fingers twitch with the urge to rip him apart, and as I turn to do just that, Balor goes tumbling to the floor. In an instant, Greer is on top of him, a knife against his neck.

Ash's hands reach out to me, and I let him help me up from the floor. Balor's hands ball into fists, and Greer presses the knife harder. "I dare you," she challenges, her tone low and deadly.

"What is going on?" Mr. Waterstone's voice echoes down the hallway, causing Ash and I to jump. Greer slowly moves off of Balor and tucks her knife away inside her boot. A drip of blood runs down his neck as he gets to his feet.

Ash is the first to answer, "Balor was attacking Talli while she was alone. Greer was protecting her."

Mr. Waterstone looks us all over carefully. "I want all of you in my office right now."

I take the quiet walk over to try to breathe through the iron grip my anger still has on me. Is the black swirling in my eyes again? What would Mr. Waterstone do if he saw it? I imagine myself mentally building a wall around the thing in my chest, caging it in as best as I can.

Mr. Waterstone orders Balor to sit down and wait while he pulls the rest of us into his office. He hands me a tissue, and after I give him a confused look, he says, "You're bleeding, Talliana." I reach up to my cheek and find a gash where my face struck the lockers. I carefully blot it with the tissue, and he asks me, "What happened?"

I carefully recall the brief interaction, and then Greer and Ash explain their side. They went to the cafeteria, and when I wasn't at the table, they went looking for me. Ash also explains how I've been bullied the last couple of weeks because of Trey's presence around every corner. That part, I could have lived without him voicing.

"Is that true? Treyton's presence is making things hard for you with the other students?" Mr. Waterstone asks me.

I nod, squeezing the balled-up bloody tissue in my hand.

"Talliana, go home and take something to heal yourself. You are excused from the rest of your classes today. I will be speaking to Treyton about his behavior. If you have any more trouble with the other students, you just let me know." He turns to Greer and says, "Greer, I understand your need to protect your sister, but putting a knife to someone's throat in school is inexcusable. I will be speaking to Aaron about an appropriate punishment. You and Asher will not be excused from your classes. Does everyone understand?"

"Yes, sir," the three of us say in unison. We exit his office and watch Balor enter it with an angry expression.

"I'm going to spread what happened across the school. I think that will help prevent something like this from happening again," Ash remarks thoughtfully.

I should be mortified at the idea of Ash sharing just how weak I am, despite all my hard work at training, but in reality, Balor is a shark going after a small fish. He is the only one that is going to look bad here. Physical bullying does not happen in this school, either. Verbal bullying is always going to exist no matter where you are, but we don't tolerate physical bullying. It's against our values as a people to bully one another. I have no doubt Ash will only have to tell one person before it spreads like wildfire through the school.

I nod, giving him the okay, and say to Greer, "Thank you for saving my ass."

"If it were anyone else, I would have let you teach them a lesson. But with Balor..."

"You don't have to explain. See you two later."

Walking out the front door of the school, I am relieved not to see Trey anywhere in sight. However, my relief is short-lived when I see Theora perched on the school's roof.

Great. Just great.

It only takes two minutes into my walk home before Trey is jogging up to me, covered in sawdust. When he is not watching my every step during the day or trying to get me to talk to him in my dreams at night, he is working on rebuilding his home with the rest of the community builders.

He stops just short of running into me and cups my cheek, looking over my injury. "What happened? Are you okay?"

I push off his touch and walk around him.

"Talli, please talk to me."

My hands start to tremble, and I tuck them into my armpits to try to hide it. I keep walking.

"Who hurt you?"

His question and the tug at our heart's connection make me stop. I turn to him and answer quietly, "You."

His face falls, and I turn back around to continue my march away from him. My heart aches. Being at odds with him is so painful, and I want to scream and rage at him all the time. This is his fault. He is so blinded by his fear that he can't see how much he is hurting me.

Trey follows me up the steps to my house, and I turn again before going inside. "You need to give me more space. If you care about me, you will do that, at least."

"Tell me what happened today." He argues.

I release a frustrated sigh. "Everyone bullies me at school because of you. They call me weak and fragile, saying that's why I need a bodyguard everywhere I go."

He drops down to the steps, takes a seat on the top one, and puts his head in his hands.

His reaction gives me the strength to add, "Balor thought it would be funny today to corner me when no one was around." Trey whips his head up to look at me. I continue, "He threw me around a bit, telling me I should scream to see if you would come running."

"That little piece of shit. I am going to kill him." Trey stands up, fists clenched.

"Greer put a knife to his throat before he could do any more damage to me. Then your dad showed up. If you try to do anything more to him, it will only prove his point. Let your dad do his job and handle it."

His head falls, and he turns back to me fully. "Did he hurt you anywhere else?"

"He took a good blow to my pride. Maybe some bruising on my wrist, but that's it. In a few minutes, I'll be healed, and it'll be as if nothing happened."

"That's not true. It did happen. You got hurt because of me."

I feel the missing "again" that he does not say. This isn't the first time he has made it seem like he was protecting me by leaving. I want to ask him why, beg him again to tell me, but I know it won't go anywhere. Instead, I ignore the anger and frustration and listen to the part of me that loves him despite it all.

Walking up to him, I wrap my arms around his neck, and hold him tight.

His arms encircle my waist, and he lifts me up as he steps onto the porch again from the top step. I bury my face in his neck and inhale the smell of vanilla, sweat, and sawdust.

"I'm tired of being angry at you," I admit into his skin.

He sets me down and replies, as if it is so simple, "Then don't be angry at me."

"That's not my choice. You decide when I can stop being angry." Stepping out of his arms, I go into the house and close the door before he can argue.

CHAPTER 34

June

IT'S BEEN A MONTH since the fire. The Waterstones' house has new walls and a roof again. Ash told me at breakfast that they will start on the flooring tomorrow. Before I know it, the house will be finished, and everything will return to normal—almost everything, anyway.

Ash is still staying with us. Dad and Mom haven't asked him to leave, and he hasn't asked to go. He and Greer have been insepara- ble, and I've been the third wheel this month. I don't really mind, but it's hard despite their attempts not to be obnoxious.

Since our argument, Trey has backed off a little. He is still always there, but at least now he isn't being so blatant about it. Instead of standing at the front door of the school, he is behind a tree a little ways away. He has also left my dreams alone, allowing me to rest without him trying to get me to talk to him. I have chosen to be grateful for those small mercies.

All has been quiet at school since the fight with Balor, which has been a relief. Now, school is finally over.

Today is graduation, and I am looking forward to the start of the summer. I will have a week's break, and then I start working at the medical center to study under Mom and Healer Weiss before college in the fall. Most of the staff who work at the medical center are educated doctors and nurses from human schools. It almost seems silly to go through so much trouble for degrees when, in many cases, our abilities are more than enough to heal effectively. But we do live in a human world, and degrees, certifications, and legitimate business practices are a must for maintaining appearances. Plus, in the case of med school, there is a lot to learn that can really benefit the way we heal.

"Ready, ladies?" Dad asks, poking his head into our open bedroom door.

I glance at Greer, who has been ready for at least thirty minutes, and then back at Dad. "Yep!" I answer and add one more pin to hold my cap in place.

Our school gowns are green. All the Order communities in the United States have green gowns. They are meant to represent our connection to nature. Granted, I think nature can be represented by many colors, but whoever decided the color must have been an Earth Elemental. I'm just grateful they aren't brown.

I slip on my silver heels and follow Dad out the door, Greer behind me. When we reach the living room, I see Mrs. Waterstone is here helping Ash put his cap on. At this point, I think Ash has three mothers now. Mrs. Waterstone, his actual mother, and mine since he has been living under our roof. Mrs. Waterstone finishes, turns to us, and declares, "Everyone looks wonderful!"

"I agree," Mom says.

"I think you all look like green blobs," a familiar voice chimes in from the dining room across the hall.

I spin and find Uncle Cyrus standing there. My day brightens tenfold at the sight of him. Careful not to trip in my heels, I hustle over to him and give him a big hug as I shriek, "Uncle Cyrus!"

Pulling away, I study my only Uncle. Uncle Cyrus is Dad's twin brother, with the same soft round face and amber eyes. He has a shaved head and a bushier beard, though. It ends about three inches below his chin and is mostly gray, whereas Dad's is closely trimmed and only sprouting a little bit of gray. I always thought that was odd, considering they are the same age, but Mom explained to me that burning out your magic too many times can sometimes age you physically a bit more than normal. That seems to be the case with Uncle Cyrus.

"Where are Aunt Janet and Penn?" I ask.

"Back at home. Penn is entering his terrible twos and it felt like a bad idea to put him on a plane full of humans." Uncle Cyrus answers. He and Aunt Janet couldn't have kids of their own, but they were able to adopt Penn as a baby two years ago from the Georgia community.

"I assume Bluebell didn't feel like coming either?" Bluebell is his bonded blue heron.

"I wanted to bring her, but apparently, you can't bring a large wild bird on an airplane. Who knew?" He gives me a teasing smile. "Now, where is your other half?" he asks, referring to Greer.

She steps up to us and hugs him as well. When she lets go, she makes a show of looking him up and down. She says, "Growing that beer belly out, are we?"

Uncle Cyrus bursts into a deep rumble of laughter. He pats his stomach a few times and answers, "I think it suits me, don't you? I'm going for that Santa Clause look."

The whole room erupts in laughter. Dad pats his brother on the shoulder and comments, "Maybe it's time to fire that trainer of yours. He's too easy on you."

We all laugh again. The joke is that Uncle Cyrus is the lead trainer for the Florida community. He is more than that, though. The Florida community is referred to as our relocation community. They handle all relocation needs for the Order. If someone wants or needs to move to a different state for various reasons, they handle the transfer. If a child loses their parents and needs a new home, they find them one. If someone is on the run as a known Hawk among the Brethren, they hide them and get them safely out of the country. Uncle Cyrus is a Shield, not to be confused with the mental ones we all create. He is a type of Air Elemental that can create a wall of wind that can withstand arrows, bullets, and anything else that gets thrown at it. It is a powerful ability that we thankfully have no shortage of. Uncle Cyrus is one of the most powerful Shields, though, and he uses it often to protect the people his community saves.

"Alright, no more time for jokes. We need to go before these three miss their own graduation ceremony," Mom interrupts.

We all head over to the school in two cars and arrive in time for Greer, Ash, and me to line up. Graduation is a whole community event, even if many families don't have kids graduating this year. Everyone shows up in support.

The ceremony begins, and we take our places in the procession. Mr. Waterstone welcomes everyone, says a few words to us, and then introduces Sarah, the class's Valedictorian, for her speech.

Ash was initially chosen as the school's top student, but he declined the honor, which was then given to Sarah who was next in line. He claimed his reasons were that he hated crowds and he didn't want to choke in front of everyone, but I suspect it was more than that. I am super happy for Sarah, though. She deserves it.

Sarah was my right-hand man for prom and has always been a nice person to everyone she meets. Growing up, if teachers didn't allow me to pair with Greer, I always paired with Sarah for projects. She is just so down-to-earth, literally, since she is an Earth Elemental.

Once she finishes her speech, we go through the tedious process of Mr. Waterstone handing all the graduates their diplomas. He then closes with some final words of wisdom, and, at last, we get to move our tassels over. To my surprise, before we are dismissed to leave, Dad goes to the stage. He has never done this at a graduation. Nerves course through me, but I focus on my breathing and wait for his words.

"Congratulations, students!" Dad's voice booms through the field. "We are all so proud of you and what you have accomplished. Looking over all your faces today, I know that our future is bright with hope and strength. I won't delay the celebrations for very long, but I wanted to take this opportunity to address the community and share some news that will be the source of even more celebration."

The crowd claps, and once that dies down, he continues, "As you all know, the Hansens are back and have resumed their work in creating tools for us to use in our war against the Brethren." More clapping. "Yes, it has been a long four years without the hope their work brings to us. I am so pleased to announce today that they have created something that will give us a huge leg up in this war." He pauses, no doubt for effect, then finishes, "Memory elixirs."

Everyone goes quiet. I suspect from confusion, like me.

"Our people have the humane opinion of not killing unless it's necessary. So what do we do when we capture Brethren? We send them away to our many prisons scattered outside this country. This uses an incredible amount of resources that we don't have, and it's no longer a sustainable option. The Hansens have created a memory elixir that wipes away a human's memory, simulating retrograde amnesia. They will not remember anything about their past, including the Brethren or the Order. Once we safely administer the elixir and ensure its effectiveness, we can simply let them go. Now, this is not the answer to ending the war, but it gets us one step closer to finding that answer."

Cheers and whistles roar from the crowd, everyone rising to their feet in the excitement.

I don't rise. I don't move. The world around me blurs out while the thoughts in my head come into focus.

Mei-Lien. What she said to me at prom about spending time in the lab. Later that night, Chief Lu talking with Mr. Hansen and the prisoners they took. They must have been test subjects. Dad and all his speeches about winning, even though we are far from it. Now that I think of it, he has always been obsessed with the compulsion ability and how it can impact memories. How long has he been working on this? Is this his end goal, or just a step toward that goal?

One step closer to finding that answer, I hear him say again in my mind.

There will be fewer killings and fewer imprisonments. We are giving the Brethren a fresh start in life, allowing them to live how they should despite what they have done to us. This is a good thing. I should be happy and proud of Dad's part in this. But something inside of me is telling me this is wrong.

"Talli. Talli. Talli?" Greer's voice pulls me back to reality. The graduates are moving to exit the ceremony. Shaking my last thought away, I jump to my feet and try to catch up with the person walking before me.

Chapter 35

"Congratulations."

I spin around, almost toppling in my heels, to find Trey behind me.

Despite everything, my traitorous heartbeat picks up at how close he is. I say, "Thank you," and then look around to try to find a way to escape.

Mom and Dad, the Waterstones, and the Hansens all set up a big graduation party for Greer, Ash, and me in our backyard. The smell of burgers and hot dogs on the grill is surprisingly comforting. It feels as if we really are all just normal humans celebrating a normal human accomplishment in a normal human way.

Trey moves his arm from where it is behind his back and produces a massive bouquet of flowers. I can't help the smile that graces my face. I slowly take the offered flowers from his hand. They are beautiful and my favorite. Peonies. Instantly, I know they are from his mother's garden by how vibrant the different shades of pink are. The sweet fragrance fills up my nose without even having to bring them close.

"They are beautiful, and that was very sweet of you. Thank you." I genuinely mean it. Trey is always thoughtful, even when he knows I still want to strangle him.

"I see your Uncle Cyrus is here. It is always refreshing to hear his dad jokes, lightening the mood around here. Weirdly enough, I always miss them when he is gone."

I want to laugh, but I can't help but feel irritated when I remember the last time we spoke of Uncle Cyrus. "Did you already set up some kind of plan with him to grab me and lock me up in a high tower for my safety?" I ask, arms crossing over my chest. This position feels awkward with the flowers in my hand, so I uncross them again.

"If I knew you would go without maiming your favorite uncle, then I would have. But as we have established over this last month, you are too stubborn to know what's good for you."

I narrow my eyes at him. "You know what I have learned this last month? Being stubborn is not a character flaw. In fact, I think it's my best quality. So, thank you for the compliment." I turn my nose up at him, spin on my heel, and walk away.

It does no good because he quickly catches up to me and halts me in my tracks. "Talli, what are we doing?"

"Well, I have been ignoring you, and you have been driving me crazy."

Trey groans. "I mean this. This whole breakup is stupid. I miss you. Our lives will probably be too short to be wasting time like this."

"Like I told you last time we spoke, you decide when I stop being angry."

He seems to war with himself for a moment and then says, "Okay."

"Okay?" My heart rate kicks up a notch.

"Start walking to our spot at ten o'clock. No earlier."

"This isn't just some plan to seduce me into forgetting everything, is it?" I've learned my lesson over these last few months. He is very good at that, and I am a sucker for it.

"No. I promise. I will bring your favorite drink and something for us to eat, though."

Once again, I narrow my eyes at him, unsure I believe him.

"I'll even let you throw your drink in my face if that earns back your forgiveness for what I have put you through."

That breaks the stern look on my face, and I laugh. "That would create such a beautiful movie-magic moment. But I won't do that to you. I can be impulsive at the best of times, but I will restrain myself."

Trey feigns letting out a held breath. Before I can move, he leans in, placing a hand on my lower back, and his lips are to my ear as he says, "Oh, and wear that dress, please. You look enchanting in it."

My cheeks flush, and the place between my legs starts to throb as he walks away.

I'm screwed.

At exactly ten o'clock, I open the back door and walk across the backyard to the trail entrance, still in my graduation dress as requested, minus the heels, but stop short. To my disbelief, fireflies light up the path to the lake.

Liar. He is absolutely going to try seducing me back into his arms. He knows I am a hopeless romantic at heart and will exploit that weakness for all its worth.

I start to walk carefully down the path so I don't disturb the fireflies. Their dance is mesmerizing to watch, how they gracefully swoop and twirl. I long to join in and shine as bright as they do against the darkness.

I give in and twirl with them. My thigh-length aqua-blue dress spins easily with me. The movement feels silly but immensely freeing, like I am just a young girl again playing in a pretty new dress.

The fireflies seem to spin with me, welcoming me as their dance partner. I laugh and leap over the tree stump I have stepped over so many times. I continue to twirl, leap, and lose myself until I spin right into Trey's awaiting arms.

I'm breathless as I stare up into his dark eyes.

After a long moment, he says, "You shine brighter than any firefly ever could."

"I wish that were true." The words tumble out before I can stop them.

"Just because you don't see it, doesn't mean it's untrue. Your heart is pure and good. There is nothing you could do that would change my mind."

A tear slips free, and he wipes it away with his thumb. If only he knew. If only he saw what was really inside of me. I feel it taking over more and more each day, like a spreading fungus. I don't know how much longer I can keep it hidden from those I love.

I swallow hard and take a step out of his arms. "How did you learn to talk to fireflies?"

He laughs softly. "Neat trick, huh? Theora asked them for me. Most bonded birds can speak to insects."

"Wow. The things you learn. Maybe one day I will bond a bird too so they can ask all the icky insects to stay away from me."

He laughs again and leads me to where he has set up a blanket under our tree, wrapped with white fairy lights. I take a seat next to a tray with a charcuterie board full of assorted cheese and crackers. Two wine glasses are filled with…I pick one glass up and give it a whiff. Yep, my favorite. Raspberry lemonade.

I take a small sip, and it's perfect—sweet and tangy. I close my eyes and appreciate it for a moment before setting it down and looking over at Trey who is sitting on the other side of the yumminess.

"I have something for you." He pulls out a small box from his pocket and continues, "I missed Christmas and your birthday and, technically, our one-year anniversary last month. I couldn't miss your graduation as well."

"Trey…"

"Even if you decide not to forgive me tonight or ever, I still want you to have this. Accept it as a gift from a friend if that makes you feel better."

He pushes the gift into my hands. It's a small dark-blue box with a curly silver bow affixed atop it—our colors from prom. I give him a small smile and then turn my attention back to opening it.

Carefully, I lift the top off. Inside is a necklace with a long silver chain and a pendant made from a white crystal that I recognize but can't quite place. I pull it out of the box and run a thumb over the smooth, soft stone that reminds me of milk.

"It's moonstone," Trey offers. "I asked a friend from North Carolina to find it in one of their mines. I thought it would help you with your nightmares."

My eyes dart quickly to him. "How…" I swallow hard. Of course, he knows about my nightmares. Or should I say, nightmare—the one with the fire and the shadow that still plagues me most nights. I haven't told anyone about it, not even Greer. I guess I like to keep secrets, too.

I close my hand around the crystal and pull it close to my chest. Our people commonly wear or use crystals and gemstones for their magical properties. Elementals, in particular, often claim that they can enhance their abilities. I've never paid them too much mind, but I do believe in their magic.

"Thank you, Trey. This was an incredibly thoughtful gift," I tell him sincerely. "Help me put it on?"

Trey smiles and nods, pleased that I'm accepting it, then reaches across the tray of food to help clasp it around my neck. His fingertips gently brush against my skin, and I shiver. When I feel the weight of the crystal resting fully against my chest, I turn back to him. The smile he had a moment ago is gone and his face is now a mix of emotions, reminding me exactly why we are here.

"Alright, I'm listening."

He takes a moment to collect his thoughts. Then he catches me completely off guard when he starts, "Your broken arm wasn't an accident."

I still, the piece of cheese I was about to bite into hanging between my fingers. I lower it to the tray, no longer desiring to eat anything.

He continues, "It was a tactic to get to me. I wouldn't cooperate, so they threatened you." He looks away across the dark lake.

"I take it, it worked."

"It did. I went with them to protect the community, but I did what they asked to protect you." There it is. Exactly what I suspected.

"What was the cost?"

Silence.

"Trey, what did they make you tell them in exchange for my life?"

He finally looks at me, and with pain in his eyes, he admits, "I'm under orders not to tell anyone. Not even you."

I huff. "How convenient. Are the elders ever going to tell us what this new possible threat might be?"

"I don't know. I didn't give them any information that we can't defend. It could just make things more complicated."

Because we need more things to make our lives difficult. Annoyance and despair fill my chest, but I try to stay focused on this conservation.

"What really happened the night of prom? Why did they come after you?"

"The Brethren are petty as much as they are violent. They want me to pay for escaping, and fortunately for them, they know all of my weaknesses. What happened at prom was a message meant to scare me into running back to them."

"But you didn't."

He shook his head. "No, I didn't. I knew that if I did, they would only burn everyone I love to ash, regardless. All that can be done is try to keep everyone safe and prepare for whatever they might do."

"You can't keep everyone safe, Trey. There is only one of you," I point out.

"Do you see me following anyone else around except for you? They know Talli. They know that all it would take is grabbing you, and I would give them anything. That is why I locked you in the school that night. I thought they were going to try to take you."

His admittance tears at me. I want to ask him why. Why would he give up everything for me? I am just one person out of many. I am not worth the cost of a thousand of other lives.

I don't voice any of that, though. I don't question or protest because, deep down, I know I would do the same. I *have* done the same with Greer's life. Ash's parents lives, too, if I'm keeping count.

So, instead of all that, I apologize. "I am sorry I have been so hard on you. You carry a lot, and I didn't understand."

He grabs my hand from my lap and says, "I didn't let you understand. I don't really care to share what happened to me there, but if you insist on asking, I will tell you."

I shake my head, "I don't need to know. Between feeling your pain that night and that scar on your bicep, I can imagine well enough."

I gently touch his arm, right where I know that scar is. I've done my best to pretend that it doesn't exist. It hurts seeing something I can't heal, but it's a part of him, and it's time I accept that.

He moves the tray of food and our drinks out of the way and pulls me to him. We lie down on the blanket, wrapped in each other's embrace. I rest my head on his chest, relieved to be back in his arms again. Relieved to let go of the anger I've been holding onto toward him.

One heartbeat. Four heartbeats. Six heartbeats pass and he says, "There was this one guard, though, I think he actually had a tiny shred of decency. He used to make things up about his meals, claiming the meat was bad or not cooked right, and then he would bring his plate to me saying 'only the trash is worthy of this food.' Funny thing is, there was never actually anything wrong with it. It was so much better than the mystery stew and stale bread they usually gave me. A few times, he even made a show of being disgusted by my smell and forced me to get cleaned up. The other guards knew what he was doing, but no one questioned him."

The knowledge that someone showed him a shred of kindness is a balm to my aching heart. I tilt my head back and kiss him as if we were never apart. Trey pulls me on top of him to deepen the kiss and I sweep my tongue into his mouth. He sucks on it and it tears down all the restraint I have built when it came to staying away from him.

I spread my legs out and tuck my heels underneath his calves, effectively wrapping myself around him with my arms under his neck. His hips lift and I feel every inch of his arousal press against me through our clothes. I moan into his mouth and grind myself against him in desperate need. Grabbing the bottom of my dress, he pulls it off in a swift movement, causing the moonstone pendant to thump against my sternum. Left in just my underwear against the cool air, I shiver involuntarily, and my nipples harden as the wind dances over them. He sits up a little to grab a folded blanket and covers me from where I am straddling him. Then he takes me in.

"So enchanting. So beautiful. So stubborn," he teases.

I laugh, throwing my head back and almost losing the blanket over my shoulders. Trey fully sits up now, wrapping his arms around me. He pulls me to him until his mouth closes over one nipple. I squeak in surprise and then melt as it feels like pure ecstasy—his warm breath against the sensitive peak. The warmth moves from one breast to the other until I feel it pool between my legs. I tangle my fingers into his short hair, pushing him to my chest even more, encouraging his touch. He switches to the other nipple, and my head falls forward on top of his.

Concluding his feast, he lifts his head and captures my mouth again. We work off his shirt, then his pants and underwear, with my flimsy scrap of fabric following suit. He places the blanket back over my shoulders, but it's no use. As soon as he places me on top of his hard length, I shrug it off. My skin is so heated now that the cool breeze is a blessing.

Trey places a hand on each of my hips and moves me up and down until I get the rhythm and take over. He groans, the sound rough and deep. Then, he meets my eyes and gives me a small nod. What is he... The breath is torn out of my chest as I sense him. *Feel* him. His pleasure is in every nerve and cell in my body. He took down his mental shield for me.

"Don't stop," he grounds out.

I lost track of what I was doing in my surprise, but quickly resume my movements at his prompting. Trey closes his eyes, and I do the same. I focus on what I sense from him and what I feel for myself. I keep them closed until we both come undone together. Then, we spend the rest of the night under the stars, healing the tattered strand between our hearts.

Anger, hate, lust, greed, fear, sorrow, and grief are all catalysts for darkness. We must not fall prey to those dangerous emotions. Darkness is always lying in wait for us to allow it in, and even if only a sliver of it is permitted, it will take over and consume until all of the light within us is gone. No one has ever come back from this.

- The Great Hawk & Our Call to Order

CHAPTER 36

July

"GIRLS! TALLI! GREER! WAKE up!" Mom's voice is panicked. My eyes fly open, and I see her rooting around in our dresser drawers.

"What's happening?" Greer is on her feet helping Mom find our fighting leathers and boots.

Oh god. My heart pounds.

"We just got word that a large group of Brethren have broken into the northern gate and are marching this way through the forest. We don't have much time."

I'm on my feet, yanking off my pajamas and pulling on my leathers.

The northern gate is the farthest gate away from houses, right in the middle of the northern border of our community. Depending on how fast they are going, we have maybe two hours before they are at our doorstep.

"How many is large?" Greer asks, already dressed and lacing up her boots.

"The guards estimated five hundred." Mom stops her frantic work getting us dressed and carefully looks at us. Greer and I stop as well. The three of us are frozen in the reality of what is about to happen. Our community is made of four hundred and fifty Hawks roughly. That is counting our elderly, disabled, and children.

"That is an army, not a large group," Greer replies, barely-masked dread in her tone.

"Has there ever been an attack of this size before?" I ask, but I already know the answer.

Greer looks at me, expression pained. "No. Fifty is the largest ever counted. They aren't here to burn down our houses and take a few of us out, they are here to slaughter all of us."

How did they get five hundred men here without state police or any other humans noticing? Not to mention, how would they explain an entire community just being wiped off the map out of nowhere? They are risking exposure by bringing an army to our doorstep.

"New Hampshire, Vermont, and New York are all gearing up to come help," Mom offers, but it's of little comfort. The battle will already be raging by the time the closest of them arrive.

We finish getting ready and collect all our weapons. My nerves are enough to knot up my stomach more than I ever thought possible.

"Greer, go to the community center. Talli, you and I are going to help gather all the children and get them into the bunker," Mom instructs us.

The bunker is an underground safe house made of rock and metal. It can hold about two hundred people and is hidden behind the community building on the other side of the range. Once it's locked, it can only be opened from the inside.

Maybe I'm brave. Maybe I'm an idiot. Maybe I have zero value for my own life. But my intuition opens my mouth and I say, "I want to go with Greer. I want to help fight and heal those who fall during the battle."

A tear rolls down Mom's cheek, and she races toward me. I'm enveloped in her arms, and she squeezes me while saying, "I will not lose you today." She pulls back and hugs Greer next, adding, "either of you." She lets go, then looks at us both, as if for the last time.

"I love you girls. Be strong and remember light always wins." She turns and rushes out the door of our bedroom.

Realizing I am also crying, I wipe away the tears rolling down my cheeks and look at Greer. "If something happens..." I start, but she cuts me off. "If you fall, I will fall with you."

There it is. Greer's greatest fault and my greatest fear—loyalty—something I don't deserve or want from anyone anymore. It's my choice to risk my life, but it's this choice that may cause Greer to lose her life as well.

She heads out the door, not giving me a chance to say anything else. The hundreds of thoughts rushing through my head all disappear until I'm left with only one: *who I am now will not be who I am at the end of this.*

As soon as we walk out the front door, Ash is there with his parents behind him. He moved in with them last month after graduation, deciding that it was time to rebuild a relationship with them.

"Greer! Talli!" he cries out. Greer nearly tackles him to the ground with her hug.

Mom rushes to Ash's parents, saying, "Killian, Stella, follow me to the bunker. We need you two to survive this."

Mom's right. Even if our community is wiped out today, they will need to continue their work if the Order has any chance of surviving.

My focus returns back to Ash and Greer. With a fierceness I've never heard in his voice before, Ash says to Greer, "I'm not leaving you."

Greer hesitates, then grabs his shoulders, pulling him in hard for a kiss. "I'm so sorry," she softly whispers once their lips part. After a moment, Greer pulls away and presses a spot on his neck causing Ash to go limp. She holds him up until Mr. Hansen hurries over to pick up his son.

"Thank you," Mr. Hansen says, and Mrs. Hansen nods with tears in her eyes. They rush off with Mom toward the bunker. My chest is tight for not getting a chance to say goodbye to him, but it's for the best. It would have only made things harder and delayed us getting ready.

I place my hand on Greer's shoulder, giving it a squeeze. She takes a deep breath, and we jog to the community building.

We find Dad in the training gym standing on a bench, barking orders at everyone. On his orders, a wave of people—mostly Earth and Fire Elementals—run out of the gym. They are heading out to be the first wave of defense to help slow down the Brethren.

"Girls!" Dad shouts and steps down off his perch, walking toward us.

He locks eyes with me. "Are you sure?"

"Yes. I want to help heal."

Dad nods. "Go to the medical center, get yourself a bag and elixirs. Once you are done, take up a station at the school. Rescue the fallen and stay behind the worst of the fighting. Greer, you are her *shadow*. Watch her back while she works. If it gets too bad, I want you both to run. Forget your bravery and forget your loyalty. Get as far away from the community as possible until it's all over. Do you understand me?"

We both nod.

"I won't leave her side," Greer promises.

Greer and I both hug him tightly and head to the medical center. It takes all my willpower not to break down watching all the scrambling children and mothers trying to get themselves to the bunker. Few have the capacity to maintain their mental shield right now, so the amount of fear spilling into the air, making it thick and hot, is almost unbearable.

We quickly stock up on elixirs, taking everything that's left—not much, but enough to fill a Healer's messenger bag. I also find a spare leather belt that can hold three elixir vials on the strap and a small hip bag that can hold four more. I fill it as well, knowing the quick access will be handy.

On the way over to the school, I ask Greer, "What would happen if they succeed and kill all of us? The government would have a field day if they stumbled upon a community missing hundreds of people."

She swallows hard, the only sign of her nerves, and answers, "They would likely leave the Order to clean up the mess. The other communities would move people around and rebuild as fast as possible to make it look as if nothing happened. They may claim a large forest fire to help explain some deaths, but I'm honestly not sure. If they succeed, though, it will no longer be our problem."

"We aren't going to listen to Dad's order to run, are we?"

"If you run, I will run with you. But I know neither of us have any real intention of it."

She's right. I don't. My hands clench onto the strap of my Healer's bag in an attempt to steady myself. I decide not to say anymore. We are clearly on the same page.

When we get to the school, Greer announces that it has been an hour since we woke up. They have to be getting close.

The school has been turned into a makeshift infirmary since it is more easily defendable and very hard to burn compared to the actual medical center. Four teams of two, one Healer and one fighter, are set up to retrieve the injured and get them to safety. Greer and I are one of those teams in position and ready to go.

"Talli?" The shock in his voice makes me cringe. I've been searching for him around every corner and hoped to find him, but I didn't think about the consequences of it if I did. I turn around to see Trey running full speed toward me. He grabs my upper arms. "Why are you out here? You should be at the bunker. There might still be time..."

I cut him off. "No, I'm where I am needed." His eyes widen, and I know what's coming. Before he can argue, I continue, "There isn't time for this Trey. I can fight, and I can heal. I can save lives out here."

"At the cost of your own?"

"My life isn't worth more than anyone else's."

"It is to me! I've sacrificed so much to keep you safe. You're throwing that all away!"

This again. I suppress my groan. I thought we were past this a month ago.

"I never asked you to! This is my choice, Trey!"

His grip tightens on my arms, bruising me. I don't back down or show a hint of pain.

"I have her back. But bruising her will not help her survive this," Greer says, placing a hand on his arm.

Almost like he has been shaken out of a trance, he looks at her and then at his hands. He lets go quickly and says, "I'm sorry. I'm so sorry."

"Treyton! Time to go," Mr. Waterstone calls out to his son. Trey looks at me desperately. I can see the war behind his eyes. He grabs my cheek gently and kisses me, my willpower wavering like a weak tree in a storm.

He pulls away and whispers, "I love you."

"I love you too."

He pulls his hand away and runs to his dad, and then they head to wherever they are stationed for this.

This battle.

This slaughtering.

Swallowing the lump in my throat, I grab an arrow from my quiver strapped to my back. Greer unsheathes her sword.

Then we wait.

CHAPTER 37

FOR EVERY LIFE I have saved, I have equally taken.

We made a special trip away from the school once already to retrieve some of my arrows from where they remained lodged in lifeless bodies. I wish more than anything that I could say I feel remorseful each time I let an arrow fly, but I don't. All I feel is hate.

Disarming and disabling are not an option today. Any life I spare of theirs, I could be risking one of ours. I believe many of us are of the same mind, despite our knowledge of the memory elixir, which many of our Healers have already started producing in mass quantities for shipment to other communities.

"On your left!" Greer calls, and I duck. She swings her sword and slices right into a man's arm, leaving it hanging off by only a tiny shred of skin and tendons. He screams, and Greer plunges her sword into his heart, instantly cutting off his pain. I look down at the injured Hawk lying on the ground and quickly get to my knees. I know him. Gage is a new guard. He graduated with Trey last year, and he has been stationed at the Hansens' house lately.

I place my hand on his forehead, even though I can see the problem. His side is sticky with blood—a gunshot wound. I rummage through my Healer's bag for the right elixir and tip it into his mouth.

"Just hang on, Gage. I'm going to get you to safety, but I'm going to need your help."

He nods.

"What I just gave you will stop the bleeding, but I have to get you back to the school so they can get the bullet out and heal you. Okay, you're going to have to try and stand up, but I will help you."

He grits his teeth and then nods again. I help pull him straight up with minimal flexing to his abdomen. Then, putting his arm around my shoulder, I swiftly half-walk, half-drag him back to the school while Greer watches our backs.

One of the other teams spots me struggling under his weight and races to us. They take him from me and carry him the rest of the way. I let out a sigh of relief. My body aches, and my muscles feel like they will give out at any minute. There is a faint glow on the horizon; the sun will start to rise soon.

"Talli, let's go inside and get some water," Greer suggests.

I want to protest. There are so many more injured that need to be rescued. Greer grabs my arm, though, and pulls me with her, the protest dying on my lips before I can speak the words.

Water. Water will help. Then I can keep going.

I only allow us to stop for five minutes before we are back outside, rescuing more of the injured. Three more Hawks saved, and three more Brethren killed.

"Greer! We need your help!" Greer and I both turn in the direction of the outcry. Two of our own are getting surrounded by five Brethren. Greer looks at me and then back to them.

"Go! I'll get back to the school," I say quickly and run in that direction, arrow at the ready.

Out of the corner of my eye, someone falls back. A Brethren with his sword raised high. I aim and let my arrow fly. It lodges in his back, and he falls right onto the Hawk, who is beneath him. I don't hesitate, running toward them to help them get up.

Reine, a Fire Elemental from our year. Aside from Greer and me, I have only seen one other from our year. Now two.

I pull the man off her while she pushes. She jumps to her feet. "Thank you, Talli."

"Why didn't you blast him with your fire?" I ask.

"I ran out of fuel in all my lighters. I think my magic is also starting to fizzle out." Fire Elementals can't create fire out of thin air—no Elemental can. So, they carry around lighters to create the fire for them to manipulate.

"Get back to the school. I think you've fought enough."

She nods and limps in that direction, her sword back in her hand and ready. I move to follow her but freeze as I sense someone behind me. I jump to the right, narrowly avoiding the flaming torch that almost burns my shoulder. When I reach for another arrow, I end up grasping at air. Quickly backing up, I reach for one of the knives strapped to my thigh. I hold it with a tight grip, looking for a way to run. Two more Brethren join the one who has me cornered, blocking my route to the school completely.

"Looks like you are trapped and all alone, little witch," the one with the lit torch taunts.

I take a deep breath and do the only thing I can do at this point. Run. I hear their laughter behind me as they pursue me.

Maybe I can lose them in the forest. I make a hard right turn and head to one of our trails. There is one that runs between the school and the community building. It's my best bet. If I ran deeper into the fighting on the street, I could run into more of them and not find help.

The idea forces me to pick up speed. I reach the trail entrance and move light on my feet, hopping over the fallen branches, tree roots, and rocks. I rarely take this path, but I know most of these paths by heart from running through them as a child.

I run and run, not daring to look behind me, but I still hear their grunts and huffs as they try to keep up. I should have lost them by now, but they are persistent. The sick bastards are probably enjoying the chase, and I am losing energy fast. Time to change tactics. The path forks, and I take the path on the left, knowing it will take me somewhere I might have an advantage.

Before I know it, I see the lake in the distance. While still running, I remove my empty quiver and toss it with my bow and bag. Placing my palms together over my head, just like I learned at swimming lessons as a kid, I jump off the bank and dive right into the deep spot of the lake.

I swim, trying only to use my arms to pull me through the water since every muscle in my legs burns. I hear a splash behind me and turn to see one of the Brethren swimming toward me. I turn back around and keep swimming.

One of them calls out to him, "She's not worth it, Ed!"

"Well, I say she is. General doesn't want anyone left," he calls back. "Move over. I'll make this quick."

BANG.

A yard to my right, the water explodes, spraying me in the face. I turn back around, and one of them is holding a gun.

Fuck.

My eyes widen, and I almost inhale water from my gasp. I spin wildly and dive, swimming as low as I can. Another bullet sinks into the water two feet away from me. I swim in the other direction. My lungs start to burn until I am forced to go up for air. I surface, and water explodes to my left. I take another deep breath, but before I can submerge again, I hear a loud *HOOT*. I halt and look toward the forest. Trey knocks the gun out of the man's hand and pierces him in the gut with his sword.

Relief floods me at the sight of him. I'm safe. He's safe. The man with the torch is suddenly behind him, singeing his side with the flame. His leathers don't catch since they are fireproof, but I have no doubt he will still have small burns underneath. Trey punches the man square in the nose, and he goes sprawling onto his back. With a lightning-fast swing, Trey brings the sword down, severing the man's head from his body.

Suddenly remembering that I'm halfway across the lake, I start swimming back to Trey. As I reach the bank, he is standing there waiting for me. He looks awful. He has a black eye and is leaning all his weight onto one leg. From here, I can sense that his left hand is broken, and his right ankle is twisted.

"You're hurt!" I exclaim as I pull my body from the water.

"I'm okay."

"No, I dropped my bag right at the clearing. I should have one elixir left." I race over to where the brown leather bag rests on a bush. Lucky throw. I fish out my last elixir and start to run back.

"Talli!" I turn to look over my shoulder, and searing pain slices through my side. A Brethren comes out from the trees, knife in hand. A wicked smile across his face. He cut through my leathers, right into one of my intercostal muscles between my ribs. I try to swallow down what is rising in my throat as I do everything I can to hold my side together with my hand.

BANG.

Blood splatters my face as the man falls straight back with a bullet between his eyes.

I turn, but as I do, a cry escapes my lips, and I fall. Trey catches me, easing me slowly down. He pries the elixir from my hand and pours it down my throat before I know what's happening. He studies my wound to make sure it closes. But it doesn't. I know it won't because it's only a freeze elixir, which will only keep my wound from getting further damage or bleeding out. It's not a tissue restitch elixir.

"Shit Talli. You don't have anything else that can close this?"

I shake my head.

"Why didn't you save some more elixirs for yourself?"

"I wasn't planning on needing them." I try to laugh but instantly regret it as it jostles my side. The wound is okay to walk with safely, but it will hurt like hell.

Trey places his arms underneath me, pulling me to him, and rises to his feet, lifting me with him. He groans from the weight when his body is already so tired, but his hold on me is firm. He slowly limps toward the trail that leads to my backyard. That direction should be safer.

"We've got to get moving, it's not sa…" His words cut off abruptly as he whirls, putting his back now toward the trail. He falls to his knees, and I slide out of his arms, falling on my wounded side. My head spins wildly from the impact. Once my vision clears, Trey is hovering over me with his hands braced on the ground. I scream, now feeling his pain coupled with my own. I scoot my body out from under him, and once I am free, he drops, and my heart plummets with him. There is an arrow protruding from his back.

I scream again, this one echoing through the clearing. It's not a scream of pain but one born from rage. I don't have to time to analyze what the *thing* inside of me is doing right now, but its ready to consume everything as I watch the man who shot the arrow run in the other direction, back down the hill. Coward.

I work to see Trey's face, and it's not good. His breathing is shallow and hard. Panic takes hold of me. My bag. All my elixirs are gone. Even then, basic emergency elixirs wouldn't be able to do much for a wound like this. It's already done irreversible damage. As soon as that arrow is moved, he will die.

I can't move, and I can't speak. I look at him in shock, trying to run through my mind any possible way to save him. If I scream for help, I risk more Brethren coming down on us.

"How bad is it doc?" he asks, and I know he is trying to lighten the mood. He knows how bad it is. He can sense my panic and fear. When I don't reply, he says, "Talli, I..."

I cut him off. "Don't. Don't even think about saying any sort of goodbye. It cannot end this way." My tone starts sharp and ends in a plea. A plea to whom? I don't know—anyone or anything that could change the reality in front of me. Perhaps to the Great Hawk. It is powerful enough to fix this, but no one knows if it still exists.

My pain multiplies tenfold as I suddenly realize, this is my fault. If I hadn't gotten myself into this situation or if I had just gone to the bunker like he asked, this wouldn't be happening. He saw that arrow aimed at me and took it himself to save me.

Trey pushes himself up onto his elbows and eases himself so he is sitting up. He scoots back up against the tree behind him, taking care to only lean with his unobstructed side, the arrow jutting out beside the tree. His face is contorted in pain. I look up, and my breath catches. We are at our tree.

That is it. I don't fight the tears anymore. I let myself cry. He reaches out and cups my cheek.

"Talli," he says softly. "My only regret in life is that I didn't see you sooner. I didn't discover my feelings for you sooner. You made my life complete. I love you so much. Don't ever lose sight of that." He wipes a tear from my eyes.

"I love you. You can't leave me. This isn't fair," I gasp out between each sob.

"Promise me. Live your life, and follow your dreams for both of us. If you ever need me, look inside yourself, and you'll find me. I'll never leave you." He pulls my head down and kisses me softly, sweetly. It's a goodbye.

He moves back and continues, "I realize now that I was wrong. You are meant to fight, and you are meant to win." He coughs, and blood splatters onto his lips.

"Trey..." I breathe in a whimper.

"Someone is waiting for you. It's time that you meet her." He points his gaze behind me.

What is he talking about? Who is she? I turn, and then I see her.

At the edge of the lake, there is a. Oh my god...It's a dragon.

THE DRAGONS ARE MORE ANCIENT THAN THE GREAT HAWK HIM-SELF. THEY WERE THE ORIGINAL PROTECTORS OF NATURE AND MASTERS OF THE ELEMENTS. DRAGONS, AT THEIR VERY CORE, ARE VIOLENT AND EMOTIONAL CREATURES WHO WALK A FINE LINE BE-TWEEN LIGHT AND DARK.

NATURE THEN CREATED THE GREAT HAWK, WHO BESTOWED A SPECIAL CONNECTION TO NATURE UPON OUR SHOULDERS. DRAGONS TRIED TO BOND WITH MANY OF US, THE BOND CREATING EXTRAORDINARY POWER INSIDE THE HAWK. BUT AS TIME WENT ON, LESS AND LESS BONDED UNTIL DRAGONS WERE NO LONGER SEEN.

- BONDED CREATURES: SPECIES VOLUME I

CHAPTER 38

HER BODY IS LONG and thin with scales that are iridescent and absolutely mesmerizing. They are blue, green, and purple, each one shifting between the pastel shades as she moves. I've never seen anything like it.

"*Hello, Talliana.*" I hear her in my head. Her otherworldly voice is like a warm blanket covering my cold and broken body.

"You...You know my name," I manage to say.

"*Yes, Talliana, I do. Although, I think 'the sad one' suits you better at the moment.*" She almost sounds sad herself. Like my pain is causing her pain. There is something about her voice that I can't quite place, like I've heard it before in a dream.

"What do you want from me?" I ask, trying to wipe away as many tears as possible from my face.

She slowly walks out of the lake. Her four legs are thin and end in wide webbed feet. I don't miss the click of her claws on the rocks as she moves out of the water to come closer to me. Her hair, a pale green, encircles her face and flows around her like waves in the water. Two horns, slanted back and pointed at the ends, part her hair on either side of her head. Her eyes are the deepest blue, almost black at first glance. They are unsettling to look into.

She's a water dragon.

Her head tilts to one side, and she looks past me. *"He's gone."*

It feels like a dagger just pierced my heart. Our connection, our link, our string, snaps, and all the air is forced out of my body from the impact. I start to hyperventilate, trying to take in air too quickly. I get it under control, and I whip my head to where Trey lies in front of me. His heart is no longer beating. A screech echoes through the trees from a little ways away. Theora.

"No. No. No!" I cry as I press my face into his chest, letting the tears flow free once again. The dragon gives me a moment to grieve. Though we both know that I will be grieving this loss for the rest of my life. It could be a minute or five or twenty before she speaks again.

"I am sorry for the loss of his life today. He is at peace now. Dying to save the one you love is the greatest sacrifice, and he will be awarded for that in his eternity of rest."

"He deserved a full life, not one that was cut short. He died because I allowed myself to be cornered and injured. I should be the one dead, not him," I spit while still holding onto his lifeless body.

"Torturing yourself with blame is not what he would have wanted, but if you insist on it, save it for another time. Your life is still in danger, and there is work to be done. He is past saving, but there are lives in this battle that still can be saved. We can save them together."

I lift my head off Trey's body to study her again. She is standing fully out of the water now. She is so much bigger close up. Being a water dragon, she is still intimidating, but really, she is just magnificent to gaze upon, and all fear one should have when looking at a dragon is forgotten. I stand up, wincing at the sharp pain still in my side, and meet her stare head-on.

"Again, I ask, what do you want from me?" There is a fierceness in my tone that I don't recognize. I feel the thing I have been pushing down and hiding for too long start to rise to the surface. It shoves and claws at the barrier I have tried to build around it.

"*Your bond.*"

My jaw drops. "There hasn't been a bond with a dragon in three hundred-something years. Why now? Why me?" I question in astonishment.

"*Three hundred and eighty-four, to be exact. Now, because I am tired of watching all the suffering and you because together we are going to bring it all to an end.*"

Not *we could*, but *we are*. Her certainty brings hope and fear to my chest. I am not worthy of this dragon, not in the slightest. But we are taught that to the creature, a bond is something never offered lightly, and to disrespect their request may get you killed. A choice that really isn't a choice if you value your life.

"Why do you feel familiar?" I decide to ask.

"*I have been with you since the first time you came here with your love. I chose you on that day, but waited until you were ready to have me. Now is that time.*"

It dawns on me, then. "You're the little blue lizard I kept seeing, aren't you? That's your smaller form?" I had heard of dragons being shape-shifters, but I thought it was just a myth. Dragon lore is so widespread and varied, it's hard to know what's true and what's made-up.

"*You are correct. Though our bond hadn't formed yet, I wanted to help you and watch out for you.*"

"You led me to Trey that day in prison." I take a deep breath. "Thank you for that."

She dips her head, and I realize I am ready for this. I have to be. This is my destiny, and I will seize it. I will seize it for Trey.

Another realization hits me, though. "The water. I thought I felt Trey's pain when he was a prisoner that one night I was near it."

"You are a Water Healer. When you are near the water, it amplifies your healing abilities. When you are in the water, you are even more powerful. Once we bond and are both in the water, no one will be able to match our combined power."

A shiver runs up my spine, but I clench my teeth against it.

"What is your name?" I ask, goosebumps rising on my neck.

"Coventina," the dragon answers.

"I accept your bond, Coventina."

Her head lowers in front of mine, and she closes her eyes. I mimic her movement, and together, our heads meet, signifying the bond acceptance. Normally, a big ceremony with many steps is held in the community, but only a few are actually needed: a verbal acceptance of the bond, the meeting of heads, and then a marking of the bond.

She pulls back, and her mouth opens, giving me way too close of a view of her razor-sharp teeth. A bead of water appears in the middle of her mouth and grows larger each second. Once it's the size of my head, it moves, and the ball of water touches the injury at my side, lingering for a minute until it disperses. I unzip the top of my fighting leathers and pull away the fabric from that side.

I am healed. Where my wound was, now there is a mark of our bond—scales that look just like hers. No one will believe that is a tattoo; the scales appear real.

Oh god. Please don't be actual scales. I hesitantly touch the mark, and to my complete relief, I still feel skin, not real scales. Okay, it will have to be written off as a very, *very* well-done tattoo.

Ignoring my moonstone necklace still in its place against my chest, I zip up my top again. "Tell me what to do."

"*Get on my back.*"

I think I'm going to puke.

I walk around to Coventina's side, and her back has to be at least six feet up, a few inches above my head. I hesitate but carefully touch her side, feeling her scales under my hand. They are less slimy than I imagined but still slick. I can see her wings from this angle, the same iridescent color as her scales. They are tucked up close to her body, probably making it easier to move quickly through the water.

"How do you want me to get on? Or hold on once I'm up there?" I ask, not quite sure of the proper technique for riding a dragon. They are supposed to be extinct, and it's not something covered in school.

Coventina bends down so that I can reach her back, then bends her front left leg to make a step for me. Or at least I hope that's what it's for. I use it and swing one leg over, straddling her like I would a horse.

"*If you put your hands in my hair, at the base of my neck, there are horns you can use to hold on.*"

I place my hands into her silky hair, and sure enough, I find two small bumps protruding out of her skin. These are rounded at the top and not easy to grip, considering I'm stretched out fully to reach them, but it's better than nothing. I notice now she has horns that start with the large ones on the top of her head and trail down her neck, two at a time. They get smaller and more rounded as they go down, ending with the ones I'm trying to hold onto.

"*Ready?*" she asks.

"No," I answer with fear clear in my voice. My stomach is starting to flip-flop. How am I on the back of a dragon? How am I bonded to a dragon? This is either a nightmare, or I'm going to die before I find out it's actually real. I look over to Trey's lifeless body one last time and see Theora perched beside him. I have no doubt she will keep him safe for me.

"Too bad." Coventina's tone is one of mock pity. Her wings unfurl from her sides and stretch out wide to either side. Much wider than I thought possible, considering how small they looked a minute ago. Then she launches for the sky, leaving my stomach and all hope of surviving today behind.

Once we level out high in the sky, I force myself to straighten, letting go briefly of her horns to see what's happening below us. The sun is in the sky now, and I can see the community easily. Many houses are half burned, some are entirely burned to the ground, and others are still engulfed in flames. So many bodies litter the streets below. I can't tell from here who any of them are and if they are dead or just injured. It's chaos down there.

"*I'm going to hover over the lake, and you are going to pull the water to you,*" Coventina instructs.

I didn't realize I had any shock left in me until now. "I don't have a full water ability. How am I supposed to pull it out?" My question is frantic as we approach the lake.

"*You do, you have just never practiced. Concentrate. Will the water to come to you.*"

We hover over the water, and I'm willing, holding my hands out like I've seen Elementals do, but nothing is happening, not even a budge. I squeeze my legs tight, trying to use them to hold me to Coventina while she circles back around.

"*Try harder,*" she grounds out.

313

I try again with the same result. Panic forces its way into my throat as I yell, "It's not working! You picked the wrong person!"

"*Use it! Use your panic. Use your fear, your sorrow, your anger! Use them to fuel your magic! If you don't, more will die!*" she screams at me in my head.

I let all of those things flow through me, and when they are not enough, I focus on Trey. They took him from me twice. Those men wanted to hurt me. They killed him. They want to kill me. They want to kill my family. They want us all dead.

I think about the man I killed at the prison. He tried to strangle me, and I killed him. I killed so many men today, and I will kill all of them for this.

For Trey.

For my family.

For me.

I will end this.

The *thing* inside of me breaks through all that's left of my paper thin barrier, shattering it into tiny glass shards, and I welcome it. I allow it to fill every empty crevice of my being and coat all the broken pieces inside. My vision darkens at the corners like I am looking through a tunnel and I know it's a part of me now.

I am the darkness, and the darkness is me.

I let out a scream as I thrust out my hands at the water and pull it toward me in one massive raging sphere. Coventina flies up and goes back to the fight. When we see the street again, I know what to do.

Willing the water, I disburse it into a blanket of a million raindrops. It soaks everyone underneath it. Instinctually, I know it's healing all of our people—my people. My chest feels tight as it fills with power, and immediately we get more water to cover all the houses and douse the flames.

Two more spheres to heal more of the injured. But it's still not enough.

One more—I need one more, but it's too much power. Even though it is water Coventina and I are wielding, I feel like I am burning up on the inside. We get the last sphere of water, and I push myself to will it to the forest, where I know the rest of the fighting is.

"*You're using too much. You must stop,*" Coventina commands in my head, urgency in her tone. I barely register it, as I keep willing the water. We are almost done. I must keep pushing.

"*Stop now! Your body is not prepared for this kind of power yet.*"

I want to tell to her that my body isn't prepared for any kind of power, but I can't. My mouth is too dry. Actually, my whole body feels dry, like I am draining all the water out of myself in the process.

Almost there...

I see black spots in my vision, and I know I am losing my grip on consciousness. I sway suddenly. Coventina dives downward. Then I fall.

Chapter 39

My eyes flutter open—and, oh god, why is it so bright? I press my hand to my head and close my eyes again.

"She's awake!" I hear someone call to the right of me. Ugh, that was loud. Greer. It was Greer that was too loud. I groan and try to crack one eye open this time. Her face hovers over mine, her forehead creased with worry, and she looks tired. Why is she so tired?

Hearing someone else run into the room, I try cracking the other eye open, and now I see Mom replacing Greer in the spot next to me.

"Sweetie, can you hear me?"

I groan audibly from the noise. "Yes, can you stop shouting?" I ask, half-realizing that my words are slurred and mumbled.

She grins at me and replies, "I was speaking at a normal volume. You are likely experiencing something very close to a hangover, but it will pass soon." She must be whispering now because the level is much more tolerable.

"What...what happened?"

"The battle," Mom keeps talking and explaining, but I stop hearing her. Everything comes flooding back to me in a rush: Trey, Coventina, falling...My heart races and my breathing becomes labored.

"*Calm yourself. All is well.*" I hear Coventina in my head. I will myself to take in slow, steady breaths, then try to sit up. That was a mistake. The room begins to spin, so I plop back down, returning my hand to my head.

"Trey. He's gone. You need to find him and..."

"We already retrieved him," Mom reassures.

Tears flow down my cheeks, and I try to take another breath as a fresh wave of grief hits me.

"How long have I been out?" I wheeze.

Greer hesitates and looks at Mom. "Two weeks," she says solemnly from the foot of the bed.

"Two weeks?" I exclaim.

"Yes, but don't worry about any of that now. You only need to rest and eat. We will catch you up, and you will catch us up soon. Starting with your bonded dragon," Mom says, gently pushing me back down and wearily eyeing the little blue lizard on my side table. I reach out my hand to Coventina, and she climbs into it without hesitation. I bring my hand to my stomach, and she dismounts my hand, settling down comfortably on top of my purple duvet. It's a good thing it isn't blue, otherwise I would lose her.

My stomach growls, and my mind goes back to the offer of food.

"Food would be good, please," I say.

Mom nods once and heads out of the room. After I watch her go, my gaze shifts to Greer, who looks stoic on the outside, but I sense the waves of confusion and anger coming off her. She must be too tired to maintain her shield. I wipe away the tears from my face. I need to focus on the now and my sister.

"How's Ash?" I ask.

"He's okay. He started out pissed over what I did. Then it quickly faded after he learned what happened to..." She trails off before saying the name. The name that will bear a mark on my heart for the rest of my life. There is no bringing him back this time.

"How many?" I venture, knowing she'll understand what I am asking.

"The number would be triple if it weren't for you."

I meet her eyes, asking, *begging* her to tell me. "Just over one hundred," she relents.

I release a choked sound, and my stomach plummets. We had almost three hundred members out on the battlefield, and lost a third of them. But if what Greer is saying is true, if it weren't for Coventina and me, we would have lost entirely, and we could all be ash right now aside from those safe in the bunker.

"That rain, Talli...It healed people on the literal brink of death. They are calling it more powerful than any elixir ever brewed. You are..."

"I have food," Mom cuts off Greer's urgent tone.

It is obvious that she has done this intentionally, as she hands the tray of food to Greer and says, "Make sure she eats and drinks lots of water. Then you," she points at Greer, "need to get some rest in your bed. You both need to get more rest."

"Yes, ma'am," we say in unison. In silence, Greer hands me food and water while I dutifully eat every bite.

I eye the water wearily before I attempt a sip. It feels strange knowing that I can control it. The urge to test it comes over me, but I suppress it when I see Greer watching me. Instead, I grab the cup and gulp down the contents. A weird sensation fills me, and I focus on it. I can feel the water move through my body, from my esophagus to my stomach, to my intestines, into my blood, through my organs, and into my cells.

"I...I need to take a shower," I say quietly, slowly getting out of bed.

"You should rest more first," Greer argues.

"I need some space to process, and I want to do it there."

She doesn't stop me, she just watches me as I painstakingly half-drag myself to the bathroom. I didn't realize how weak I would truly feel. It's painful to move a lot, but I need to see it.

"Be careful. Don't overdo it," Coventina warns.

I pull off my shirt in front of the mirror and turn sideways, looking for...Oh my god.

Coventina's bonding mark is still there, but somehow, I don't remember it being this large. The mark is about the size of my hand, stretching from the top of my hip bone to well over my ribs. I touch it again, and it still feels like skin. But what is...I run my hand over the entire thing, and it feels raised in the middle. I look down and see the faintest shade of white poke out from under the scales—the knife wound. It's still there. The smallest trace of it, but it's there—a reminder of what put me on this path. Trey.

I completely unravel. Turning from the mirror, I fall to my knees and hold myself as I allow everything to hit me. Pain. Grief. Fear. Heartbreak.

Tentatively, I look inside of myself and find my heart. Our connection, the strand between our hearts, is lying limp. Still there, but broken. Another scar to remind me.

They took him. They took so many. They will pay for this.

Anger embraces me like a familiar friend, and I turn my attention away from my heart toward the darkness inside. Pulsing and ready for a fight. The inky blackness fills up all the space inside of my body—every crack and crevice. My heart is the only thing left that is not fully covered by it because it's the only place left with a little bit of light still inside.

The darkness calls to me, telling me that vengeance will be mine.

Good.

I stand up from my huddled position, mentally burying that sad, grieving girl under layers of darkness. My legs now steady and strong, I get in the shower. Once my body is thoroughly hydrated with warm water, a stark contrast to the chill inside of me, I lift my hands on impulse. The water stops midair around me until I will it to gather in my palm and form a tiny sphere. It spins wildly, and then I stop it again, willing it into the shape of a dagger. Then, an arrow. Then, a spear. I grab onto it and hold it firm in my grip. Instinctually, I blow out some of the chill inside of me, coating the tip of the spear in a frosty cloud. The water turns to ice before my eyes.

Water and Ice then...Two different Water Elemental abilities. Slowly, I touch it with my pointer finger and feel the bite of its sharp point.

I'll never be helpless again.

Leaving the bathroom, I'm not surprised to see Greer sitting on the edge of her bed, waiting for me. Her face is pensive, with deep creases between her brows.

"Ask it," I say out loud, startling her. Her eyes widen at me, then she hesitates for a moment before asking, "What did you do in order to control that much power?"

Without flinching, I answer, "I bonded a fucking dragon, Greer. That's what I did."

"I don't think that's all."

"I did what I had to."

320

She explodes, "You almost died. You should have died. Why would you wield so much power and push yourself too far like that? How could you be so reckless?"

I throw up my hands and say, "So many people were killed, and more were dying. Coventina and I could save them."

"By sacrificing yourself? On the same day, you bonded with the most powerful creature this world has ever seen. Those people knew the risk of the battle and chose to fight. You could have pulled back once it got to be too much."

Disbelief almost knocks me over, and I pin her with a glare. How dare she berate me for saving lives, whether I risked my own or not? It's not up to her to decide when I should or should not risk my life for others. Trey sacrificed himself for me. Why shouldn't I sacrifice myself for so many others?

She continues, "You told me you were going back to the school to wait for me. I wanted to fall on my sword when I couldn't find you. Then suddenly, you were in the sky doing the impossible. People who were taking their last breath only a moment before were rising to their feet, picking their weapons back up. I was confused and terrified. When I found you again in the sky, I saw you fall. I ran as fast as I could, but by the time I got to the lake, Coventina had you slung over her back coming out of the water. I found Trey and I thought you were dead, too."

"You thought I deliberately pushed myself too far because I lost him?" I ask, understanding now why she is so angry.

"Yes. I didn't think you could bear losing him again," she breathes.

Everything inside of me deflates, and my legs grow weak again. I walk slowly back to my bed and climb in. I couldn't bear it. I can't bear it. But there is more that needs to be done. I need to end this for him first.

Finally, I tell her, "Coventina told me that she and I will end the war one day. I need to see that through before I can think selfishly again." Her eyes sharpen and lock onto mine. "Will you help me, Greer?"

Her mouth falls open, but she doesn't say anything. Suddenly, I am very tired. I lie down and pull the covers over me, closing my eyes.

I barely register her voice when she answers, nearly to herself, "I'm supposed to help *you* change history."

Chapter 40

THE NEXT MORNING, I feel strong enough to make it downstairs with some help from Mom. I am relieved to see Ash sitting at the table with Greer. Their chairs are right up against each other with the entirety of their sides touching. Ash lifts his head to meet my gaze and a smile spreads across his face. He quickly gets out of his seat and meets me halfway to the table, pulling me into an embrace.

"I love you, Talli." My heart melts as I hold onto my best friend.

"I love you too, Ash."

Greer helpfully adds, "He has been very generous with his use of that word lately. I'm starting not to feel so special anymore."

Ash pulls away and helps me to the table as he says, "Life is short, and I want to ensure everyone important to me knows."

"Well, it brightened my day. Thank you," I assure him.

He smiles at me and takes his seat next to Greer again. The front door opens and closes. Dad walks into the room, and pulling my chair out carefully, leans down and gives me a hug while I stay seated. He presses a kiss to my head and says, "You had me so worried."

Blinking away the water that builds in my eyes, I manage to say, "I'm okay."

Dad takes a seat next to me. "You're not only okay, but you are the hero of this community."

"Dad, I..."

"Listen to me. I know it is hard to hear, considering what's been lost, but you must understand what you did. The people outside of our door understand it. It's taken all your mother's and my energy to keep them off our doorstep with their eagerness to come see you and say thank you." Despite the thoughtfulness behind Dad's words, they don't carry the same vigor of his normal speeches. I look him over and notice more gray hair starting to creep in at his temples. He continues, "Sweetheart, you performed a miraculous thing. You bonded a dragon. You have developed as a Water Healer, unlike any we have seen since the first one in our history, and word has already spread throughout the communities. There is no downplaying or hiding this. So, I need you to rest to your full strength and prepare to face it."

Mom comes through the door with a plate full of French toast. "What your dad is trying and failing to say is that things are going to change, but we will go at whatever pace you need."

Dad smiles lovingly at Mom as she gracefully moves around the table, dumping food onto everyone's plates.

"Okay. After breakfast, I think it's best if we talk. I need to be caught up on everything that happened and I think it's important for me to share a few things with you all," I announce, even though unease courses through me.

"If you feel ready," Dad offers.

I nod and focus on eating my breakfast.

"*Are you ready?*" Coventina asks.

It feels unnatural, but I focus on replying to her in my head. "*No one needs to know the how, but I think…I know they need to know about the future and what it could mean. What you said we would do together.*"

"*What did I say?*"

"*That we would end the suffering together,*" I answer hesitantly.

"*Good. Just making sure you heard me.*"

Snarky dragon.

"*And I heard that!*"

"*My first goal is to learn how to not share every thought with you.*"

"*I think you will find that is way too challenging of a path.*"

"*Why? Other Hawks can do it with their bonded creatures.*" It's a form of shielding. It makes it easier for the bonded creature to distinguish between what's inner monologue and what's actually meant for them.

"*Dragon bonds are different.*"

"*Why am I not surprised? I have a feeling you will defy what's considered normal at every step.*"

"*You are right about that.*"

One week later, I am completely healed and back to full strength. Physical strength, anyway. Today is Trey's funeral. The Waterstones decided that they could not lay their son to rest without me in attendance. I appreciate their decision, but I would be lying if I said I didn't wish I could avoid the whole thing.

Throughout the week, I have been fully updated on all the details of what happened during *The March on Massachusetts*, as everyone is calling it. We completely lost thirty houses, and another fifteen took a lot of damage. Those still with houses standing took in who they could, and then the school was converted into a shelter for the rest of those displaced. Hawks from other communities came flooding in to help us bury our dead and dispose of the bodies of the Brethren. Many of them stayed behind to help us clean and rebuild. The Brethren left us with a huge mess to cover up quickly or risk our entire existence becoming known to the human world. It's a complex process of creating fake death causes, changing people's places of death to other community medical centers, forging false accident reports, and more. For the Brethren, we burn all their bodies and let their leadership explain all the disappearances. Despite being each other's enemies, neither group wants to be discovered. Granted, this whole thing makes me question if their opinion on that has changed. Nonetheless, we have to assume and hope they will do a count of their people and handle everything accordingly.

The one hundred and six deaths on our side were nothing compared to the loss the Brethren took. The healing rain I created did not heal them like it did our people. So, despite the hesitation most Hawks have toward killing, many not having killed before, only a hundred and fifty Brethren survived and were imprisoned until they could have their memories wiped by the Hansen's new elixir. Another fifty escaped during the confusion of the mysterious rain.

Between the injured being healed by the water and some Brethren running, it was enough for us to take the upper hand we needed, and the battle ended shortly after that.

In all the debriefing and different accounts of the battle, including Coventina's, I found out that I did fall from her back, but she caught me with her claws until she could hover over the lake and drop me in. I was so far gone, I should have died, but the water from the lake healed me enough until I could be properly treated for magic depletion. According to Coventina, I can self-heal in water. My desire to always shower or take a bath when I don't feel good makes a lot more sense now.

Getting used to her being in my head is going to be a challenge for sure. She loves to chime in with her snarky, soft voice and give her two cents whenever she sees fit. I can't tell either if Greer is annoyed by it or jealous every time I go quiet to have a conversation with Coventina in my head. Usually, it happens when we're in the middle of a conversation ourselves. I've been trying to figure out how to ignore her until Greer and I are done, but there is no such thing as ignoring a dragon in your head.

My parents also explained to me that not everyone saw me and Coventina flying over the community. Apparently, we were glamoured in a way so that anyone without a bond themselves could not see us while we were in the sky—dragon magic. However, even though only about half of the community saw us, word of what happened spread quickly.

"Are you ready?" Greer asks, standing in the doorway to the bathroom. Pulled from my thoughts, I look at her and blink for a minute before replying.

"No, but I can't avoid it forever."

"We'll get through this together."

I nod, extending my arm out for Coventina. She climbs onto my shoulder, her new favorite spot, and I follow Greer out the door.

We do, in fact, get through it together—Greer, Ash, and I. I even managed to stand up at the funeral and explain to the crowd how Trey saved me in the end. It hurt, and guilt kept creeping up my throat, threatening to choke me, but I pushed through. His was the last funeral of all the ones held over the previous few weeks, and it's the only one I have been able to attend.

They decided to lay Trey to rest by our tree, where he died. It's what he would have wanted, and it warms me a little to think of him being buried in his favorite spot. *Our favorite spot.*

The funeral was my first real outing since everything, and I had a constant stream of people coming up and thanking me for saving them or their loved ones. I am grateful that we could save so many, but it doesn't make up for the fact that we couldn't save Trey or the others.

Once each thank you feels like a weight getting added to my chest, I hear Coventina remark softly, "*I think that's enough gratitude for the day.*"

Greer and Ash notice me trying to leave and take up a place beside me, walking quietly. Once we are out of sight, Coventina jumps from her place on my shoulder as a lizard and shifts into her dragon form.

Greer and Ash have both seen her a few times in person, but it seems that for everyone except me, it will take some getting used to. Weirdly enough, it feels right having her with me, like she has always been there.

After a few moments of walking together, Greer breaks the silence. "You know you both looked totally badass, flying together, sending water down, saving lives and stuff."

Even though there was no hint of it in her tone, jealousy pours off her. I have difficulty suppressing my laugh as I ask, "Is that jealousy I sense?"

Greer sighs loudly and says, "Maybe! You not only bond before me, but you bond with the biggest, baddest creature ever. At this rate, I'll be lucky to bond a squirrel."

Her whine causes us both to laugh, but to my surprise, Ash isn't laughing. He looks serious.

"What is it, Ash? Afraid you'll have to share a bed with a squirrel one day?" I ask, giving him a little nudge.

The corner of his lips does lift a little, but then he turns his serious expression to Greer. He asks her, "Greer, you saw them during the battle?"

"Yes. I've told you that a few times," she answers.

"But how? You're not bonded. Only bonded Hawks were not affected by the glamour." His confusion is palpable.

"*I'm going to call him the smart one from now on. I told you that dragon bonds work differently. Our connection starts the moment we choose you; the bond acceptance and marking are only formalities,*" Coventina chimes in my head.

"What does that mean, Coventina?" I ask my question out loud for the sake of Greer and Ash. We all stop and look at her.

"*Well, jealous one, he's not a squirrel, but my brother would like to meet you.*" By the look on Greer and Ash's face, Coventina spoke to all of us, not just me.

Coventina lifts her gaze to the sky, and...there...coming toward us, is a dark gray dragon.

"No...This can't be real," I hear Greer say to herself.

The dragon's wings are massive, much bigger than Coventina's, but his scales shimmer in the sunlight just like hers. He looks much more like a traditional dragon you would see depicted in a fairytale terrorizing some helpless village, with a more proportioned body and no flowing hair. He is not a water dragon like Coventina, not at all.

"Meet Draven. He's a shadow dragon."

Maybe it is my imagination, but I swear the ground shakes when he lands in front of us.

KEEP READING FOR A BONUS CHAPTER IN GREER'S POV.

GREER

June

GRADUATION WAS NOT AS dull as I thought it was going to be. Dad's speech was surprising in what he said but not surprising in that he made a spectacle of it. Intelligence. The internal scoff echoes through my head. They are always so dramatic. It's like the Great Hawk wired in the trait with the abilities that fall under the classification. It's one hell of a package deal. Talli's reaction to it concerned me. I would have thought that she would have been thrilled at the news, but she was worried. Something is going on with her, I can feel it.

I look down at my raggedy black leather boots, the toes gently brushing against the grass as I swing slowly back and forth. Talli tried to hide them this morning so I would wear something nicer with my graduation dress. I admire her for always trying, but I know all her hiding spots.

I grab the worn-down chain of the swing and push myself a little harder. It will never fail to surprise me that this old swing set Dad bought for Talli and me after my adoption is still standing. It is coated in rust from years of the elements taking their best shots at it, but still, it stands. Maybe that's why I like it so much. Like my old boots, it's resilient.

I look up and see everyone socializing. That's something I don't like, all these people milling about like there is nothing more important to do. I spot Ash where he is with his parents. He's going to move in with them soon. He hasn't spoken that out loud, but I know it will happen. I sensed it last week. I'll hate it, but if it makes him happy, then I'm happy for him. If I had the same chance he does, I would take it without a thought.

"Greer, would you stop looking like a rain cloud and let people congratulate you?" Talli lectures. She sounds more like Mom every day. I snicker at the thought but reply, "People can come over here if they want to congratulate me for doing the bare minimum in school."

She scowls at me and retorts, "You did not do the bare minimum. Should I remind you of your GPA?"

"No need. I couldn't care less about an imaginary number."

Talli laughs. "Alright, you do you, but don't say I didn't try."

"Talli, no one could ever accuse you of not trying."

"Thank you! I'm getting so many good compliments today." She beams.

I raise a brow at her in question, and she waves a hand, "Don't worry about it."

"I will say that I am worried about your reaction to Dad's speech earlier."

Talli's smile falters. "Just a bad feeling."

"That intuition of yours again?"

"Yeah, but I'm not sure that is the proper name for it anymore."

"What is?"

"I'll tell you when I am sure." Then she walks away back to her mingling. I smile, though, appreciating her always checking on me in social settings.

I am only granted another moment of silence before Dad's shadow hovers over me. "Careful, people might think you are enjoying your-self. Your reputation might never recover." Dad's smirk is infectious, but I drop my smile to pretend that it isn't. He knows I did it on purpose.

"Can I talk to you for a minute? I have a graduation gift for you inside," he asks.

"You and Mom already gave us our gifts," I point out.

"This is different. Come on."

I follow him through the back door and into his office. He shuts the door behind him, and we both sit on opposite-facing chairs. Melisan-dre is curled up in the corner of the office, lying on a plush bed with the sunlight pouring out onto her from the window.

This office used to be my biological grandfather's. This whole house was his because it is a designated elder's house, and he was the community's mayor before Dad. It was a Meyer who led the Order from Scotland to America, and a Meyer has always served as an elder for the Massachusetts community. Until my father ran away with my mother, that is.

"You know that your father and I were friends," he starts. I nod as he expects, outwardly remaining calm, but nothing inside of me feels calm. "I would like to tell you more about him, if you're up for it."

Nodding again, I brace myself. I have thought about my father today. I think about him and my mother most days. I would give so much to know what they would think of me right now.

My mental shield must have wavered because Dad says, "He would be so proud of you. You are a lot like him, actually. He hated crowds, was quiet, and fiercely loyal to those who were important to him. You also have his dark hair, which is a Meyer family trait. Oh, and he loved to draw. He always had pencil lead smudged on his hands."

My heart warms, and my stomach settles as I focus on each of his words, determined to commit them to memory.

"I met him when I first moved to the Massachusetts community. I won't bore you with all the details, but we became as close as brothers. We agreed on everything except for the future of the Order. Your father believed that humans could protect nature on their own and had governments set up now to prevent too much evil from gaining power. He believed that the solution to the war was to disassemble the communities and mix with humans until all the magic in our bloodline was gone."

That surprises me. Dad had mentioned before how my father was averse to fighting, but I didn't realize he was *that* averse to it.

"So, the contingency plan I heard about a few months ago for the communities to be disassembled was originally my father's plan?" I ask.

Dad gives me an assessing look. "Do I want to know where you heard that from?"

I shrug. "Mom mentioned something to Talli." I don't have to say the rest—that Talli told me. There is an understanding in this house and among many who know us that if one of us knows something, so does the other.

He sighs and continues, "In opposition to your father, I believe that humans do still need our help, and if we weren't meant to help them still, then our magic would have faded a long time ago on its own. The Great Hawk would not let us walk around with abilities if they weren't necessary."

I agree with him. There is more work to be done.

"Despite our difference in opinion, he was still my best friend. Your grandfather, the old hateful man that he was, groomed your father to become the next elder as was tradition, all while your father was passing everything on to me. He was happy to hand off the responsibility, and I was happy to take it." Dad laughs, then says, "I found Rose and got married, all while your father had been engaged to a girl from the Vermont community for half his life. A month before the wedding, your father told me he had found the love of his life in a human, and he was going to run away with her and his child that she was pregnant with. Imagine my surprise at his admission, because it was the first I had heard of this human girl. I told him I would help him on one condition: he had to let me meet her."

I scoot to the edge of my seat, and he continues with a smile, "She was beautiful. She was a nature photographer and she traveled all over the world to take pictures for different magazines and such. Her intentions and love for your father were pure, and I helped the three of you vanish. Your grandfather was like a wrecking ball afterward trying to find him, but he never did. Instead, he ended up dying of a heart attack about a year and a half later. Your father actually came back for a couple of weeks to help deal with your grandfather's affairs. He did bring your mother and you with him. I suspect he never went anywhere without you two. I had become an elder and had Talli. She was about nine months old, and you were a little over a year old. You both immediately hit it off. You would march around with her crawling behind you in her diaper. You always tried sharing your crayons with her, but she was always too busy playing with her toes to care."

Dad smiles again, this time bigger, clearly remembering how we were. He shakes his head. "Anyway, I begged your father to return to the community for good and give you a permanent home, but he always said no each time I asked. He wanted you to have a normal life, and I respected that, as much as it hurt to see you all go again. The next time I saw you was when I picked you up from the police station to bring you home."

Dad's smile is gone, replaced with a sorrowful look. I also feel sorrow and grief for what could have been if my father had listened and stayed here.

"Well, I didn't tell you all this to make you feel sad but to give you some backstory before I give you this." He gets up from his chair and goes around his desk to open a drawer, where he pulls out a sealed envelope.

My breath catches, and Dad explains, "It came with instructions to give it to you when you needed it the most once you became an adult. I intended to give it to you for your eighteenth birthday, but things were a bit crazy around here in October, so I saved it until the right moment. Today felt like that day."

He hands me an envelope that reads, "To Greer."

"I'll give you some time alone with it. I have no idea what it says, but if you have any questions after, I'll see what I can do." He turns, then spins back around to face me again, "Before I go, let me just say, Rose and I love you so much. You are our daughter as much as Talli is, and we are so proud of you."

Climbing out of my seat, I wrap my arms around his neck. He gives me a firm squeeze and a kiss on the forehead before letting go. Dad leaves the office with Melisandre on his heels, then shuts the door, leaving me alone with a racing heart. I go back to my seat and settle in, tucking my legs beside me. I carefully break the seal on the envelope and undo the tri-fold in the paper. I start to read.

My daughter,

I entrust this letter to my close friend Aaron because, in our world, we have to expect the worst to happen. I hope I give this to him only for him to have the privilege of shredding it one day when it's unnecessary, but in case something does happen to me and your mother, I know my friend, with as many lives as that cat of his, will protect you until he takes his last breath.

You are only one year old as I write this, but even now, it's evident who you will grow up to be. You are clever, strong, and beautiful. You will also be brave, much braver than I could ever wish to be. Greer, your path will lead you to do amazing things. I saw it last night in a dream. I can't share the details, as you should know the rules by now of our foresight, but you will help change history. I fear that I have made the wrong decision by taking you away from where you belong, but going back risks us losing your mother, and I'm too much of a coward to risk that. I hope you can forgive me for it. I know, though, that one day, you will find your way to the Order and the destiny that awaits you. I never felt like I had any kind of destiny growing up in our family's shadow, but I know now that my destiny was bringing you into this world so that you can make it a better place.

There isn't much advice I can give you because I have little wisdom to pull on. But I will tell you that being a good soldier in this war will not get you where you need to be. Only you can lead yourself there. Trust yourself and your closest allies, but be wary of everyone else. We have incredible gifts, but they cannot protect us from everything. Keep your shields strong and ensure the right person is always at your back.

Your mother and I are so proud of you, and we love you more than you could ever know.

With all the love in my heart,

Papa

I carefully fold up the letter and wipe the tears starting to well in my eyes. Then I do my best to quietly slip out of Dad's office so that no one is alerted to my presence. I don't want anyone interrupting my escape to my bedroom.

I peek around the corner of the hallway, and all is clear. I dash up the stairs on light toes, but as I reach my bedroom doorway, Ash walks out of it.

"Oh, hey. I was looking for you. You ran off. Though, I shouldn't be surprised." Ash laughs quietly.

"Sorry, Dad needed to give me something, and I got caught up." I do my best to suck in the tears and will them not to fall.

Ash squints his eyes at me. "Greer, is something wrong?"

"Nope. Nope. I'm...fine." I struggle through the words, and my voice cracks at the end, giving me away.

Ash has me in his arms in less than a second. "I have you. Let go."

I do as he says and release all the tears I've held back. Talli is the one who always cries. Not me. But fuck does this feel good. I hold onto Ash harder, and he takes it, along with the onslaught of emotions I am feeling right now. He knows I don't need or want to talk. I just need him and that comfort thing he is so good at.

When the stream of tears slows, he leads me to the spare room where he is currently staying. Not that my room doesn't work, but there is not much privacy from Talli there, and I only want to be with Ash right now. I will share the letter with Talli tomorrow.

Ash shuts his door behind him, and we curl up in his bed, where he holds me and kisses away all the heartbreak I feel from missing my parents.

ACKNOWLEDGEMENTS

I have had Talliana's story in my head for over fifteen years and have always wanted to write it. I never thought I would have the opportunity to, but life has a funny way of giving you exactly what you want in a way you didn't want it. I've learned in this experience that the key is not to squander it by focusing on the path that led you here but to seize it before it's too late. So this is me, seizing my opportunity with a grateful heart for those who helped me get here.

To my husband, Tom, none of this would be possible without you. I couldn't even begin to guess how many times you told me, "I got it. Go upstairs and write." Even in the beginning, when this book started as something I was writing only for myself, you knew I would take this all the way, and you supported me at every step. You are my light, and I am so grateful to have you as mine.

To my daughter, Emmalyn, thank you for always pulling me back to the real world when I get lost in my head. You are my heart, and I could never ask for a more awe-inspiring daughter.

To my best friend and biggest hype woman, Marci, thank you for the long video calls that kept me sane when spiraling with ideas. You have held me accountable when I didn't do enough research and have been a stickler for making me answer the silly questions that make my writing better. Thank you for putting up with my quirks and reminding me that it is okay to be human.

To my book bestie, Pattie, thank you for all your detailed feedback on my initial drafts and for answering every random message asking for your opinion on any number of things. Your opinions and feedback have been invaluable, and your support has meant the world to me.

To all my other family and friends who have encouraged me through my journey, thank you for being there for me with excitement and promise to share my work with anyone who would listen.

To my wonderful editor, Haleigh St. Paul at Page Perfectors LLC, when I was searching for an editor, I thought I was looking for someone to correct my mistakes. I never imagined finding one so enthusiastic about my work that I felt excited for their feedback. You made me feel like my story was special through every edit, and you knew just how to polish it up to make it the best it could be. Thank you for all your hard work and passion for perfecting a story.

To my cover designer, Moonchildreams. You took my idea and brought it to life in gorgeous detail. I am honored to have your amazing art depict my story. You are truly great at what you do. Thank you for working with me.

ABOUT THE AUTHOR

C.L. Sharp considers herself a firm believer in happily ever after and loves writing stories with bumpy roads and banter-filled dialog.

When she isn't writing in her East Coast home, she loves spending time with her husband, daughter, and two dogs. She enjoys working with her hands for many different hobbies and is a frequent visitor to zoos, aquariums, and theme parks, where she insists on riding every roller coaster.

If you enjoyed Blind Thoughts, be sure to join her mailing list and follow her on social media for upcoming titles!

Website: www.clsharp.com
Instagram: @c.l.sharp_author
Facebook: Pages/C.L. Sharp